"If I go home, I will be forced to marry a man I loathe."

"Is that all?" Robert asked her.

"All? That is a great deal. And I assure you, I have tried to convince my uncle that I cannot and will not marry the man he wants me to, but he will not listen."

Robert heard her sincerity, her determination and, beneath that, the thing that touched his heart: fear. Despite that fear, however, she was so desperate for her freedom, she would risk danger to achieve it.

She was not a fool. She was brave.

"As a solicitor, I know many things about marriage—and how to avoid it. Come with me out of the chill night air. Perhaps I can help you."

"If you can offer me an honorable way out of my predicament, I am willing to listen," she said.

And Robert Harding held out his arm to escort this unknown, brave and desperate young woman away from the dangers of the riverbank . . .

Other **AVON ROMANCES**

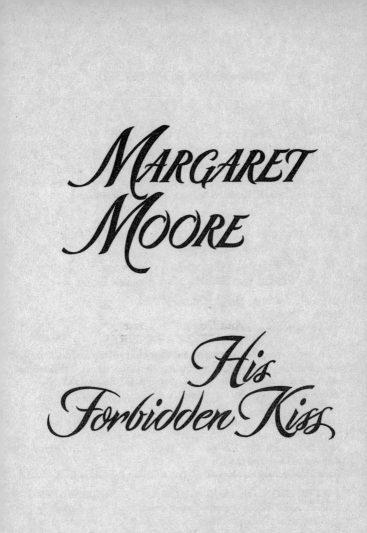

Margaret Moore

His Forbidden Kiss

AVON BOOKS
An Imprint of HarperCollinsPublishers

AVON BOOKS
An Imprint of HarperCollins*Publishers*
10 East 53rd Street
New York, New York 10022-5299

Copyright © 2001 by Margaret Moore Wilkins
ISBN: 0-380-81335-1
www.avonromance.com

First Avon Books paperback printing: March 2001

Avon Trademark Reg. U.S. Pat. Off. and in Other Countries, Marca Registrada, Hecho en U.S.A.
HarperCollins® is a trademark of HarperCollins Publishers Inc.

Printed in the U.S.A.

10 9 8 7 6 5 4 3 2 1

Chapter 1

London, 1663

Robert Harding strode through the narrow alley in Bankside, that part of London south of the Thames. At a scurrying sound, his brisk steps slowed, until he spotted the rats fighting over a piece of rotting cabbage.

Deftly avoiding them, he hurried onward until he came to the end of the alley. The street adjoining it continued to the wharf and water stairs. From there, the Bankside denizens could cross the river to the richer parts of London, or those from the richer parts could disembark, ready to risk Bankside for their sport, whatever it might be.

As he got closer to the river, creeping fog began to obscure his vision, the feeble October moon doing little to provide illumination. The fog hung heavier at the wharf overlooking the dank waters of the Thames, and the moist air seemed more laden than usual with the scent of mud and decay.

A man lingered in the shadows cast by a torch stuck near a piling, the sharp stench of pitch joining that of the mud.

Alert for danger, Rob continued to walk boldly forward, his gaze trained on the man, making it clear he was not a fop or aristocrat lost and alone. The fellow slid back into the darkness, and Rob made a small, grim smile of satisfaction.

Then he saw the woman.

Shrouded in a dark cloak, she stood on the brink of the wharf, her slender form bent forward as if peering down to the murky depths below.

As Janet had probably done on the last night of her life. Was this unknown woman intending to end her life in that same watery grave?

This place was hardly conducive to soliciting business if she was a whore, and even less suitable for a clandestine rendezvous with a lover.

Perhaps if someone had come upon Janet as she stood on the wharf waiting to end her life and spoken to her, she would still be alive.

Not wanting to startle the woman, for the stones were wet and slippery and a sudden movement might make her slip and fall, he moved cautiously toward her.

"Madam," he said, his voice low and gentle, "do you require assistance?"

She quickly turned around and thrust out her hand to ward him off. "Stop!"

She had nothing in her hands: no baby to abandon or drown like an unwanted kitten.

Suicide, then, like poor lost Janet.

"Leave me alone," she ordered.

She did not sound desperate, yet her imperious words and manner did not dissuade him. This could all be bravado, a show to make him go away so that she could finish what she had come here to do.

"Madam, I cannot." He took another step closer. "It is not safe for a woman to be alone in this part of the city, especially at night."

"I will be safe enough once you have gone about your business, whatever it may be in this part of London at night."

Although he could not see her face because of the shadow cast by the hood of her cloak, her voice belonged to a young woman of about twenty, he would guess, and well-to-do, if her accent and that fine cloak were anything to go by.

Spurned by a lover, perhaps.

He took another step forward. "You must allow me to escort you wherever you wish to go."

"Escort me?" she demanded skeptically. "How do I know you will not murder me? If this place is not safe, what are you doing here but mischief?"

"I give you my word that I will not hurt you. I am a solicitor, with chambers in the city."

"An attorney who does business in Bankside?"

"If my client is a poor honest widow who is being cheated out of her inheritance by her late husband's dishonest partner and can afford to live nowhere else, I do."

"So, if I believe you—and I assure you, sir, I am no babe in the woods to believe everything I hear—you are an honest man here on honest business. If so, I thank you for your chivalrous, if misplaced, concern, and now you may go on your way."

"I will not leave you here alone."

"Sir, I do not require any assistance," she repeated.

This time, he heard the slight quaver in her voice. Determined not to abandon her, he took another step forward.

"Stay back!" she cried, again holding up her hand.

Then she lost her footing on the slick stones. Her arms flailed as she tried to regain her balance, and in that instant, Rob darted forward. He grabbed her and pulled her back from the edge with so much force, she collided against his muscular chest with a dull thud.

"Good God, I nearly fell in," she panted, clutching his upper arms and steadying herself as she looked back over her shoulder into the dark water.

Rob's heartbeat thundered in his ears as he held her, acutely aware of the sensation of the voluptuous young woman in his arms. She smelled of roses and the fine fabric of her cloak slid softly under his hands.

And he could finally see her face beneath her hood.

Each dark eyebrow rose to a point in the center, as if she were some kind of questioning imp. Small, delectable little curls lay on her forehead, and longer curls bounced over ears bearing very fine earrings—an excellent night's take for a brigand. Half parted, her lips enticed him, and her skin . . . her skin looked even softer than her cloak.

A rendezvous with a lover now seemed the more likely explanation for her presence here, and given her pretty face and shapely form, he could envy her lover, as well as curse him for putting her in such danger.

As he held her, he wondered if a woman of her obvious social status had any real conception of the danger facing a lone woman in Bankside, or anywhere else, for that matter.

"You made me slip!" she charged, pushing him away. "Let go of me!"

He did at once. "I didn't mean to startle you."

"Go away!"

"Please, madam," he coaxed. "Forgive me if I frightened you. I mean only to help—and I will not leave you here alone. It is too dangerous. Your cloak alone makes you a target for a thief, and if so, a swift slitting of your throat could prove to be a blessing."

She raised her chin and regarded him with a mixture of defiance and incredulity. "Don't you think I know that? I am not a fool who has wandered here by accident."

"Then what are you doing by the river?"

"That, sir, is my own business. However, I assure you that I value my life as much as anyone." Her eyebrows drew together as she frowned. "Besides, if I had determined upon such a sinful course, throwing myself into that cesspool would not be the way I would choose."

So, she was not like Janet, who had drowned herself rather than come back to him.

She owed him no explanation for her presence here, and yet he felt disappointed when she did not offer one. However, it was still a dangerous place for a lone woman, for any reason. "If you would keep your life and your honor, you must not be in Bankside by yourself. You have already had one narrow escape tonight, and I do not mean falling into the river. There was a man watching you before I came upon you."

"What did he look like?" she demanded, looking around as if expecting the man to show himself. "Was he a gentleman?"

"I didn't see him clearly, but I am quite sure he was no gentleman. Were you here to meet one?"

She took a deep breath and fastened her steadfast gaze upon him. "No. I came here to get away from one."

"Then it is even more imperative that you allow me to escort you home."

"You misunderstand me, sir. I fled my home."

"What can await you there that . . . ?"

He suddenly realized what *could* be awaiting a vulnerable young woman in her own home. He moved closer to her, bending his head and speaking in the low, sympathetic whisper he had often used when Janet was upset, before she left him for another. "Are you mistreated there?"

She drew back. "Do you mean beaten? No."

Again, he spoke with gentle sympathy. "Or otherwise mistreated? By your father or brothers, perhaps?"

She gasped. "No!"

He sighed with relief. "Then I think you should return home. Whatever your troubles, they cannot be worth endangering your life."

She frowned and her brows lowered. "If I go home, I will be forced to marry a man I loathe."

"Is that all?"

"All? That is a great deal. And I assure you, running away from my home is no impetuous, childish act. I have tried and tried to convince my uncle that I cannot and will not marry the man he wants me to, but he will not listen. I have reasoned, cajoled, pleaded and finally begged him to listen to me, all to no avail."

He heard her sincerity, and her determination, and beneath that, the thing that touched his heart: fear, and the vulnerability that accompanied it. Despite that fear, however, she was so desperate for her freedom, she would risk danger to achieve it.

She was not a fool. She was brave, as brave a woman as he had ever met.

He would do his best to encourage her to return home, because there was another way out of her dilemma that he could offer her. "As a solicitor, I know many things about marriage law and property settlements—and how to avoid them. I would be glad to offer you my legal advice."

Her beautiful eyes widened.

A door banged loudly close by, and she jumped, then shivered.

"Come with me out of the chill night air," he offered. "There is a tavern nearby where we can talk."

She regarded him steadily for what seemed a long moment, with a measuring gaze that reminded him of another person's scrutiny many years ago.

Then she nodded. "If you can offer me a way out of my predicament, sir, I am willing to listen."

More pleased than he had been in many a day,

Robert Harding held out his arm to escort this unknown, brave and desperate woman away from the black water of the river.

As Vivienne Burroughs allowed the stranger to lead her through the dark and foggy streets, her whole body trembled with suppressed fear. Her bravado had been an act, a desperate attempt to make a stranger leave her alone so that she could escape from her uncle, her unwelcome suitor and even London itself.

Surprisingly, he had been most determined to offer his assistance and protection, whether she wanted it or not. Even more surprisingly, she was willing to accept it.

From the first, his deep, kind voice and obvious concern had lessened her terror, and then he had saved her from falling into the Thames. If he had not pulled her back from the brink, she would have drowned for certain. She was wearing several layers of clothing—not wishing to have to carry any obvious baggage—and her wet clothing would have dragged her beneath the water as if she were weighted with stones.

She well remembered the taunt bulge of muscle in his arm as she had held on to him. He could have forced her into a dark alley and she would have been powerless to fight him off.

Therefore, she reasoned, he was either a truly chivalrous gentleman . . . or he had his own reasons for luring her away from the river.

She stole another glance at her silent companion, wondering if she should put her faith in a man she had never met before. Perhaps she should run away from him, too.

But what if he really was a solicitor and there was a way to avoid marriage to Sir Philip Martlebury that didn't involve having to flee her home and be at the mercy of a world that had little use for women on their own?

They came to a brighter thoroughfare. Lanterns, hung outside the houses and shops by order of law, illuminated her companion's face. His dark hair was brushed back from a wide, intelligent forehead. His nose was straight, his jaw strong, and his cheekbones prominent enough to cast a slight shadow. Despite the lean and angular nature of his features, his lips were full and remarkably sensual, as if there were a passionate portion in the man beside her. He was also younger than she had thought. She would put his age at about thirty.

She scrutinized his clothing. Living with her uncle, a silk merchant, all these years, she had learned much about fabric. This man's jacket and breeches were made of coarse, dark wool. His linen, while apparently clean, was very plain. He may be a solicitor, but he was certainly not well-to-do.

Nor did he sound like any gentleman she knew. Of course, he might have been raised in the country, where there were any number of dialects.

"Here is the tavern," her escort said as they reached a building with a sign above its entrance, rocking in the slight breeze off the river, declaring it to be the Bull and Crown.

She hesitated.

"What is it?" he asked, regarding her with his mysterious dark eyes, so hidden beneath black brows, she assumed more than knew that they existed.

"I have never been in a tavern before." *And what if this is just a ruse, and once I am inside . . . ?*

"Ah. If you would rather not go in—"

"As you said, Bankside is a dangerous place. Perhaps I am wrong to trust you."

"Perhaps," he calmly agreed. He slowly crossed his arms. "If you leave me here, what will you do?"

"What I was going to do before—leave London."

"How? By stealing a boat?"

She didn't answer.

"If that is what you intended to do, I may have saved your life in more ways than one. Have you any idea what would happen to you if you were caught stealing?"

"I would be arrested," she replied, trying to sound matter-of-fact, even though that possible fate terrified her. She had never been inside a prison, but she had heard about them, and it was enough to turn one's stomach.

"You would be taken to a prison little better than your idea of hell and, if convicted, branded, transported or perhaps even hung. And what of the boat you stole? It might be some poor man's only means of earning a living."

"I had not considered that," she confessed.

"I thought not."

She did not need him to criticize her, too. Her uncle did that quite enough. "Then what am I to do? Marry a man I hate? I would really rather die—or try to fend for myself."

"It is an easy thing to say one would prefer death to a less-than-ideal fate, yet I think you would answer differently if it truly came to that." He lowered his voice, and a quiet calm infused his tone as he gazed into her face. "At least, I hope you would. A comfortable life is not something to be thrown away. And your family is not something you should abandon without better cause."

"My uncle will abandon me if I continue to oppose his plans. He will surely cast me out of his house into the street with nothing but the clothes on my back."

"Then why run away?"

"Because this way, I can . . ."

She fell silent. She had more than a few clothes on her back, and all her pin money and jewelry hidden upon her, too. "Have you ever been forced to do something you hated," she asked, "something that seemed against your very nature?"

He nodded slowly, and a strange, world-weary expression flitted across his features as he regarded her with his dark, intense and inscrutable eyes. "Many times."

Before she could speak, he went on. "I am not ignorant of desperate situations, mistress. Please allow me to give you my professional advice. You will be safe with me, I promise you."

Could she trust him?

How could she be sure he was even a lawyer at all?

In the end, all Vivienne could do was rely on her instincts. "Very well, sir, I will hear your advice."

Chapter 2

⌒◡◠◡⌒

As she entered the tavern, Vivienne's eyes stung from the sudden assault of smoke. She blinked and squinted as she tried to distinguish the shapes barely illuminated by cheap candles. Some were men sitting at tables, hunched over their drinks. Dogs wandered about, sniffing and snuffling along the floor. One or two people moved swiftly; by their curved bodies she guessed they were serving wenches.

"This way," her companion muttered, taking her hand and leading her through the maze of benches, scarred wooden tables and drunken patrons.

She could see better now, yet wished she couldn't at the sight of the filthy, curious or leer-ing faces. They made Sir Philip's lustful looks seem the height of propriety.

Her companion ignored them all as he made his way through this place as if he were the king of it, or as if he were oblivious to anything but the object of his quest, the empty table at the far end of the room.

When they reached it, he gestured for her to sit on the rough wooden bench nearest the wall. "This is as much privacy as a tavern such as this safely affords," he said.

He waited until she had settled herself before sitting opposite her. Although she could see the rest of his face better now, the single candle burning feebly in its holder on the table did not do much to light his dark eyes.

"What is your name?" she asked.

"If I am to give you legal advice though I am not in your pay, I think it would be best if I do so anonymously," he said, sounding very businesslike—or like an attorney, she supposed. "Nor should you tell me your name, or that of any of the parties involved."

A serving wench appeared at the man's elbow. She ran a curious gaze over Vivienne, then grinned. "Been a long time, my buck."

Vivienne stiffened.

"The courts not keepin' you busy enough?"

She breathed again.

"He's somethin', ain't he?" the woman continued, grinning at Vivienne. "Brains in that handsome head o' his and shoulders on him, eh? Not too many solicitors from this part o' the city, but he done it."

"Polly," the solicitor said evenly, turning to look at her and giving Vivienne a better view of his remarkably fine profile, "this is business. Wine, if you please. Your finest—and not watered down," he added.

"Nothin' but the best for you, o' course!" the wench said. She laughed and displayed black teeth as she winked at the lawyer. "She's a beauty, I must say. And business, is it? I'll wager it is! There's a room upstairs for your business, if you like."

Vivienne flushed hotly. "I am not a harlot!"

"No?" the woman replied with a hint of amusement. She addressed the man. "Jack said you give that up, but I didn't believe him. Guess he was right, after all."

"Polly, just fetch the wine," the man replied in a low voice.

"Aye, I will," she replied, still chuckling as she sauntered away, hips swaying.

"She is a friend of yours?" Vivienne inquired coldly, all the heat of shame at being thought a harlot gone as she wondered what kind of man was sitting across from her.

His brows contracted and suddenly he reminded her of a painting of the god Mars she had seen once.

Dread again threaded down her spine and she searched through the smoke for the door. She wished she had not taken him up on his offer, even if he really was an attorney.

She splayed her hands on the table and began to rise. "I think I have made a mistake—"

He covered her right hand with his. "Lawyers are not born lawyers," he said softly, his sincere gaze searching her face. "I know Polly because I grew up not far from here."

"Yet you would have me believe you are a solicitor? How do I know you are not in league with that woman, that this is not some ruse?"

"To what avail?"

"To rob me, or worse. First you gain my confidence, then you bring me to your lair and—"

To her astonishment, he laughed, a low, deep sound that seemed sad, somehow, too. "My lair? I assure you, madam, the only lair I possess are chambers near Chancery Lane." He sobered, and regarded her with more respect than ever Uncle Elias or Sir Philip had. "I see I was quite wrong to think you were foolishly naive."

"I told you, I am not a fool."

"Just desperate."

Vivienne sat down. "Yes."

The serving wench returned with the wine. As she set down two pewter mugs, she gave Vivienne a warm smile. "Whatever you're up to, take care of him, won't you, m'dear? He's a good friend to me and mine. Sees to all the legal troubles for lots of folks'd be taken advantage of otherwise."

Vivienne didn't respond as her companion paid for the wine. "Thank you, Polly."

Mercifully, an impatient customer shouted drunkenly for more ale, causing the woman to hurry away.

"What did she mean?"

"She means, I often give advice. Now, about your problem," he replied, once more the cool, efficient advisor. "When is the wedding to be?"

"The arrangements have not reached that stage yet."

One of his eyebrows rose questioningly.

"But they will," she affirmed. "My suitor," she said, her tone sarcastic in the extreme, "has apparently made his intentions clear."

"Apparently?"

"To my uncle, not to me. Indeed, they both act as if I have nothing to do with the marriage at all, except to be there in body."

"Your uncle is your legal guardian?"

She nodded. "My parents died five years ago. I came to live with my uncle then."

"It could be that your uncle and your suitor consider the business side of a marriage not of interest to a young woman."

"It is not the 'business side of a marriage,' as you call it, that I object to." Vivienne leaned forward, more into the light, trying to see him better. To see his eyes. "It's the groom. I don't love him, and he doesn't love me. He doesn't even like me, except that he would like me in his bed."

The very notion of making love with Philip made Vivienne shiver with disgust. She couldn't even imagine kissing him on the lips.

Kissing *this* man, however . . . suddenly it was very easy to imagine pressing her lips to his, their breath mingling, his powerful arms tightening about her . . .

She forced that image out of her mind. "Unfortunately, my uncle sees marriage only as a business proposition. I am the object to be sold, and my suitor has the appropriate payment."

"What is the payment?"

"A title." Vivienne wrapped her hand around the cold pewter mug. "The man my uncle wants me to marry is a nobleman."

The lawyer's eyebrows rose and she could finally see that his eyes were as brown as his hair. "You are not titled?"

"No, I am not," she replied, a little flattered by his surprise. "Nor is my uncle, or any of my family."

"You do not want a titled husband?"

She sighed with exasperation. "If I loved him, a title would be a charming addition. However, I do not love him, so if he were the king himself, I would not want to marry him."

"That is a very unusual attitude."

"Perhaps, but it is mine. My uncle doesn't care at all about my happiness. You see, if we wed, my uncle gets a title in the family and an introduction to the court, which he can use to his advantage in business. He does not think of me at all."

"Is the bridegroom ignorant of your true feelings?"

"Even if he were the greatest dolt in England, he could not be. I have given him no encouragement at all. Unfortunately, my uncle is well-to-do, and the groom, for all his breeding, is not overly wealthy. I will be my proposed spouse's way to regain a squandered fortune."

"Did *he* squander it?"

"No. Not even a title would overcome that deficiency in my uncle's eyes. My suitor plays the much-put-upon heir to perfection."

"Are there other objections?"

She ran her finger around the rough edge of the mug, then raised her eyes to look at her companion. "Need there be more? My parents loved each other and they were very happy. I want to marry for love, too, not gain or social position."

"I gather your uncle does not consider your reason sufficient impediment?"

"No. He will not listen to me at all."

The solicitor leaned back and regarded her thoughtfully. "Then what you need to do is change *his* mind about your suitor. Search out those things most likely to upset your uncle, not you. Debts your suitor has kept secret, for example, or liabilities he has not spoken of."

At once Vivienne saw the wisdom of his advice and realized she had been trying to discourage her uncle in the wrong way.

He was a man of business, and it was business, not emotion, that he understood best.

"Or . . ." the lawyer began. Then he hesitated.

"Or?" she queried, wondering what else he could suggest.

He shifted forward, bringing more of his face into the candlelight.

She had never seen lips like his, full and yet with no hint of softness about them. They were undeniably masculine. Virile. And incredibly alluring, so tempting she could scarcely attend to his next words, which were spoken softly, in a low, confidential whisper. "Has your would-be groom ever behaved improperly toward you?"

"Only by persisting in his suit."

"He has not tried to seduce you?"

If Philip had used that tone of voice, and looked at her with such intense, dark eyes, and possessed such lips, she might have been tempted.

"Forgive the personal nature of my questions, but has he ever done so?" her companion repeated.

Vivienne forced herself to concentrate and answer him. "Thankfully, no."

He looked relieved a moment, before his face assumed its usual serious demeanor. "Is there nothing else you can say against him? Does he gamble? Drink to excess? Wench?"

She shook her head. "I have heard nothing of any indulgence in serious vices."

"Then I must say you have very little with which to condemn him as unworthy."

"I will not marry without love," she reiterated.

"And obviously, you are so adamant about this, you will risk your life."

"Yes."

He took a sip of wine, then very slowly and deliberately set down his mug and raised his eyes to regard her steadily. "Then my advice is, go home."

"But—"

"Allow me to finish," he commanded, and in such a tone, she did. "Return to your home and find ways to delay the proceedings."

"Delay?"

"Yes, and while you do, try to find out all you can about the proposed groom."

"I don't want to know more about him," she murmured, realizing she would much rather know more about the man facing her.

"It is your best chance. Every man has something to hide."

"Even you?" she blurted.

"We are not discussing me."

She flushed hotly. "I'm sorry. How am I to discover such things?"

He immediately continued as if she had not made her impetuous remark. "There is always gossip," he said, and she thought his jaw clenched a bit. "You must find something to make the groom less appealing to your uncle."

"Yes, I understand."

"If things progress to the point of discussing a marriage settlement, there can be many questions and items to dispute during the negotiation of that legal document that will provide extra time for your investigation, as well."

"I understand," she said, nodding. Then she frowned. "I am ignorant of the law. How would I know what to query?"

"Query everything and anything. Ask all the questions you can possibly think of. If I guess aright, at least a few will give your uncle pause. He may begin to ask other questions, or doubt some of the language of the contract. I assume he will want it all to his advantage, or as much as possible."

"He will." She toyed with her mug. "He may tell me such things are none of my concern."

"He may not if he is pleased by your interest."

"I can try," she conceded.

He looked around the tavern, and Vivienne

realized it wasn't as crowded as before. "The hour grows late," he observed. "You must go home, and you must not think of running away again. Although now you think your family is being most unreasonable and even cruel, I'm sure they would be very distressed if anything were to happen to you."

"I am not so certain."

He reached out and cupped her chin in his long, lean fingers. His dark eyes seemed to be full of sorrow, a sadness that made her own heart ache, although she could not say why. "Trust me, they would."

He let go of her, and got to his feet.

This place stank worse than a abattoir, but she didn't want to leave. Not yet.

"Have you ever participated in plans for a marriage where a woman was obviously not willing?" she asked, making no move to go. "Or the groom?"

"No, although I have seen many where affection appeared to play little part in the planning."

"To be in such a marriage must be a miserable existence."

He held out his hand, obviously expecting her to take it, and stand. "They seem able to cope."

"Yes, by taking lovers or gambling or drowning in drink," she said, still delaying. "As I said, I do not wish to live that way. I want to have the kind of marriage my parents had, a marriage based on love."

"They were fortunate."

"And your parents?"

"I never knew them," he said coldly.

He was shutting her out. For whatever reason, he had decided the conversation was concluded.

Reluctantly, she placed her gloved hand in his bare one and rose, noting the stains of ink on his right hand. Could he not even afford a clerk? she wondered as she reluctantly let him lead her from the tavern.

"We are in luck," he observed as a hackney coach lumbered toward them.

She did not think so. She would think herself lucky if they had to walk back to her uncle's house together.

He raised his hand and the hackney rolled to a stop beside them. As it did, he reached into his jacket and pulled out his purse.

"There is no need for you to pay for the coach," she said. "I have money."

"I cannot allow that."

"I thank you for your generosity, sir, but truly, I would be ashamed to be any more indebted to you."

"You owe me nothing."

"I owe you a possible path out of my predicament."

"I will pay for the coach," he said as coldly as if they had not just spoken for all that time in the tavern. As if he had not come to her aid. As if he had not tried to save her life, whether from a watery grave or an abhorrent marriage.

"May I truly not know who has been so kind and generous to me, and given me such sage advice?" she asked softly.

"No."

"There must be a way I can thank you."

"Your words are enough."

"I think not."

"I am glad I could be of service to a woman in distress."

He smiled, and she realized just how handsome he was, as handsome as any man she had ever seen.

And he was certainly kinder than most.

"The coachman is waiting," he whispered.

"Yes," she murmured, her heart thrumming with an emotion she had never felt before.

She didn't move. She wanted to express her gratitude, and mere words seemed pale and insufficient.

With a different sense of desperation, she suddenly pulled him close and kissed him.

Not on the cheeks, as anyone might do in parting, but full on the lips, leaning into him. Passion and desire flared within her at the touch of his lips on hers. The sensation reached into her body and demanded more—more fervent excitement, more passion, more communion.

She had never kissed before, nor had she ever

imagined that the melding of mouth to mouth could be so intoxicating.

His embrace tightened about her and his mouth moved over hers with equal passion. Insistent need exploded within her when his tongue pushed against her lips. She eagerly parted them and let him enter, as willing and full of fire as he.

Sweet heaven, she didn't want to stop kissing him. She only wanted more.

He held her so close, she could hear his heart beating—or was that her own?

" 'Ere, enough o' that. Are you going to get in or not?" the coachman grumbled.

The lawyer abruptly stopped kissing her and stepped back.

She almost moaned with dismay.

"She will tell you where you are to take her," he said.

He sounded so calm, while her heart hammered and her blood throbbed and every sense seemed more alive. Then she saw that his face was flushed.

He pressed his purse into her hand. "That should be enough," he murmured. "Farewell, and Godspeed."

With that, he turned on his heel and disappeared into the fog like some sort of phantom.

She might have doubted he had existed at all, except that she could still feel his hot kiss on her swollen lips.

She had behaved like an utter wanton, kissing him like that. She should be ashamed of herself, and sorry.

But she was not.

She only regretted that she did not know his name or have any idea how she could meet him again.

Chapter 3

Seated at his desk, Rob rubbed his eyes, then tried to concentrate once more on the document before him. He hadn't had a decent night's sleep in a week, ever since that night in Bankside.

Against his will, his mind's eye conjured a pretty, smiling face and beautiful blue eyes. Blue like the sky if one were out of the city, with its coal-smoke-tarnished air. Blue like the velvet coat King Charles had sported as he rode past Robert's office a few days ago.

He assumed she had arrived home safely and had sufficient money to pay the coachman. He had given her all that he had, but it was not much.

Perhaps he should have gone in the coach with her, told her his name, asked her what hers

29

was, found out where she lived—but surely that would have been unwise. Judging by her garments and accent, she was far above him. What could he ever hope to offer a woman like her? Chambers he owed back rent on, and not even in Chancery Lane like other solicitors. A bevy of poor clients who were very grateful, but could not afford to give much cash for his services. The few secondhand furnishings he owned, some well-tended clothes.

And his reputation—the good and the bad.

No, he could never be anything more to her than a nameless solicitor who gave her some advice.

Yet every time he spared a moment from his work since he had met her, or when he tried to sleep, he had seen the unknown beauty's face, and even more vividly remembered her kiss.

He had never known such a kiss, full of vibrant ardor and desire. His surprise at her unforeseen act had immediately given way to a thrill of delight and growing excitement.

How wonderful her lips had felt against his own, and how astonishing her passion. To think a woman like her, in a fine soft cloak, by her voice well born and well bred, who could surely have her pick of men—provided they met her uncle's approval—*she* had kissed him.

To be sure, he had been kissed before, especially by his lost, beloved Janet, until she had the chance to be a rich man's mistress and to leave behind their wretched poverty for something better.

Sadly for Janet, her opportunity had only led to her miserable death.

At times in the tavern, with her head demurely lowered and her dusky lashes fanning her rosy cheeks, the young woman had reminded him of his sweet and gentle Janet.

At other times, she most definitely did not. She met his gaze straight on, her full lips pressed together, her very attitude one of purpose and determination.

Perhaps that was another reason she haunted his dreams, where she was always waiting for him. She stood in a luxurious bedchamber, a large room lit by several candles, the bed wide and covered in pristine linens.

She wore a simple white garment, like an angel, her hair loose about her shoulders, and her eyes shone with welcome. Then she smiled and came toward him slowly, until she was close enough for him to take in his arms.

How he kissed her then! The scent of roses lingered about her, growing stronger and stronger as their kiss deepened. With impatient desire he picked her up and carried her to the bed.

Light in his arms, she laid her head against his chest as if she knew he would always protect her and never, ever abandon her.

Not like Janet.

With a sigh, he once more forced himself to

study the contract before him. He could not help Janet anymore. Nor could he help the unknown beauty.

But he could help Mistress Dimdoor. She had been abandoned by her husband, who had sailed to the New World. One of the husband's former associates claimed that he had also left a sizable debt unpaid, and he was suing Mistress Dimdoor to recover it. It was not difficult to see why Mistress Dimdoor was in difficulties. The promissory note before him held more prevaricating language than he had yet encountered in his career.

Fortunately for her, the signature of the creditor at the bottom was clear enough, indicating that the debt and all the interest had been paid in full. At least her husband had not abandoned his debts along with her when he had sailed.

Sighing again, Rob leaned back in his chair, the wood hard against his shoulders. Would that everything in his life could be so easily concluded and he could forget the past.

The singular smell of goose grease made him open his eyes.

Bertie Dillsworth's deferential face appeared around the door, his hair sticking up as it always did, despite the goose grease he insisted upon using in his vain attempts to get it to lie flat. "There's a man here, Rob—Mr. Harding," he sheepishly corrected, remembering that Rob had instructed him to use a formal address when there were clients to hear, "and if you please—"

"Of course he pleases," a languid, upper-class voice drawled. "I'faith, man, I'm bringing him some business, so he better damn well please. And what in the name of St. David is that stench?"

Bertie's head disappeared abruptly and the door flew open, revealing Bertie staggering back as if he had been shoved while another man, the very picture of a well-dressed, well-fed, well-wined courtier, sauntered into Robert's office, regardless of the other people waiting to see him in the anteroom.

As Rob rose, the man looked around, his expression one of mild disgust, before his blood-shot gaze settled on Rob. "You are Heartless Harding, I presume?" he asked in that same languid voice, as if speaking were really too, too much trouble.

Or perhaps it was only so when he was addressing his social inferiors.

A vein in Robert's forehead started to throb; otherwise, he gave no outward sign that he was even slightly disturbed by the fellow's haughty attitude. "I am Robert Harding. Dillsworth, please ask Mistress Dimdoor if she would mind waiting a moment."

The arrogant stranger looked at Rob as if he had uttered blasphemy, while Bertie quietly spoke to the middle-aged seamstress waiting on a bench. She looked at Rob and nodded her head, eliciting a rare smile from him that made her flush to the roots of her hair.

"Since Mistress Dimdoor is so good as to accommodate you, please sit down," Rob said.

"You *are* the chap who arranges such wondrous contracts and settlements and wills," the fashionable fellow replied. "Ironclad and faultless, so I've been told."

"So some people claim. I do my best."

"Of course you do. Your servant." The man swept the broad-brimmed, plumed hat from his head, which sported one of the more extreme style of wigs currently in fashion among the court. The dark curls extended well past his shoulder, over his embroidered scarlet velvet jacket.

Rob wondered what color his hair really was, for he suspected the black was a compliment to the king's own fulsome—and natural—locks.

"Your servant, sir," Rob automatically replied.

The man's superior smile seemed to indicate that he took that social pleasantry for truth before he sat in the chair opposite Rob's desk.

"Dillsworth, be so good as to close the door," Rob said, glancing at his inquisitive clerk and incidentally all the rest of his clients, who were listening with unabashed interest.

The man opposite him twisted slightly in his chair and watched as Bertie obeyed, giving Rob another chance to scrutinize him.

He had a long thin face with a slender, aquiline nose, a thin upper lip above a fuller lower one, and narrow eyes overshadowed by brows that Rob guessed had been dyed to match his wig, for the shade was unnaturally dull. His complexion also seemed unnaturally pale, as if he rarely saw the sun. He sported small patches of black taffeta cut in the shapes of diamonds and circles on his chin and cheek. Judging by the red skin at the edge of the one on his chin, they were there both because they were fashionable and to hide blemishes.

As for his clothes, they were not quite so fine upon closer examination. The embroidery had obviously been mended and his gauntlet gloves and hat were far from new, although Rob thought the plume had recently been replaced.

So, he was not as wealthy as he would like people to believe. That was unfortunate.

After Bertie closed the door, the man turned back to Rob. "I am Sir Philip Martlebury," he announced, by his air suggesting that Rob must have heard of him.

He had not. Still, a nobleman was a nobleman, and he might know yet more noblemen in need of a good solicitor. "How may I help you?"

"I am about to become engaged to the niece of a canny old buzzard and want you to negotiate the marriage settlement for me."

As Sir Philip steepled his fingers and smiled with smug satisfaction, Rob commanded himself to betray nothing.

Not surprise. Not dismay. Not envy.

After all, there was nothing—nothing at all—to indicate that this had anything to do with the young woman he had met in Bankside. No doubt there were many young women in London who were in a similar situation.

"You say nothing, Mr. Harding."

"I am taken aback, Sir Philip," he replied, trusting that the man before him would apply his own flattering interpretation to that remark.

Judging by Sir Philip's widening smile, he did. "I gather you don't get many men of my station coming to you on such errands. Still, I hear you are the best, and if you *are* the best, I certainly shall not be the last. I have several influential friends at court."

"May I ask, Sir Philip, how you came to hear of me?"

"The whole court was buzzing about how you outsmarted that playwright when he married the rich widow."

At the recollection of the marriage settlement between Sir Richard Blythe and Elissa Longbourne, Rob's lips twitched. He had indeed drafted a very one-sided document which the groom had signed without reading. Despite his amusement, he kept his voice carefully level when he replied. "I understand they are very happily married."

Sir Philip had one of the most disgustingly evil chuckles it had ever been Robert's misfortune to hear, and he had heard several evil chuckles. "He's happy bedding her, no doubt, as I will be when I take my bride."

It was all Rob could do to keep his lips from curling with scorn. Rob had known men who lived in filth and poverty who would never speak of a woman with such disrespect.

Rob wanted to tell him to get out, but Sir Philip's next pronouncement made him hold his tongue.

"There will be a fine fee in it for you, of course, for it will likely take several hours of work. Her uncle is the kind to haggle for days over something. Still, if all turns out as I plan, there will be a premium in it for you. I wouldn't be surprised if you earned over fifty pounds."

Fifty pounds. That was nearly as much as Rob had made in the whole of the previous year. He needed the money this man was offering, and he would surely benefit from a pleased nobleman's reference.

As for his personal aversion to the man, he had searched through the stinking muck of the Thames to earn his bread once; surely he could put up with Sir Philip.

It would be even more ridiculous to turn him

down on the remote possibility that the man was going to marry a woman Rob had only met once, if memorably. "I accept your offer."

"Excellent!" The nobleman reached into his jacket and pulled out a white piece of cloth, which he sniffed delicately. The scent of a heavy, flowery perfume made Rob want to cough.

"I shall, of course, require a portion of the fee today," he said.

Sir Philip frowned. "How much of a portion?"

"Generally, I ask for a sovereign upon commencing."

Sir Philip snorted most inelegantly. "Gad, man, is that all? I thought you were going to ask for half!"

"Then obviously you will have no trouble providing the sovereign. My clerk will be happy to take it."

Sir Philip reached into his jacket and pulled out a rather tattered purse. He fished around for a moment, then tossed a gold coin on the desk. "There you are, my man."

"I said you may give to my clerk," Rob reiterated, making no move to touch it.

With a sour frown, the nobleman's hand darted out and he took it back again. He rubbed it between his fingers.

"Perhaps we should celebrate your good fortune with a drink?" he proposed, his gaze surreptitiously scanning the room, no doubt for a bottle or decanter.

The need for a drink might also explain his nervous twisting and turning of the coin.

"I think not."

Sir Philip reared back in astonishment. "Gad, are you a Puritan?"

"No. However, I keep no wine or spirits in my office, and I have no time to visit a tavern today." Rob gestured at the document still on his desk.

"Oh, I see," Sir Philip grudgingly replied. "I have a meeting with my bride's uncle, Elias Burroughs, tomorrow afternoon. Sup with me at noon and we can discuss the terms to offer. We'll go to see him afterward."

"Very well," Rob agreed, rising.

Sir Philip likewise got up. "I live in the Strand, Martlebury House." He chuckled his nasty chuckle. "I can hardly wait to see Burroughs's fat face when he finds out I have Heartless Harding in my purse."

Holding his hands stiff at his side, his fingers slowly curving into fists, Rob made a small bow and watched as the nobleman sauntered out the door as if he owned all of London and a good portion of England besides.

"Bloody jackanapes," Rob muttered under his breath as he returned to his desk and once again silently vowed to forget a beautiful young woman with lively blue eyes and passion in her kiss who refused to marry to a man she did not love.

Chapter 4

"**S**o there I was, my dear, absolutely bank- rupt and not a farthing to my name and Edmond glaring at me in the worst way," Lettice Jerningham said as she put another French bon- bon in her bow-shaped mouth and giggled. " 'But Edmond,' I said, 'I thought I was going to win!' I mean, really, Vivienne, what else did he think I was betting for?"

Vivienne nodded absently as she sat beside Lettice in the Jerninghams' drawing room and watched Lettice consume a plateful of sugar- covered confections.

Lettice Jerningham was the daughter of one of Uncle Elias's business associates. She had married a minor courtier, of nearly the same age as Uncle Elias, and been presented at court last year. She rarely mentioned her much older husband, preferring to talk about the court and especially the king.

She also apparently found some compensation in eating bonbons while petting her spaniel, Lord Bobbles, whom she had purchased in imitation of King Charles, who was known to adore his dogs.

Normally, Vivienne avoided Lettice as much as she could. Unfortunately, she had not been able to find out much at all about Philip in the past week, and so had come to Lettice as a last resort. Even more unfortunately, although she had come to visit Lettice for the sole purpose of asking about Sir Philip, the very notion of giving the loquacious Lettice even a hint of Sir Philip's intentions was so distasteful, she hadn't yet been able to mention him.

Nevertheless, the mysterious solicitor had been right—she had been going about dissuading her uncle from making the match the wrong way. She had been trying to force him to see things her way, something that was utterly impossible. Instead, she must discover things about Philip her uncle would find objectionable. Ever since she had returned home on the night she'd tried to run away and climbed back into her room, she had thought of little but the solicitor and his advice. He even haunted her dreams.

In those dreams, she was always running down a dark and foggy street. At first she was frightened, sure she was being chased. She would see the handsome solicitor standing in a blaze of light and her fear would disappear. She ran into his arms, feeling cherished and safe.

Then they were magically in her bedchamber. In her bed. Naked. Together.

He would caress her body and kiss her with his marvelous lips, and she would touch him, feel his flesh hot against her hands—

"Would you like some wine, Vivienne? It *is* a trifle warm in here," Lettice said, yanking Vivienne from her reverie.

"No, thank you," she replied, commanding herself to remember why she was here, and to forget her dreams.

Vivienne made a small, companionable smile and shifted away from Lettice and Lord Bobbles, who was shedding all over her skirt. Uncle Elias would not be pleased if she returned home with her pale pink gown covered in black hairs. "I thought your husband didn't approve of gambling."

"But everybody gambles! The king gambles," Lettice declared with a shake of her blond head that set her ringlets bouncing, as if that decided the matter.

"The king does many things many people do not approve of."

In the act of lifting another confection to her lips, Lettice halted and stared at Vivienne. "You sound just like one of those horrid old Puritans!" She giggled again. "And your expression is just like one of the queen's ladies-in-waiting."

"I have heard they don't approve of the English court."

"I should say they don't," Lettice agreed with disdain as she popped the confection in her mouth and spoke while delicately chewing. "They refuse to learn even a word of English, they wear nothing but black and their expressions are so sour and their gowns so old-fashioned, they look like effigies. They should all be lying on a tomb somewhere. Indeed, I always have to assure myself they're actually breathing! And they are so very proper, it's . . . well, it's ludicrous. They say they won't sleep in any bed a man has *ever* been in."

"Given what I have heard of the court, they must had had to order several new beds."

Vivienne immediately wished she hadn't mentioned beds, because beds made her think of her dreams, and the lawyer's hands, and his lips, and their passion. . . .

Lettice giggled her agreement and brushed a bit of sugar from the lace around the curved neckline of her satin bodice. "That is a very pretty gown."

Vivienne was glad of the change of subject. "Do you like the color? It is one of my uncle's new dyes."

"No lace?"

"You know he does not deal in lace, so I never wear it, Lettice."

"You should be glad he sells such lovely silk and ribbons, though," Lettice noted. She examined the silk damask and nodded her approval. "Very pretty. Lady Horrace was wearing something rather similar in court."

"Have you been to court recently?"

Lettice preened a little as she put the last bonbon into her mouth. "Just last week, for a masque. It was very exciting. And oh, how handsome the king looked! I swear to you, Vivienne, he is the finest-looking man in the kingdom."

Vivienne had serious doubts about that, unless the king resembled a certain solicitor of her acquaintance.

"To see King Charles dance! And his legs, my dear." She leaned forward again. "His legs are really quite muscular."

Vivienne wondered about her solicitor's legs. In her imagination, they were as muscular as the rest of him.

"There's no need to blush, my dear. I assure you, we were all properly attired, some more than others, though," she finished with another giggle. She lifted her dog and rubbed his nose against hers. "Isn't that so, Lord Bobbles? Didn't your mama have on a very lovely dress?"

That was it. Embarrassment or no embarrassment, Vivienne couldn't stand this much longer.

"Lettice, what do you know about Sir Philip Martlebury?"

Lord Bobbles fell back to his mistress's lap with such unexpected swiftness, he yipped.

Lettice moved forward and smiled broadly. "I was wondering if you were ever going to mention that," she said, stroking Lord Bobbles's head.

Vivienne didn't hide her surprise. "You have heard that he wishes to marry me?"

"He talks about you quite often. He thinks you're very beautiful, you know. He is very eager to make you his wife."

And get the dowry, no doubt, Vivienne thought with a sigh.

Lettice eyed Vivienne. "I should think you would be delighted. He's a good-looking fellow and a nobieman, too."

"I am suspicious of his attention," she answered with cautious truth. "After all, what have I to offer him?"

"Oh, you mustn't underestimate the power of beauty, my dear," Lettice said with a companionable smile.

Lettice herself was quite pretty in a florid sort of way. Nobody would ever overlook her in a room full of women. "He brags of you, you know. Well, not to me, but to other men, or so I've heard. You're going to be a very lucky woman. To be sure, he's not the king, but then the king is already married," she finished with yet another giggle.

The fact that Charles was married probably wouldn't bother Lettice if the king invited her to his bed.

"Yes, Philip is a good-looking man," Vivienne agreed. *For an overdressed courtier.* "That is partly what troubles me. Have you heard . . . do you know . . . does he have a mistress?"

Lettice smiled with genuine kindness and stroked Vivienne's hand as she had her dog's head. "Not recently."

"Who was she?"

"Oh, I forget. But it was over weeks ago. He has been quite the footloose fellow since."

Obviously, she wasn't going to get more out of Lettice on that subject, and it wasn't one likely to dissuade her uncle anyway. Money was Uncle Elias's Achilles' heel. "I know everybody gambles. Does he, too?" Vivienne asked, practically gritting her teeth as Lettice continued stroking her hand.

"Not overmuch. Indeed, I have seen him leave the table while he was still winning, which, I assure you, is something I would never do. Why, just the other night I said to Lady Rowhampton, 'I shall likely have to pawn my jewels one day,' and she said—"

"Lettice?"

"Yes?"

"Are you very familiar with solicitors?"

Lettice regarded her as if she had suddenly sprouted an extra nose. "Solicitors? Whatever would I have to do with one of them?"

"They, um, they prepare marriage settlements, do they not?"

"Oh, of course!"

"Have you ever met any?"

Lettice gave her a knowing smile. "Need one, do you?"

"Not yet, but perhaps soon," she prevaricated.

"Well, my dear, you must try to engage the one they call Heartless Harding. He's quite the marvel when it comes to property law. His marriage settlements are legendary. Well, one, anyway, for that playwright fellow, and what a rogue he was, if half the stories are true, and I daresay they are."

"Why do they call him 'heartless'?"

"Because he doesn't appear to possess one. Nothing but a legal brain, or so people say who've met him."

Vivienne thought of the man she had kissed. He had been kind and sympathetic and so much more; there could be no doubt he had a heart. Indeed, she had felt it beating when he held her in his arms. "Do you know of any others?"

"I don't even know him, except by reputation," Lettice said, obviously affronted by the notion that she would consort with mere solicitors, who were, after all, not barristers. "My dear papa oversaw my settlement," she continued, "and I am glad he did. I would have been bored beyond belief with all that legal talk."

Deciding she had spent quite enough time being bored herself, and without learning anything helpful about Sir Philip, Vivienne rose. "Oh, dear! I just realized how long I have been here."

That wasn't exactly a lie. Every minute had seemed an hour. "I had best be on my way."

"There is no need to rush off," Lettice protested. "I have yet to tell you what dear Lady Rowhampton said. It is so very droll!"

"I'm sorry, Lettice, but I really must leave."

Vivienne hurried to the door, wishing she had spent an hour on the rack instead of coming to visit Lettice.

As it was, she had endured an afternoon of giggled gossip and thinly disguised boasting to no avail.

Rob scanned the large withdrawing room belonging to the uncle of Sir Philip's intended bride, a room that was above a large and bustling silk business.

Rob's gaze roved over the fine dark furnishings newly made, probably in the Netherlands. It would take two men to carry the sideboard. One could likely manage the chairs. The family portraits on the wall were worthless to anybody but the family, while the silver candlesticks on the mantelpiece could fetch twenty-five pounds at least. A thief could pocket those and be out the mullioned window in an instant.

The windows sported excellent locks, though, which said something for Mr. Burroughs's intelligence, as the size and furnishings of this room did for his wealth.

A family of ten paupers would account themselves lucky to have so much space, Rob reflected as he glanced at his client, who was impatiently pacing up and down the carpet.

Even now, Rob could not get used to seeing somebody step on a carpet as if the expensive item were not there.

A door beside the mantel opened, and a man every inch the prosperous tradesman entered. He wore a jacket and breeches of a navy blue fabric that gleamed in the light. Silk, probably, Rob thought, although he himself had little knowledge of such a luxurious fabric. The man's jacket sported no trim, except for large, no doubt expensive silver buttons. His peruke, the hair glossy brown and curled, framed a plump face that bespoke fine meals, and none ever missed.

His shirt and hose were gleaming white, and his shoe buckles also made of silver. One of them could probably feed that poor family of ten for weeks.

"Ah, Sir Philip!" the man cried as he came forward and bowed to his guest. "Delighted to see you again, sir, *de*-lighted!"

Sir Philip surreptitiously tugged his jacket

sleeve over his dingy cuffs as he made a considerably smaller bow to the taller man. "Your servant, sir." He turned toward Rob and gestured for him to come forward. "Mr. Burroughs, allow me to present my solicitor, Mr. Robert Harding."

"What, not Heartless Harding?" Mr. Burroughs cried, his tone pleasantly surprised—but there was no corresponding delight in his eyes.

Because of Rob's reputation in legal matters, or something else?

"I heard about you after you got that hundred pounds out of Millton," Mr. Burroughs said after Rob endured another moment's scrutiny.

"Mr. Millton was in breach of contract."

"So you say."

"So the law says, sir."

"Well, so the judge decided, at any rate, and Millton was most put out about it, most put out."

Rob said nothing. What was there to say? He had won the case, and Mr. Burroughs's friend had lost.

"As I have said," Sir Philip said smoothly, "I like the best. Given our conversation the other evening, I thought to save us both some time by having my solicitor draw up the first draft of the settlement."

Mr. Burroughs's lips twitched in a little smile, and Rob realized he wasn't taken in by this explanation. Sir Philip wanted to make the preliminary agreement to give him the advantage by committing the first negotiations on paper. Once things were committed to paper, Rob had discovered, many people considered them sacrosanct.

Not him, of course, and he doubted Mr. Burroughs would think so, either. Rob suspected it would be a rare fellow who ever got the better of Mr. Burroughs in a bargain. The negotiations were Rob's job, however, and he also suspected that Mr. Burroughs would very likely underestimate him. Most men who knew of his history did.

That was their error. There had been days when a ha'penny was worth an hour's haggling to him, and so he had learned to bargain well, a talent which stood him in good stead in his profession.

Let Mr. Burroughs beware, and his solicitor, too, who was probably the person opening the other door this very moment.

Rob half turned, wondering who his legal opponent was going to be.

The first thing he saw was a gown of pale pink fabric, like the bud of a rose. And then her face, the unforgettable face of the young woman he had kissed in Bankside, with her periwinkle blue eyes and memorable, delightful, querying eyebrows that now rose with blatant surprise.

Chapter 5

It could not be! It *must* not be.

Maybe she was not the bride. Maybe the bride was a sister or cousin or friend. Please let her be a sister or a cousin or a friend!

"What do you want, Vivienne?" Mr. Burroughs demanded.

Vivienne. Her name was Vivienne.

"I told you Sir Philip was coming," Mr. Burroughs continued, obviously putting his own interpretation on her reaction as Rob struggled to regain his inner equilibrium.

And control the blood coursing through his body, rampaging in his veins.

Sir Philip smiled at her in an insolent, possessive way that made Rob want to strike him, then said, "Your uncle has given me leave to talk of a marriage settlement, so I have brought Mr.

Harding, my solicitor. I am counting the hours until we can be wed."

Oh, dear God in heaven, she was the bride. It took every measure of self-control to keep Rob from groaning with dismay.

He immediately considered excusing himself from this business. For heaven's sake, he had advised the bride on how to delay and possibly avoid the marriage entirely.

And they had kissed—oh, how they had kissed! He could not bear the thought of her marriage to a man like Sir Philip Martlebury.

But if he excused himself, he would have to say why. What might happen to Vivienne then, if they heard she had tried to thwart their plans? He could guess, and it would not be good.

He thought of giving another reason to be excused. Or giving no reason at all. He could simply say he was unable to continue as Sir Philip's solicitor.

But again the question of Vivienne's fate arose.

Even as his heart bemoaned this horrid twist of fate, he realized there was one thing he could do for Vivienne Burroughs.

He could make sure she had a good marriage settlement. Otherwise, how long would even a large dowry last in Sir Philip's hands? A year, maybe two, unless it was protected by the law.

He had no qualms about doing that, for he believed in fairness, not the sort of legal maneuvering aimed at vanquishing the other party completely. He had seen too many people left ruined and destitute by such legal wrangling, often because they were too ignorant and poor to be able to fight for what was theirs by right of law.

Burroughs was a well-to-do merchant; surely there would be enough money to satisfy Sir Philip and provide for her separate use, too. He could see that it was so.

If, in fact, the marriage took place at all. He could believe that Vivienne Burroughs was quite capable of following his advice, so perhaps all talk of a marriage settlement would prove to be moot.

Sir Philip would be out of pocket for the time Rob had spent on the settlement to that point, but the man could always use it as a rough draft the next time he sought a young woman's hand in marriage, so he would not be paying for nothing.

"Your solicitor?" Vivienne Burroughs repeated, turning to regard him gravely.

"Sir Philip engaged my services yesterday."

"Ah, only yesterday?" she said as a beautiful smile of comprehension dawned on her face.

He noted with relief that she was acting as if they had never met, which was the best thing for her to do. "Are you the one they call Heartless Harding?"

A hope he had not dared to acknowledge slowly died within him. If she knew what people called him about the courts, what else did she know about him? "Yes. You have heard of me?"

"I was talking with a friend about solicitors, and your name was mentioned."

He would have given all he had to know exactly what had been said about him. The truth was bad enough; the rumors and gossip infinitely worse.

"As I told your uncle, I like the best," Sir Philip remarked.

"So you keep saying, and I gather Mr. Harding is."

"I do my best for my clients, mistress."

"I'm sure your advice is excellent." She turned toward her uncle. "I was not aware we had reached this stage."

"I am impatient to become your husband, my love," Sir Philip said.

Her eyes flashed angrily as she looked at him. "I am not your love."

"Leave us, Vivienne," her uncle commanded.

Her expression altered to one of apparent contrition—but the anger still smoldered in her eyes if one looked for it. "Forgive me, Sir Philip. I should say, you do not love me *yet*." She faced her uncle. "Shouldn't I stay for this discussion? It is my marriage settlement, too, after all."

Rob was glad to hear she was following his advice.

"It's business, and women have no need to

listen to business," Mr. Burroughs declared with obvious finality.

"Very well, Uncle," she said, wisely not pressing the issue.

She was as intelligent as he had believed that first night.

"It is a fine afternoon," she said, "and I believe I shall take a stroll around the mercer's garden. Perhaps Sir Philip might find a moment to join me there? You can tell me all about your estates in the country and your friends there."

Wise woman, to think of finding out about his acquaintances outside of London, too.

"I'm sure Mr. Harding doesn't need me at this point in the discussion," Sir Philip said as he hurried toward Vivienne and captured her arm. "We have already talked about the settlement. Come along, my dear."

He led her from the room and Rob told himself that was for the best. He needed to concentrate on the business at hand, and he could not do that while she, and her rose perfume and soft pink dress, were in the room.

"Let's go to the offices below," Mr. Burroughs suggested. "That's the place for business."

"Even this kind?"

"Especially this kind," the silk merchant replied with a throaty chortle. "I leave the sentiment to the couple. It is my job to consider the practicalities, and I always do that better below."

Rob nodded his acquiescence. No doubt there

would be no lingering scent of roses in the offices, either.

"Enough!" Mr. Burroughs declared some time
later. "I am famished and dying for a drink of
wine. Will you join me in the withdrawing
room?"

He put his fleshy hands on his desk, which
was covered in receipts, swatches of fabric and
bits of ribbon, and heaved himself to his feet.

"I thank you for the invitation, Mr. Burroughs," Rob said as he carefully sprinkled sand
over the portions of his notes where the ink was
still damp, "but I should return to my chambers.
I have other clients to see today."

And the less time he spent near Mr. Burroughs, the less he was likely to encounter Vivienne. He must avoid her, and the feelings she
aroused that had no future, at all costs.

"I have enough with the first draft of the settlement," Rob continued. "When I have com-
pleted it, Sir Philip will read it and let me know
what needs to be amended. Then I shall return
to you for more discussion. Or perhaps I should
consult with your solicitor?"

"I don't intend to pay one of your fellows for
this. I know how to read a contract, by God."

Judging by what had just passed, Rob could
believe he did indeed know as much about contracts as any solicitor.

"If you change your mind," Mr. Burroughs

said as he went to the door, "ask one of the clerks to show you upstairs."

Rob nodded and began to gather his things. As he put them in his worn leather pouch, he surveyed the silk merchant's office. His gaze passed over the whitewashed walls decorated with small pieces of silk affixed with sealing wax, the shelves bearing bolts of unfinished material, the dyed bolts leaning against the wall and the black and gray fabric farther back upon the shelves, a reminder of the grim days of Cromwell, perhaps. He couldn't see any sign of light pink fabric.

Then, as if his thoughts had somehow taken material form, he smelled roses. Straightening abruptly, he saw Vivienne standing on the threshold.

She wore a cloak, the same cloak she had worn that night in Bankside. The hood was up around her face, but now that he had seen her, he could perceive her features in the shadow it made.

She smiled. "Mr. Harding, I am delighted to see you again, even under these unusual circumstances."

As she came inside, he made his face as stern and cold as he could. There could never be anything more between them. "Your uncle has gone upstairs to the withdrawing room, mistress."

She drew back her hood.

He wanted to pull her into his arms and kiss

her with that same passion they had shared before.

But he could not. He didn't dare touch her ever again. Simply being in the same room with her was torment enough.

He was basely born and poor. She was neither.

He could only ever be a solicitor who helped her, and he must do so in secret, for both their sakes. Nobody, and especially not Sir Philip, could ever know his feelings for her, or what he had done because of those feelings.

He couldn't even run the risk of having her inadvertently betray him. If necessary, he must drive her away.

"Where is Sir Philip?" he asked calmly, his years of self-restraint standing him in good stead.

Vivienne came farther into the office. Mr. Harding, her savior, stood as stiff as a soldier on guard duty, and she smiled to put him at his ease. "This is a very troublesome situation, is it not? Imagine Sir Philip engaging my advisor."

"An unforeseen but not insurmountable difficulty," he replied.

How stern and forbidding he seemed! She might think "heartless" appropriate, if she had not met him under other circumstances.

"It is inappropriate for you to be here alone with me, so I must ask you to leave."

Halting abruptly, she searched for signs of her kindhearted benefactor in Mr. Harding's hard dark eyes. "As you may have realized, I sometimes act inappropriately—but I hope you do not think I go about kissing strangers all the time."

"It matters not to me what you do."

"I thought it might."

He regarded her with grim resolution. "No, it does not. Other than to express my regret about your previous behavior, there is nothing more I have to say to you."

"*My* previous behavior?" she demanded incredulously.

"Yes."

"You would tell me you did not return my kiss?"

"If I did, it was because you caught me off guard."

Vivienne was astonished by his words. "Do you always kiss so passionately, then?"

"How I kiss, or when, or whom, is none of your business." He straightened his shoulders, almost as if he were squaring off against an opponent. "Mistress Burroughs, I am sorry if I have led you to believe that there was anything more between us than a single kiss and some advice dispensed when I was ignorant of your identity. However, Sir Philip has hired me since then. It is my duty and my intention to do the best I can for my client in the matter for which I was hired."

"But you did not know who he intended to

marry then, and now you do," she protested, unwilling to believe what he was saying in that deep, cold voice. "Knowing that I hate him, surely you cannot continue to represent him?"

"He is paying me. Surely you are intelligent enough to discern that I could use the money. I have no well-to-do uncle to support me."

"For money you will help that odious creature marry me?" she cried incredulously. "You will sell my happiness for money, too, like my uncle? Good God, sir, you gave me cause to expect better of you!"

"Listen to me, Mistress Burroughs, and listen well," he said severely. "You have money and position and beauty and all the power that goes with it. To be sure, you would prefer to choose your husband. Who would not wish to have some choice in their fate? It cannot be so for most. Not the infant abandoned in an alley on a dung heap. Not the whore poxed before her fifteenth birthday. Not the soldier wounded and forgotten by the government he fought for. Before you bemoan your fate to the heavens, give some thought for those less fortunate than you. Be glad you have a chance for honorable marriage and don't have to sell your body in the street. Be happy that you have money to save you from begging or thievery and the noose."

Her steadfast gaze, which had been trained on his face the whole time, did not falter, nor did she move to wipe the single tear that rolled down her cheek. "I may not be a whore, Mr. Harding, but my body is being sold nonetheless. At least a poor man can work to change his lot, as you apparently have, whereas I have no such opportunities. You are right that I am more privileged than many, but I will not think it a crime to want to be happy. If I have done anything wrong, it is to misjudge you, and that is what I regret. So now I give you good day, sir. I hope I never see you again, and may you enjoy the money Sir Philip pays you."

She turned on her heel and marched toward the door. One hand on the latch, she hesitated and glanced back at him.

Her gaze faltered, then she opened the door and slammed it shut behind her, and was gone.

Gone forever. Driven away. By him.

He had to do it. Beautiful, spirited Vivienne Burroughs must not be stained by her association with a gutter-born bastard said to have achieved his current success by the most vile of means.

Chapter 6

Sitting at her dressing table, Vivienne stared unseeing at the mirror and absently shredded the velvet ribbon in her hand.

She was utterly confused and confounded by Robert Harding. That first night, he had been kind and generous, willing to help. Today, he had been harsh and cruel, and when he had ruthlessly chastised her, his words had cut her to the quick.

Perhaps she didn't understand poverty, but she did understand loneliness and unhappiness. If she married Sir Philip, she might as well be alone, and she would most certainly be unhappy.

Nevertheless, despite Mr. Harding's harsh remarks, when she had looked at him there at the last, she had seen in his eyes a look of need and anguish at odds with the grim, hard line of his lips.

Did he not mean all that he said, then? Was there any cause to hope that he might yet come to her aid—or was she better off trusting in her own efforts to save herself from a loveless marriage?

What would his continuing representation of Sir Philip mean to her? He had told her how to avoid marriage to his client. He would know what she was trying to do if she asked many questions. Would he tell Philip?

Surely he would not wish to tell his client what he had done, even though at the time he hadn't known who she was. Whatever the circumstances, that would not endear him to Philip.

No wonder he had acted as if they had never met, and that might explain why he was so cold and cruel.

She sighed wearily. It was as if there were two different Robert Hardings, one a cold-hearted solicitor, the other a passionate, chivalrous gentleman.

She rose and went to the window, looking down at the roof of the stable that abutted the back of the building. If she had to, she would go out that way again. The next time, however, she would avoid Bankside altogether and go straight for the Oxford road.

The door to the dingy dwelling hit the wall with a bang as sharp as the report of a pistol.

The young woman in the fusty bed gave a scream as Jack Leesom scrambled off her and reached for his knife. Then he glared at the man who had entered the room in so noisy a manner.

"Bloody hell, Rob," he growled as he put his knife back on the bedside table. He covered his naked torso with the threadbare sheet. "I coulda killed ya."

"Good evening to you, too," Rob said, surveying the well-known room and breathing in the familiar odors of ale, wine, sweat and dirt. "Polly said she thought I'd find you at home, and not alone. Is that Nell Gwynn?" he asked, nodding as the pretty young woman, unabashedly unclothed, sat up and stared at him. "Given up on the theater, have you?"

"No, I ain't," she retorted, grinning. "Just having some fun with Jack is all, on me night off."

Rob sat on the only other item of furniture in Jack's shabby quarters, a large battered chest with a broken clasp. Years ago they had found it discarded behind a shop and lugged it here. "I'd like to speak with Jack about a job, if you don't mind, Mistress Gwynn. In private."

"Oooh, ain't he lovely with his Mistress Gwynn?" she said with a charming laugh. Her eyes shone with avid curiosity. "What job?"

"Don't you think you'd better put some clothes on?" Rob replied. "I wouldn't want you to catch a chill."

Nell threw back her head and laughed again, her pert breasts jiggling. "I'm in the bed, warm as warm can be . . . or nearly. Nice o' you to care, though, I must say. I didn't catch your name."

"It's Rob," Jack growled as he pulled on his breeches. "A friend o' mine."

"A friend of yours?" Nell asked.

"Yes. He doesn't sound like me because he had an education." He straightened and gave her a rueful smile. "I'd be careful around him, Nell. He's an attorney and can probably get up to all sorts o' legal mischief."

"Mistress Gwynn, why don't you get dressed and run down to the tavern and get us some wine?" Rob said, passing over Jack's comments.

"That's generous of you," she replied with another grin as she got out of bed and started to dress, not a whit embarrassed to do so in front of the men. "And while I do that, you two can have your talk without me about."

"Thank you very much."

"Yeah, thank you very much, Rob," Jack grumbled. "Thank you very much for interrupting. Thank you very much for making me get out of bed. Thank you very much for stopping by, old son. I should think some wine the least you could do."

Rob shrugged. Jack could be touchy sometimes.

"Oh, Jack, don't be such a bear," Nell cooed as she tied her bodice lacing, then held out her hand expectantly toward Rob. "I'm not a bit sleepy yet."

She gave Jack a saucy wink, then eyed Rob speculatively as he gave her a coin. "You should come to the theater tomorrow," she suggested with a toss of her thick, curling hair. "The king's going to be there."

She darted a secretive glance at both of them before saying with merry roguery, "And I've undone the seam of my dress right up to my hip. I hear Charles likes a nice pair o' legs, and I mean him to see mine. He will, too, unless he's blind."

"You *are* the clever one, but I don't think they're your best feature," Jack noted.

"They're the best one he can see from a distance," she retorted.

Jack grabbed her by the waist and pulled her to him. He nuzzled her neck, working his way toward her breasts as her trill of a laugh filled the room.

"Jack, I don't want to be all night," Rob said.

His friend let go of Nell. "Off you go, then," he muttered, patting her buttocks. "Don't be too long."

"Oh, I won't." With her hips swaying with outrageous—and rather effective—sensuality, Nell Gwynn left the room.

Jack sighed as he looked at Rob. "You would have to come right then."

"I'm sorry, but this is important."

"Must be, to make you go to Polly to find me." He ran his gaze over Rob. "Allow me to make an observation, m'lud," he continued, imitating an aristocrat to perfection. "You look like you could use a stiff drink and a night with a sprightly whore."

"I require neither."

Jack made a skeptical face.

"Do you want to earn some money or not?"

"Course I do."

"What do you know about Sir Philip Martlebury?"

"Martlebury, Martlebury," Jack muttered thoughtfully, rubbing his hand over his stubbled chin. "Name's not ringing any bells in the tower." He regarded Rob steadily with his dark brown eyes. "Should it?"

"He has hired me to do some work for him and I have my doubts about his financial solvency."

"You're not talking to your jack-a-dandy friends, Rob."

"I'm not sure he'll be able to pay my fee."

This was true enough, and while he believed Vivienne Burroughs was clever enough to discover anything that would dissuade her uncle from going through with the marriage plans, he was not averse to learning more about his client, too.

If Jack did find something against Sir Philip

that Vivienne did not, he would tell her and cease to represent the man.

"Now you're talking sense," Jack said. "So you want me to see what I can find out about him, eh?"

"Yes."

"And if he can't pay, want me to make it clear to 'im he should find the money somewhere?"

"No." Rob rose, signaling the end of the interview. "I just want you to find out what you can."

"Right. Besides, if there's any points need makin' in that regard, you can always do it yourself, eh?" Jack finished with a wink. "We should 'ave kept track of how many bones you broke, eh, Rob?"

Rob winced. "I do my battles legally now, Jack."

"Sure ya do, sure ya do, and right well, too, so I hear," his friend said. "Polly says if you come by, you can have a go for free."

"She always was a kindhearted, generous woman."

"Too kindhearted and generous, if you ask me," Jack observed. "You can afford to pay—but you was always her favorite."

"Plenty of the girls preferred you."

Jack's grin was devilment itself. "So they did, and right clever of them, too. Where's this Sir Philip live?"

"The Strand. Martlebury House."

Jack guffawed. "O' course. Shoulda thought o' that. But I guess we can't all be as clever as you, can we?"

"Whatever you do, don't let him realize you're interested in him or be seen following him."

"I'll be careful." Jack slid closer to the end of the bed. "Say, Rob, it ain't that late. You could get yourself a girl and we—"

"No," Rob snapped. He made an effort to smile. "I'll leave you to your sport." He reached into his purse and pulled out some more coins.

Jack counted the money. "Very generous of you, Rob, very generous. Nice o' you to think of your old friend in times of need."

Rob nodded and walked out while Jack hid his payment before Nell got back.

The next morning, Rob headed from his chambers to his office below. He could not sleep, so he might as well work. Upon opening the inner door, however, he discovered that not only was the diligent Bertie already at his desk, but somebody else was there, too.

Bertie's quill hovered uncertainly over his work, as if temporarily blinded by the clothes of brilliant blue, scarlet, green and gold sported by the round-faced, rather befuddled and forlorn man sitting dejectedly near him. Lost in his thoughts, the young man twisted the brim of a wide-brimmed hat adorned with several ostrich feathers.

Rob immediately recognized Fozbury, Lord Cheddersby, a friend of Sir Richard Blythe, and an aristocrat with the kindest, friendliest mien Rob had yet encountered. Unfortunately for the hapless Lord Cheddersby, he seemed nearly overwhelmed by his garments of fine and costly velvet. Indeed, between the clothes and his fulsome, curling wig, he made Sir Philip look like a model of sartorial restraint.

"Lord Cheddersby, is it not?"

The fellow jumped to his feet, which made his full, pleated breeches puff out like a ship's sail before the wind. He bowed with his right leg extended, bending his left knee and sweeping his hat across his chest. "Your servant, sir."

Rob glanced at Bertie, who was giving evidence that Lord Cheddersby was not the only befuddled person in the room, then addressed Lord Cheddersby. "Won't you please come into my office?"

"Yes, of course, gladly," the nobleman answered. He preceded Robert, who followed him and closed the door, all the while wondering what had brought the good friend of Sir Richard Blythe to him. Surely if a man of Lord Cheddersby's wealth and position needed a solicitor, he would use the finest in Chancery Lane.

Once alone, Lord Cheddersby stood awkwardly, still nervously twisting the wide brim of his hat in his hands.

"Won't you sit, my lord?"

"Oh, yes . . . well, no, I think I'd rather stand," Lord Cheddersby stammered. "But you sit, by all means."

"How may I be of service to you?" Robert asked as he eased himself into his chair, a wary eye on the anxious man before him.

Lord Cheddersby looked around guiltily before replying in a loud whisper, "There's a woman."

Rob raised an inquisitive brow.

"She . . . um . . . she claims I promised to marry her . . . which is an outright, damnable lie!" He seemed to realize he had raised his voice, for he flushed and continued more quietly, "And if I don't pay up, she says she'll take me to court on an action of *assumpsit*. But there was no breach of promise. I never promised her anything! I barely know her! I met her at the theater and I may have . . . that is, I'm not the most attractive fellow in London and she was very . . . very . . . willing."

He sat heavily in the chair across from Rob's desk and regarded him beseechingly. "I'faith, sir, she was downright persistent! And . . . and I must say that such . . . attention . . . is quite rare for me . . . and so . . . that is, it never entered into my head, I assure you . . ."

"You made love to her."

The unfortunate nobleman nodded mournfully.

"How much, my lord?"

"Three times altogether, I think."

"I meant, how much money will it take to prevent her lawsuit?"

"A thousand pounds, she says."

Although his expression didn't change, Rob felt as if he'd been kicked in the chest by a mule. "That is a considerable sum," he agreed. "What if you refuse to marry or to pay?"

Lord Cheddersby's face turned nearly as scarlet as his clothes. "She's made . . . threats."

"What sort of threats?"

"That if I don't pay, she'll spread terrible rumors about me." He looked about, then leaned forward and whispered, "She's going to say I have the . . . the French disease."

Richard refrained from curling his lip. It was an old ploy to threaten a rumor of a venereal disease, and that particular malady was especially heinous. "So you wish me to represent you?"

"Yes, if you wouldn't mind."

If he wouldn't mind.

This fellow could pay for the services of a hundred solicitors; Rob was in no place to refuse a commission, or he would have sent Sir Philip away at once.

"I read that marriage settlement of my friend Richard's and it was marvelous!" Lord Cheddersby continued eagerly. "Well, not marvelous for Richard, of course, not at first. He's quite happy now, though, and you never saw a man so enamored of his child . . . well, except maybe my other friend, Lord Farrington, and—"

Richard sought to steer the conversation back on course. "I shall be happy to represent you."

"Oh, wonderful!" Lord Cheddersby sighed, relief lighting his average features. "I confess I would ask my friends to help, but they live in the country now. They abandoned me here in London, and I can tell you, Mr. Harding, it is a *wicked* place!"

"Yes, it is," Richard replied, wondering if this man had any idea how really wicked some of London's population could be.

"Besides, I know I can trust you to be discreet," he added. "I'm already considered something of a fool, and this would confirm it."

Rob made a rare smile. "Your secret is safe with me, my lord. I have met this sort of woman before and know how best to deal with her."

"Oh, thank God," Lord Cheddersby sighed. "I will be forever in your debt."

Rob doubted that as he reached for a piece of parchment and a pen, which he dipped in the ink bottle. Although he believed Lord Cheddersby meant what he said at the time he said it, he was unlikely to see the nobleman again unless he got himself into another similar predicament. "If you would give me the particulars of the woman?"

"She's rather pretty, but not so pretty when you see her without her powder and patches and wig, let me tell you. Odd's bodikins, she's nearly bald. I know because her wig fell off when she was . . . when she was . . ." He colored. "She was being especially energetic."

"I meant her name and her address, my lord."

"Oh, yes. Delphinia St. Dunstan."

"Where does she live?"

Lord Cheddersby muttered an address that, Robert thought, should have given the nobleman a clue that she might not be trustworthy.

"I suppose you think I'm a great, blundering fool," Lord Cheddersby said sorrowfully. "And I fear you would be quite right—especially when it comes to the fairer sex. I am quite hopeless. I always seem to be falling in love with the wrong ones. First it was my friend's wife—not that they were married then—and then Richard's wife— they weren't married then, either—and, well, it just seems every time I see a pretty woman, especially one with lovely eyes, I fall in love and there you are! I am utterly enamored, and this time . . . when she seemed to like me back . . . Oh, I just had the most marvelous idea!"

Robert set down his pen and regarded the young aristocrat.

"It has just occurred to me that Richard has a new play at the King's Theatre this afternoon and I would be delighted if you would come with me."

"Today?"

"This afternoon."

Vivienne Burroughs was going to be at the theater today. Her uncle had mentioned it yesterday during their discussion.

Threading the largest plume on his hat through his fingers, Lord Cheddersby sighed. "Oh, well, I just thought . . . I don't have anybody to go with these days except Croesus Belmaris, and he talks through the whole performance. Plus, there's that unfortunate wart on his nose. I find myself staring at it at the most inconvenient times."

He had no appointments this afternoon, and Lord Cheddersby, a very kind and wealthy nobleman, was asking him.

"I shall be delighted to accompany you to the theater today, my lord."

After all, the theater was a crowded place. Even if he saw Vivienne Burroughs, it would be from afar.

What harm could there be in that?

Chapter 7

Rob left his chambers earlier than necessary to get to the theater to meet Lord Cheddersby. He could be fairly certain that the woman attempting to extort money from the nobleman would be in at this hour.

He easily found the rooms of the woman who called herself Delphinia St. Dunstan in a building that had obviously started out as a market stall. Some time later, the stall had been enclosed, and some time after that, a second floor added. Still later a third story had appeared, jutting over the other two.

This was not at all unusual in the city, unfortunately. Rob didn't doubt that one day, some of these cramped and ramshackle structures were either going to collapse in a pile of rubble or burn to the ground and set the neighboring houses on fire, too.

He went up to the second floor and knocked loudly on the woman's door, inhaling the stale scents that came from cramped, crowded rooms with little ventilation, yet mindful that there had been a time in his life when a room in such a place would have seemed the height of luxury.

A female voice wafted to him like the odors from the stairway. "Who is it?"

"A friend of Lord Cheddersby."

There was a sound of hasty movement behind the door, which soon swung open to reveal a woman slovenly attired in a day robe, her curling wig slightly askew and her eyes bleary enough to tell him—if her breath had not—that she had been drinking heavily.

"This is a pleasant surprise," the woman drawled, surveying him slowly and lasciviously. Her pasty brow wrinkled slightly. "So, you are one of dear Foz's friends?"

"I am Robert Harding, Lord Cheddersby's solicitor."

"What?" she cried, shoving the door closed— to no avail, for Rob's booted foot covered the threshold.

He put his hand on the door and pushed it open. The woman gasped, then grabbed her robe and pulled it tight, as if it were some kind of protective armor. "Get out!"

"I am here to discuss terms."

The fear left her face and she crossed her arms. "Come in."

Rob did so, and closed the door behind him. He scanned the room and the one visible beyond. He wondered if Lord Cheddersby had ever actually been here, or if she had insisted they go to his house, and eat his food and drink his wine.

"Terms, eh?" the woman queried.

"Yes."

"Is he going to pay?" she demanded, shifting her weight to the other leg.

"I thought you wanted him to marry you."

"He . . . he's willing to marry me?" she asked, dumbfounded.

"No."

Her eyes got a triumphant gleam. "Then he's going to pay."

Rob continued to regard her steadily. She blinked and moved slowly toward an open bottle of wine and a pewter goblet sitting on a table covered with a shabby stained cloth. "I don't expect all that I asked for, naturally. That was just an opening . . . suggestion."

"How much will you settle for?"

She studiously poured out some wine and took a large gulp. Setting the goblet down, she wiped her lips with the back of her hand. "Half."

"Unacceptable."

Her eyes narrowed. "Quarter, then."

"I think nothing would be appropriate, Mistress St. Dunstan, if that is really your name."

"Nothing?" she cried, arms akimbo and paying no heed to the comment about her name, or the fact that her gaping robe revealed nearly the whole of her pendulous breasts.

"Nothing. If you had identified yourself as a whore in the beginning, you would have received suitable remuneration, I'm sure. Since you did not mention money before the act of sexual intercourse, it was not clear that you were a whore. My client thought you were simply a generous woman. To attempt to wring money from him now under the conditions you specified is extortion. Unless you cease and desist, I will be delighted to take the case to court."

She scowled. "You would, wouldn't you?"

"Yes."

Eyes narrowing, she waggled a finger at him. "You might not be a lawyer. For all I know, you could be one of Cheddersby's actor friends from the theater playing at being his solicitor."

"You are free to think whatever you will," Rob replied, "as long as you understand there will be no money forthcoming from Lord Cheddersby, and that if you attempt to spread false rumors about his physical condition, I will have you arrested and charged with slander.

"So we understand each other, Mistress St. Dunstan, do we not? Lord Cheddersby will never hear from you again."

Suddenly the woman's eyes widened. "I know who you are! I've seen ya before! You're Heartless Harding!"

"So some people call me."

"I know all *about* you, too," she said with a sly smile. "How you was caught picking a pocket and would have hung except the man you tried to rob was a solicitor who liked the way you tried to talk your way out of it. Liked *you* so much he took into his house and educated you and let you be his clerk and so you got to be a solicitor yourself. I know how you paid him back, too, my fine Heartless Harding. Seems I ain't the only whore in the room today."

Rob crossed the room and grabbed the woman by her soiled robe. He brought his face within inches of hers, ignoring the stench of her breath. "You don't know anything about my education, but I'll tell you this. If you *ever* come near Lord Cheddersby again, you will be sorry."

"I won't!" she cried, her eyes wide with fear. "On my life I won't!"

"Good." With that, Rob let go of her and strode from the room, slamming the door behind him.

Once outside and around the corner, he slumped against the brick wall of a pawnshop.

Sweat dripped down his back and he panted as if he had run a mile in the summer's heat as he tried to control his rage and his dismay.

How long might it be before Vivienne heard the stories about him, too?

Her hand reluctantly on Philip's arm, Vivienne joined the throng entering the King's Theatre. Ahead of them, her uncle led the way through the crowd like a ship through waves, leaving them to follow along in his wake.

There were so many people here, she was rather glad of that, just as she was *not* glad to have Philip so close beside her. He pressed against her, and his wine-soaked breath was hot in her ear. "Forgive me, my dear," he murmured. "It's the damnable mob."

He wasn't fooling her with that excuse. He was trying to look down her bodice.

When they finally reached their box in the upper gallery, the noise did not diminish. People around them, as well as below in the pit, talked and laughed loudly. From this upper vantage point, the stage seemed a dizzying distance away. Vivienne's vision was not aided by the smoke from the various candles, which had little escape in the poorly ventilated building.

She pulled away from Philip and moved a little closer to the railing, scanning the crowd below rather than look at him. She spied Lettice Jerningham talking to a woman equally fashionably dressed even as her eyes roved over the assembly.

Lettice was right where she most enjoyed being, whereas Vivienne wished she were back at home reading. She spotted Vivienne and waved gaily. Vivienne made a halfhearted smile and a feeble wave.

"Good evening, Sir Philip, Mr. Burroughs."

She recognized the man's voice at once and whirled around. Heartless Harding was at the entrance to their box, wearing the same clothes he had worn before, and with an expression just as stern.

For one moment, as their gazes met and held, it was like that night in Bankside, before they had kissed. Once more he was the gallant gentleman who had come to her rescue, not with sword or pistol, but with words and logic.

While some women might admire the flash and physicality of the former sort of hero, she would rather respect one who also used his mind. And, she had to admit, he stirred her passions as much as any dashing hero might.

Then, suddenly, the gleam of emotion in his eyes disappeared. "Good afternoon, Mistress Burroughs."

He spoke as if nothing at all had happened between them. As if he had not offered his help, then withdrawn it. As if they had not kissed with so much mutual passion.

Disappointment, dark and bitter, filled her.

Who *was* this man who could be so different from one instant to the next?

What did it matter? Why should she let him confound her? He had made it quite clear he wanted nothing to do with her.

Determined to ignore him, she looked past Mr. Harding to the very stylishly attired young man with a round, pleasant face and a most outrageous hat who was standing behind him. With a very interested expression on his face, the unknown man pushed his way forward past the attorney.

Either he was here with Mr. Harding or he was one of the most blatantly nosy people Vivienne had ever encountered.

With an expectant smile, he looked back over his shoulder at Mr. Harding, who stepped forward to make the introductions. "Mistress Burroughs, Sir Philip, Mr. Burroughs, allow me to present Lord Cheddersby."

Lord Cheddersby swept his hat from his head and bowed. "Your servant!" he declared fervently, as if being their servant were the dearest desire of his heart. "Mistress Burroughs, you are lovely!"

She had been told that a hundred times by Philip, but never once with this sincerity. She smiled as she curtsied. "You are too kind, my lord."

"Your servant, Lord Cheddersby," Uncle Elias

said, a slight emphasis on the "lord." His eyes gleamed as his gaze darted between Vivienne and Lord Cheddersby.

She knew that gleam. He got that when he was contemplating a bargain likely to come out in his favor.

A bargain involving her and Lord Cheddersby?

Paying no heed to her uncle, Lord Cheddersby addressed her with enthusiasm. "I saw you from afar and asked Mr. Harding if he knew who you were, by any chance. Imagine my delight when he said he did! I insisted he do me the honor of introducing us."

"How kind," Philip muttered.

Mr. Harding turned his cold gaze onto the nobleman. "I could not deny *his lordship*, surely."

Philip scowled, but said nothing.

Mr. Harding then turned his attention to the orange girls in the pit. Their job was to sell fruit to the theater patrons, but they seemed a performance in themselves with their witty jests, blatant innuendoes, brazen smiles and the way they swayed their hips, the boxes of oranges moving from side to side.

Was he attracted by their antics, or repulsed? Did he even see them at all, or was he contemplating something else entirely?

Why should she care what he thought about the orange girls or her or anything at all? He was Sir Philip's solicitor, and nothing more.

"If you will all excuse me," Mr. Harding suddenly declared, speaking to everyone, it seemed, but her, "I believe I see a client of mine below. I should speak with him before the play begins."

"By all means," Lord Cheddersby said genially.

"No leisure for lawyers," Uncle Elias added with a companionable chortle, as one businessman to another.

Vivienne said nothing. If he had to go, goodbye and be gone, she told herself. That was better than having his cold presence near her.

Especially when she seemed to feel so hot.

"Does the famous Heartless Harding represent you, too?" Philip demanded of Lord Cheddersby after the solicitor had departed.

"Yes . . . no . . . sometimes," Lord Cheddersby stammered, looking as if he'd been ambushed. "Not exactly. Our family's had the same solicitor forever. I think the fellow must be about a hundred years old. He certainly looks it. But this . . . this was a special case, requiring, um, special expertise."

"And we know the kind of expertise he has," Philip muttered darkly. "You must be rather desperate for company to bring your solicitor to the play."

"As a matter of fact, I am," Lord Cheddersby acknowledged. "Lord Farrington and Sir Richard are apparently permanently ensconced in the country with their families these days.

Not that I begrudge them that, of course, for they are very happy."

"Is he arranging a marriage settlement for you, too, my lord?" Uncle Elias suggested.

"Oh, good God, no!"

The gleam in her uncle's eyes brightened.

"You sound as if you miss Lord Farrington and Sir Richard," Vivienne noted.

"I do. I have nobody left."

"You have Mr. Harding."

"Oh, yes, I do, I suppose. But he's not exactly a talkative chap."

"No, he's not," Uncle Elias agreed. "Still, devilishly clever, so they say."

"Have you known him long?" Vivienne asked.

"Unfortunately, I haven't, except by sight and reputation and what happened with Richard. He was Lady Dovercourt—that is, Richard's wife—he was her solicitor before Richard or I had heard of him. I gather he is very good at the law."

"I assume he is well educated?"

"Vivienne, there is no need to interrogate Lord Cheddersby," Uncle Elias growled.

"Oh, I don't mind," Lord Cheddersby replied.

"He had a good teacher," Philip interjected. "I gather they were very close."

Vivienne frowned, unsure what he meant, although it was obviously not a compliment. Rather than have him explain, she addressed

Lord Cheddersby again. "Does he have many clients among the king's court?"

"I don't believe so, no," Lord Cheddersby replied.

"I should say not," Philip seconded. "I thought I would have fleas after I left his office. Nothing but riffraff for clients. It's a wonder the man makes enough to live on. You would think he would have been delighted to see me, but he was almost rude. He actually had the effrontery to ask some old woman if she would mind waiting while he spoke to me. I'faith, I nearly walked right out."

Philip's denunciation probably meant Mr. Harding had not been sufficiently humble and deferential to Sir Philip. She also suspected that if Mr. Harding's clientele were poor, his fees were small. No doubt that was another reason Philip had chosen him.

"The play's about to start," Philip observed coldly to the young nobleman. "Should you not go to your own box?"

"Nonsense!" Uncle Elias growled. "We have room in our box for one more."

"I wouldn't want to intrude," Lord Cheddersby demurred.

"You won't be," Uncle Elias assured him. "Here, sit beside Vivienne, my lord. Sir Philip, there is plenty of room on the other side of my niece."

In a few moments, they were arranged as he proposed.

Eagerly taking his seat beside Vivienne, Lord Cheddersby said, "I can tell you something about Mr. Harding that's really rather astonishing," he began. He didn't wait for Vivienne's nod of approval before continuing with awe and admiration. "Richard told me that Mr. Harding threatened him once."

"He threatened Sir Richard Blythe?" Uncle Elias said with a gasp of disbelief from behind them. "He's only a solicitor. How dare he draw on a friend of the king?"

"Oh, not with a weapon. Richard was telling me about how he reconciled with his wife and he said that he was very upset when he went to see Mr. Harding, who had made a rather serious allegation about Richard. It all was for naught, of course, because Richard wouldn't do anything despicable, although one might believe him capable of anything if you saw all his plays and some of the characters he's created. Really, Richard does come up with the most astonishing people sometimes."

Fortunately, Lord Cheddersby paused to shake his head.

"What happened when he went to see Mr. Harding?" Vivienne asked.

"Mr. Harding told him to sit down."

Vivienne's mouth fell open in surprise, and

her uncle sounded only a little less surprised. "That is all?"

Lord Cheddersby nodded gravely. "He *ordered* him to sit down and, as angry as he was, Richard *did*. I swear, if Richard came upon me when he was enraged, I would turn tail and run. I would never dare to order him to do anything—and Richard would never do it anyway. Mr. Harding must have looked very fierce."

"It would take more than a verbal command to make *me* sit down," Philip declared, "if he even possessed the gall to try to order me about."

"Perhaps not," Lord Cheddersby replied as he gave Philip a dubious look. "Still, he is rather intimidating. I suppose if one saw him smile, one might think differently. Supposing he can smile, that is, and I'm not absolutely sure of that," Lord Cheddersby confessed genially.

She thought of the difference a smile did impart to Robert Harding's usually stern features. No, he was not intimidating then.

"Do you know," Lord Cheddersby began meditatively, "I would have liked to have been a barrister, but I daresay my father wouldn't permit it."

Although she really couldn't imagine Lord Cheddersby gainfully employed, Vivienne gave him a friendly smile for the sentiment, while Philip emitted a scornful snort of a laugh.

"You are fortunate that you do not have to work for a living," Uncle Elias said.

"Yes, I suppose so. Father's investments and estate see to that." The young lord sighed heavily. "Still, it can be quite boring, all that money."

Vivienne glanced back at her uncle. She had never seen an expression quite like the one that was on his face. It was as if he didn't know whether to be pleased, shocked or horrified.

"I hear that saucy Nell Gwynn has a part in the play tonight," Lord Cheddersby went on. "Richard was quite impressed with her and gave her a major role. Mind, she's as impertinent as they come. She nearly knocked me out with an orange once. That's how she started in the theater, selling oranges in the pit."

"Now she's on the stage instead of in front of it. I daresay she sold more than her oranges for that opportunity, and that Sir Richard was more than happy to pay," Philip muttered sarcastically.

The whole audience suddenly rose en masse, heralding the arrival of the king and his party. Charles acknowledged their greeting, then began to clap at the sight of an attractive young actress who appeared on stage to recite the prologue. The audience quickly resumed their seats.

The amusing actress was wearing what was apparently supposed to be a shepherdess costume. A side seam in her skirt had split open, and Vivienne wondered why no one had gone to the trouble to fix it.

Regardless of her torn costume—or perhaps because of it—Philip and Lord Cheddersby were obviously finding her fascinating. Vivienne, however, was not nearly so interested in the sight of a bare leg, so she let her gaze rove from the stage—and her heart seemed to stop.

Robert Harding stood in the dark corner to the left of the stage, where he was speaking to another man with long, shaggy hair and an eye patch. The stranger looked very much like a pirate, and she wondered if he was the client Mr. Harding had mentioned.

Suddenly Mr. Harding looked over his shoulder, seemingly right at her. She flushed hotly, and quickly turned away, but not before realizing his companion was staring at her.

Why should she be embarrassed? she thought wildly. She hadn't done anything wrong.

Resolving not to be embarrassed or intimidated, she looked at the corner—only to discover that Mr. Harding and his associate with the eye patch were gone, as if they had melted into the very plaster of the walls.

Chapter 8

❦

"'Scuse us, ladies," Jack said with a grin as he led Rob through the backstage warren of the King's Theatre, past a group of actresses, props, flats and several men who, by rights, should have been in the audience, not flirting with the female performers.

"Oh, we'll excuse you two, all right," one of the actresses said with a bawdy leer, while another whistled with approval.

"Here, hold your noise!" the property master hissed. "Nell's makin' her best speech."

Chuckling and regardless of the attention he had drawn, Jack continued out into the alley before he turned and faced Rob. As he did, he pulled off the unnecessary patch over his left eye, then scratched his eyelid and the red mark the patch had left.

"Are you still using that patch?" Rob asked, glad to be out in the slightly fresher air. Little daylight penetrated the shadows here, but he could see Jack well enough. "I thought it made your head hurt."

Jack's friendly smile turned into a smirk. "The ladies like it, and I was never one to disappoint the ladies."

"So I recall."

As Jack tucked the unnecessary patch into his belt, he studied his friend a moment. "Neither was you, back in the day."

"I prefer to forget those days."

"Don't I know it," Jack said. "Can't hardly get you into a tavern now. Or is it that you've got a woman and you don't want me to find out? That one Polly seen you with, I'd wager. Right skint of you to keep her to yourself if you do."

Rob had no desire to get into a discussion about women—and especially Vivienne—with Jack. "Speaking of wagers, what happened to your new jacket?"

His friend shrugged.

"Lost in a bet? What was it—dice? Bearbaiting? Cockfighting?"

"Nothing wrong with this old one, is there?" Jack demanded defensively.

"Except for the patches, no."

"There was a time, old son, you looked like a walking scarecrow and I never made sport o' you, so no need to insult me, is there?"

"No. I was merely making an observation."

"Observations, is it?"

"Yes."

"Not judgments?"

"No."

"Good, because we both know we ain't neither one of us been saints."

"I do remember, Jack. It's just that I prefer not to think too much about the past." Except when he had to, to remind himself why he must not want Vivienne Burroughs.

And never again would he give in to the temptation to see her, he silently vowed, if it could be avoided at all.

He should not have come to the theater today. It had been torment enough to see her in the gallery while he stood with Lord Cheddersby in the pit. How boldly alone she had seemed, standing apart from Sir Philip and her uncle as she looked out over the throng below. She was like a goddess in the heavens whom mere mortals could only gaze upon from afar.

But judging by more than her appearance, he knew that she was not like any other woman he had ever met. She was not willing to accept what her uncle and society demanded of her. Proud and sure of what she wanted—as he himself had been even in the gutter—she would rather defy them all and risk everything for her liberty.

He knew the extreme price such freedom

could exact, and that the ultimate end could be disaster, despair and death. That was why he still believed he was right to advise her to return home and find another way out of her predicament, a way that would surely lessen that price.

He would have to be grateful for the service he could render her, even if she never knew of it. He would help her, as he had not been able to help Janet in her hour of hopelessness and need.

With that in mind, he should have been more subtle in the theater. Lord Cheddersby had followed his gaze and asked who the beauty was.

Perhaps he should have lied and said he didn't know. But, he had reasoned, London was not so large a place that Lord Cheddersby and Sir Philip would never meet. Better to be honest.

So he had admitted he knew Sir Philip, and that the young lady was his intended bride. Then Lord Cheddersby had pleaded with him to introduce him to them.

Given that Lord Cheddersby was somewhat notorious for falling in love with amazing rapidity, Rob would have preferred not to; however, he could hardly refuse the request of a lord.

So they had ascended to the box.

For one glorious instant, as his gaze met Vivienne Burroughs', it had been as that first night, just before she had kissed him. For one exquisite moment, time had slowed. Welcome and joy shone in her eyes and it was as if there could, someday, be something between them.

Then harsh reality—if that term could ever be applied to Lord Cheddersby—had intruded and his brief delusion ended.

"So, that was her, eh?" Jack said with a grin. "Sir Philip's intended?"

"Yes, that's Vivienne Burroughs."

"And the other one? Who was he? Looks like a right fool."

"Lord Cheddersby, and I grant you, he looks an easy mark, but I wouldn't get too many ideas about that. He's a friend of the king, and a kind-hearted fellow."

"Oh, now you're making friends with the sparks, eh? Gonna leave your old pal by the side o' the road, are ya?"

"You know better than that, Jack."

"Aye, I know what I know. That Burroughs wench—she's a beauty, and no mistake, eh, Rob?"

"She's pretty enough. That wasn't what I want to discuss with you."

"My God, Rob, are your eyes goin' with all the reading? Pretty enough? I'd say she was more than that by a long ways."

"All right," Rob agreed reluctantly. "She's very beautiful."

Jack got that suspicious look in his eyes again. "Wasted on that coxcomb, is she?"

"I never implied any such thing. Now, what have you found out about Sir Philip?"

"Lots more money than you or I will ever

see," Jack answered, "but not nearly as much as he pretends. In debt, but not as bad as some. His estate's mortgaged not too bad. All in all, I wouldn't feel I was risking too much to spend a night at the tables with 'im. He's got a ways to go to be bankrupt, and he's braggin' about town about the woman he's going to marry, who's got a rich old uncle with no other relations. There ain't a merchant in the city won't give him credit if he asks." Jack looked puzzled. "I thought you'd be pleased to hear that."

"I am," Rob said, telling himself it wasn't a lie.

"He's also a right arrogant bastard, I hear."

"I agree he's not a pleasant man, but business is business."

"Any plans for this evening, Rob, old son? Nell'll be some time yet with the play. We could go to the Bull and Crown and have a drink. And more, if you've a mind."

"I don't think Nell would be pleased to find out you've been with another woman, Jack."

"Oh, Nell won't care. She's Charlie Hart's mistress, after all."

"The actor on stage with her tonight?"

"The same. She's probably letting Lacey, the dancing master, have a go or two as well. She's an ambitious girl, our Nell. I tell you, Rob, when she talks about getting the king's notice, she's not jesting. You ain't the only one got ambition."

"I know that, Jack. I know that very well,"

Rob replied softly, thinking of Janet and the end of her dreams of wealth and comfort.

If Jack realized where his friend's thoughts were tending, he didn't show it. "So for the time being, Nell's a nice bit of fun. She thinks I'm handsome, so we have a bout now and then, but there's nothing more between us, so no harm done."

Rob couldn't condemn Jack for his lack of sentimentality. Indeed, right now, he envied him. If only he could have such cavalier feelings for Vivienne Burroughs.

"Anything else you need, Rob?" Jack asked. "Anybody else you want me to find out about, or needs watchin'?"

"No." Jack caught the coin Rob tossed him. "Good night Jack."

"Good night Rob," Jack called after him as he watched Rob went back into the theater.

Alone in the dim shadows, Jack threw the coin into the air and deftly caught it, then threw it again and caught it once more.

"She's a beauty, all right, old son," he muttered as he finally pocketed it, "and if you ain't half gone over her, I'm a monkey, and if she ain't pantin' after you, I'm an ox."

Then Jack Leesom's face twisted into a scowl full of naked hatred. "You always was a lucky bastard."

* * *

When the play concluded, the audience broke into loud and enthusiastic applause. Although Vivienne had been too preoccupied to follow much of the story, she clapped enthusiastically when Nell Gwynn took her bow, for the pretty young actress had delivered her lines with a merry vitality and humorous hint of innocent innuendo that was quite charming.

Vivienne noticed the king and his party stayed a moment to clap before leaving the royal box. Lettice, who had appeared in the gallery shortly before the play began, saw her and waved again.

Vivienne wondered if Lettice would try to talk to her, and hoped she wouldn't. She had endured enough today without having to listen to Lettice's gossipy chatter.

"Good God, that was short," Philip muttered as he got to his feet, yawning prodigiously.

Vivienne refrained from pointing out that it would seem so if one slept through most of the play. However, she had been glad that he had.

"Was she not a delight? And this is Richard's best play yet!" Lord Cheddersby declared. He gazed happily at the audience, who were all applauding loudly. "He will be so pleased."

"Odd's fish, that must be Cheddersby!" a haughty, yet amused, voice suddenly announced from the door of their box. "I would know that voice and that back anywhere!"

Vivienne turned around and hurriedly curtsied, because the man standing on the threshold

of their box was none other than the Merry
Monarch himself, King Charles the Second.

"Cheddersby, you dog," the king said, coming closer, "it has been an age since we have seen
you at the tennis courts."

Her gaze fastened firmly on the floor of the
box, Vivienne saw only the buckles of Lord
Cheddersby's shoes. His feet moved, and she
knew he had stopped bowing. Should she stop
curtsying?

She had no idea what to do, and for once in
her life, she wished Lettice were with her.

"Majesty, as you know, I am not good at
games," Lord Cheddersby demurred, "and I
have not your vitality. I find it very difficult to
wake as early as you, sire."

The king chuckled, and Vivienne detected a
hint of vain pride in the sound. "Of course we
do not expect everyone to be as we are," he remarked. "Who are your friends?"

Vivienne risked raising her eyes to glance at
the king, then blushed furiously as she found his
brown eyes shrewdly appraising her, the way
her uncle examined a bolt of silk. She quickly
looked away again, at her uncle's shoes.

"I believe Your Majesty may know Sir Philip
Martlebury," Lord Cheddersby continued.

"Yes, Your Majesty," Philip interjected, and his
impatient feet came into her view. "I was at
Whitehall shortly after your restoration, and I—"

"So were a great many people," the king interrupted. His tone was not harsh, but it was obvious he didn't wish to hear more from Philip.

Vivienne subdued a grin and risked another look. Behind the king were several men. There was also one very beautiful, arrogant woman wearing much jewelry. Lady Castlemaine?

Another swift, surreptitious glance at her uncle, and Vivienne knew she had guessed right. Slowly straightening, Uncle Elias seemed torn between looking at the king and staring at the beautiful woman.

"This is Mr. Burroughs, a merchant in the city, and his niece, Vivienne," Lord Cheddersby continued.

"Mr. Burroughs, Mistress Burroughs." Vivienne saw a hand reach out and take hers, a hand with very fine French lace cuffs extending to its knuckles, and a blue velvet sleeve beyond.

She swallowed hard as the king himself raised her from her curtsy.

This close, he was not what one could call handsome. His nose was too large and his lower lip considerably fuller than his upper, a defect his slender mustache was perhaps intended to diminish. However, when he smiled, and with those merry eyes, she could see how a woman could overlook such faults.

"We are quite charmed, Mistress Burroughs, and of course, any friend of Lord Cheddersby's is a friend to us. You and all your party must come to Whitehall. Say, a week tomorrow? The

Portuguese ambassador should be on his way by then. He has the most horrible way of ruining a good evening."

"Majesty!" her uncle exclaimed. "We shall be honored! Delighted!"

"Good. Excellent." The king glanced over his shoulder. "We fear Lady Castlemaine will be out of sorts all night if we linger here another moment. Since that is not at all what we desire," he said, winking at Vivienne, "we had best take our leave. Farewell, Foz, and make sure your friends come to Whitehall. It shall be on your head if they do not!" he finished jovially.

"Oh, good God, I must sit down!" Uncle Elias declared after the king and his friends departed. He hurriedly did just that, on the back bench of the box. He fanned himself with his mouchoir, which made the whole box smell of sandalwood. "The king! Lady Castlemaine! An invitation to Whitehall!"

"Calm yourself, Uncle, or I fear you may fall ill," Vivienne said with sincere sympathy. Even though he did not listen to her wishes regarding marriage, he was her nearest relative, and she did not want him to have apoplexy.

"It isn't as exciting as all that," Sir Philip observed scornfully. "It means we get to watch him eat."

Uncle Elias frowned and his mouchoir stilled. "That may not mean much to you, Sir Philip, but since *I* have never been invited to Whitehall before, it does to me." His eyes narrowed. "I also note that you may not be on quite the terms with the king you have implied."

Vivienne subdued a pleased smile. Sir Philip might be capable of hanging himself; she may not need do more.

"I wonder where Mr. Harding has got to," Lord Cheddersby said. "I had better go and find him. Very rude of me to invite him along and then forget him, wasn't it? But that Nell—she's quite something!"

"You stupid popinjay," Philip muttered under his breath.

"I would beware what you say about a good friend of the king," Vivienne chided quietly. "He might hear you. And so might my uncle."

"I don't care," Philip snarled.

"Odd's bodikins, Martlebury," Lord Cheddersby said with a frown, obviously overhearing. "That's no way to address a lady."

"Perhaps I should remind you that I intend to marry this lady," Philip retorted.

"Perhaps I should remind you that it has not yet happened," Vivienne snapped.

"No, it has not," her uncle seconded.

Philip ignored her, and Uncle Elias, too, to address Lord Cheddersby. "Given the people you usually mingle with, I think it's vastly impertinent of you to chastise me."

Quite unexpectedly, Lord Cheddersby drew himself up with a pride Vivienne had not suspected the genial man possessed. "What do you mean by that, sir? To whom do you refer? What 'people'? I assume you do not include this lady in your description."

Philip flushed. "Of course I don't. I mean the other rogues and reprobates you consort with. I'faith, I think this lady should be embarrassed to be seen with you."

"If I am embarrassed to be seen with anyone, it is most assuredly *not* Lord Cheddersby," Vivienne replied.

Philip's face turned purple with rage. "And just what does that mean, you impertinent wench?"

"That is inexcusable!" Lord Cheddersby cried indignantly. He yanked off one of his fine kid gloves and struck Philip in the face. "You will give me satisfaction, sir," he continued, his voice trembling, "for addressing this lady in such a manner."

Vivienne stared in horror as, instead of retracting his words, Philip smiled an evil, triumphant smile. "I will be happy to do so."

He was probably already picturing Lord Cheddersby dead at his feet.

As she was. Surely the kindhearted, bumbling young man could be no match for him, or any man, in a duel.

"I'm sure you need not fight over this," she pleaded to Lord Cheddersby.

"He has insulted a lady and must be taught a lesson."

"Oh, yes, by all means, try to teach me," Philip jeered.

"My lord, Sir Philip—" Uncle Elias said helplessly.

Vivienne regarded Lord Cheddersby beseechingly. "My lord, it is not worth the risk. *I* am not worth the risk."

To her shock and chagrin, his adamant, yet half-fearful, expression didn't change. "I think you are, and as I am a gentleman, I am bound to uphold your honor."

Regardless of Philip, she took Lord Cheddersby's hand and grasped it in her own. "My lord," she said with quiet fervor, "I would be very unhappy if you were to suffer doing so, especially when I do not . . . My lord, I don't think I ever will . . ."

"Mistress Burroughs, he must be taught a lesson."

"But not by you!"

He smiled wistfully. "Do you think I am that incompetent?"

"Please, Lord Cheddersby, please, I beg of you. Do not waste your efforts trying to teach this fool anything."

"When we marry, I will remember what you called me," Philip muttered.

She whirled around to face him, her legs shaking with rage. "Do you think I will ever marry you now? You are the stupidest of fools if

you think so! I would rather marry Lord Cheddersby!"

"Really?" he gasped behind her.

She spun around to look at the dumbfounded
nobleman. What the devil had she just said?

Philip grabbed her arm roughly. "I don't
know what game is afoot with you and your
uncle—"

"Unhand me, you snake!"

As Vivienne twisted out of Philip's grasp,
Lord Cheddersby drew his sword with a surprisingly accomplished and fluid motion, making the startled Uncle Elias jump back so fast, he
nearly tumbled over the railing into the pit below. "I am a bit of a bumbler, Martlebury, but
I've had the very best teachers, and trust me,
they can work miracles with even the most incompetent of swordsmen, so I suggest you apol-
ogize immediately."

Philip stared at him incredulously. "I haven't
drawn my sword."

"Please do."

"This is ridiculous! We cannot duel in the theater."

"If you say you're sorry, that will be the end
of it," Lord Cheddersby offered hopefully. "I
hate to fight, although I will if I have to, you
see."

His face scarlet with mortification, Philip's
mouth worked a moment before he spoke. "I'm

sorry for my hasty words," he mumbled after a moment.

"And insulting a lady," Lord Cheddersby prodded.

"And insulting a lady."

"Excellent!" Lord Cheddersby cried, quickly sheathing his sword. "I'm satisfied. Are you, Mistress Burroughs?"

She was so relieved that there was to be no fighting and no duel, she could only nod.

"Now I had better find Mr. Harding. Good evening, Mistress Burroughs, Mr. Burroughs," Lord Cheddersby said genially as he bowed. He glanced at Philip. "You will forgive me if I pay you no compliments, sir," he said as he left the box.

"Come along, Vivienne!" Uncle Elias barked, taking her arm.

Glad to get away from both Sir Philip and the curious crowd, Vivienne eagerly followed her uncle. As they made their way forward, she glanced back over her shoulder to see Philip standing where they had left him, an angry scowl upon his face.

Chapter 9

"**H**ow can you be so pleased?" Vivienne demanded as she sat across from her uncle in their coach on the way home. Her voice quavered both from suppressed emotion and the fact that they were going over some particularly bumpy cobblestones. "Sir Philip insulted me, and it is only because I begged Lord Cheddersby not to fight that they didn't duel about it. Philip might have killed him."

"That would have been most unfortunate, of course."

"Unfortunate? I thought you liked Lord Cheddersby. I thought you would were already hoping he would be interested in me, for he is much richer than Philip."

"Naturally, if he had made me an offer for

your hand, I would have been greatly upset. However, he has not, and Sir Philip has."

"Philip is also rude and insolent and disgusting."

"He's in love, Vivienne. He was jealous, that's all."

"I keep trying to tell you, Uncle, he's in love with your money. As for being jealous, he is like a spoiled little boy."

"Sir Philip has gone so far as to involve his solicitor," her uncle reminded her, as if she needed reminded that Mr. Harding was Sir Philip's agent. "All Lord Cheddersby has done is sit beside you at a play."

"He defended my honor."

"I agree that is a most promising beginning."

"But I don't want Lord Cheddersby!" she protested.

She didn't want a man who didn't excite her. Who roused nothing but a genial sort of affection, the same kind Lettice had for her dog.

She wanted a man who loved her passionately. Who needed her. Who loved her. Just as she passionately loved, needed and wanted him. She wanted a man who stirred her soul and made her feel cherished and safe.

A man like Mr. Harding, or at the least the Mr. Harding she had met that night in Bankside.

"There is no need to get so agitated, Vivienne," Uncle Elias chided. "Lord Cheddersby has made no serious offer and might never do so. Besides, there may be some cause not to encourage Cheddersby. You have heard Lord Cheddersby himself speak of his friends—a playwright and Lord Farrington. They are hardly paragons of virtue.

"However, he is also rich and titled, so of course I will not discourage him, and you shouldn't, either."

"I am to encourage him in spite of what I feel? To play the hypocrite? That, Uncle, I will never do."

"Vivienne, this is the way the world works," Uncle Elias explained wearily. "We have one solid offer that is not yet binding. We may have another potential suitor, who may or may not prove acceptable. There is still time to cast our net."

"Cast our net? It is not enough that I have one suitor I do not want, and perhaps another?"

"The more bidders, the higher the price."

"How could I forget that maxim?" she mused sarcastically.

"You would do well not to," Uncle Elias retorted. "Especially if the quality of the bidders continues to improve."

Her eyes narrowed. "I have no idea what you're talking about, Uncle."

He gave her his most patronizing look. "Think, Vivienne. If there was one man in the kingdom worth having, who would it be?"

She knew that the answer which immediately came to her mind would not be the one he was thinking of, so she didn't reply.

"Come, come, girl! Surely you are not that stupid. We met him tonight."

"Not the king?" Vivienne said with a gasp. "Surely you cannot be aiming that high!"

"Why not?"

"Because he has a wife."

"He is the king of England."

Vivienne straightened her shoulders and raised her chin defiantly. "If Charles were to ask me to be his mistress, I would refuse."

"Vivienne, cool your blood. He has seen you but once, and nothing more may ever happen. If it doesn't, we will take the best offer, and so far, that belongs to Sir Philip—but that doesn't mean we cannot hope for better. Now I will hear no more complaints. Gad, you would think I was trying to palm you off on some pauper in the streets."

"If I loved the pauper, you could do so with my blessing, Uncle," she replied.

"Do not tempt me, niece," he muttered as he raised the window covering to look out onto the dark streets, indicating that this discussion was obviously finished, as far as he was concerned. "Do not tempt me."

The next day, Vivienne hurried through the crowded streets near the Inns of Court, surreptitiously looking over her shoulder nearly every time she took a step. Fortunately, her ancient maid, Owens, had either not yet missed her, or she had gotten far enough away that the woman's hue and cry were not likely to cause her any troubles.

If Owens even raised a hue and cry. This was not the first time Vivienne had slipped away from the slow-moving servant, and if her luck held, Owens would assume she had gone home, then simply return there herself. If her luck were really with her and Mr. Harding was not too busy, she might even be back before Owens.

Despite the risk of yet another berating lecture from her uncle, she had to do something to protect the bumbling Lord Cheddersby from Philip's animosity. Unfortunately, the only thing she could think of was to send Lord Cheddersby a warning through Mr. Harding.

Nevertheless, despite her fears for Lord Cheddersby's safety, she had nearly turned back a hundred times after slipping away from Owens at the milliner's. Given Mr. Harding's changeable attitude, from chivalrous savior to coldhearted mercenary, coming here might prove to be a fool's errand.

She hesitated, unsure which building in this cramped and crowded little street housed Mr. Harding's office. She would never have gotten this far without asking a multitude of livery boys and laborers and peddlers if they knew the solicitor Mr. Robert Harding. Fortunately, he seemed very well-known to the local folk, who all spoke of him with respect and even something akin to awe.

She spotted a small brass plaque beside a plain door across the street. She hurried across and saw that she had found what she sought.

Taking a deep breath, she cautiously opened the door and went inside. The anteroom of the simple whitewashed offices overflowed with people, several of them elderly, all of them simply dressed in rough, serviceable clothing.

A youth sat on a high stool behind a higher desk and she supposed he was Mr. Harding's clerk. She addressed her query to him as she closed the door behind her, while every single inhabitant in the room turned to stare at her. "This is Mr. Robert Harding's office, is it not?"

"Aye, it is," the youth said as he hopped down from his perch. "I'm Dillsworth, his clerk."

"Is he in?"

"Aye. He's with another client at the moment. If you'd care to take a seat, I'll tell him you're waiting. Who should I say it is?"

"I am Vivienne Burroughs, but please, don't interrupt him if he's busy. I can wait." *A little*, she added inwardly.

An old man who smelled of tallow made room for Vivienne at the end of the bench beside him. His scarred fingers and hands, as well as the odor about him, told her he was probably a candle maker.

"Thank you," she said as she pulled her cloak tighter, so that she took up less space.

The door to the inner office opened and a woman of middle years exited, wiping tears from her cheeks. She paused on the threshold and looked back into the inner room.

"Thank you very much, Mr. Harding," she said in a heavy Yorkshire accent. "I thought that money gone forever."

Mr. Harding came to the door and gently steered her out. "It was my pleasure. It is no more than you deserve, and they should have paid your back wages years ago."

Vivienne's heart beat faster, for she recognized that tone of voice. The knight in shining armor *did* exist.

But not only for her.

That was good, she told herself. She had not come here on her behalf, after all.

Mr. Harding glanced at the waiting people. "Dillsworth, who's—"

He fell silent and his eyes widened when he saw Vivienne.

She half rose. Then, embarrassed and blushing, she sat back down.

"I will see Mistress Burroughs next," he announced, all hint of warmth gone from his voice. He turned on his heel and went back into his office.

But she had heard benevolence in his voice again, and she would take heart, she vowed, as she hastily rose and hurried after him into the most spartan office she had ever seen or imagined. "I don't mean to take you away from your clients, but—"

"How may I help you?" he demanded, turning to stare at her without a sign of welcome, as if she were a complete stranger to him.

"I have come about Lord Cheddersby."

"Did you come here alone? I cannot believe your uncle would allow it."

"He didn't. I escaped from my maid."

"You seem to have a propensity for sneaking about London."

She would not be dissuaded by his cold and indifferent tone. "I know Sir Philip is your client, but I believe Lord Cheddersby is your friend. You must tell Lord Cheddersby to stay away from me, or I fear Philip might hurt him out of jealousy."

"So, you are here as His Lordship's advocate?"

"Without his knowledge, yes. I am afraid for him."

"Charming sentiment. However, I believe His Lordship well able to look after himself. Therefore, I give you good day."

She would not give up, not when she remembered the look on Philip's face when they left him at the theater. "You were not in our box at the end of the performance, so I daresay you are not fully aware of how serious the situation is. Lord Cheddersby challenged Philip to a duel af-

ter Philip insulted me. Fortunately, Lord Cheddersby was very quick to forgive Philip for the
insult.

"Unfortunately, Philip is a jealous, greedy
man. He might hurt Lord Cheddersby—maybe
even kill him—if he thinks Lord Cheddersby is a
rival for my hand. As you are his friend, you
must make him understand that."

"I am not Lord Cheddersby's friend, and I
must say I think he would be more likely to listen to you."

"I'm sure he would listen—"

"Mistress Burroughs, I do not wish to be involved in your lovers' quarrels."

Righteous indignation rose in Vivienne, especially when she considered how he had behaved
toward her in Bankside, and toward the woman
she had just seen. "I daresay you might feel otherwise if Lord Cheddersby were standing on the
banks of the Thames in the dark of the night.
Then you might find it in your heart to help him,
or is it only women who inspire such chivalry in
you?"

"You cannot know what motivates me," Mr.
Harding muttered, turning away.

"I had hoped kindness and concern for a
friend would motivate you, or even simple human decency. All I ask is that you speak to him.
At the very least, I should think you would be
upset at the prospect of losing a client."

He flushed, and she pressed on. "If I can risk my uncle's wrath by sneaking away from my maid to see a solicitor who is doing his very best to help a man I detest make me his bride, can you not say a few words of warning to Lord Cheddersby?"

Mr. Harding winced.

Sweet heaven, he winced. She was finally making him see her point of view.

When he looked back at her, however, that wince might have been no more than a trick of her mind. "I doubt Sir Philip will go to such an extreme."

"I hope for all our sakes you are right, because *I* would hate to have any injury to Lord Cheddersby on my conscience."

Mr. Harding didn't answer, nor did his expression change. "Please, Mistress Burroughs, leave me."

He sounded different, almost as if he were pleading with her to leave him—because he knew she was right to be worried about Lord Cheddersby, or was there more?

"Not until you tell me you will help."

"Mistress Burroughs, I have an anteroom full of clients who, while they may not be well-to-do, are deserving of my attention and aid, so I must ask you to leave."

She gazed at him just as intently as he had looked at her. "Your voice betrays you, Mr. Harding, and your eyes. I think you do care about Lord Cheddersby."

"As you say, I would regret losing his business."

"No. It is more than that."

"Mistress Burroughs, please go."

"You feel guilty, I hope. After all, you introduced us. You bear some responsibility—"

A sudden wild notion popped into her head, something that was not at odds with her first impression of him. "Why did you go to the theater?" she demanded.

He hesitated before responding, and that gave her cause to think she was on the right road. "I hardly think I need answer that."

"Then I shall simply have to guess."

"Is a lawyer not allowed to go to the theater?"

"Of course he is," she replied. "Indeed, I am very grateful you went to the theater with Lord Cheddersby. Now Philip is going to have some competition for my hand, and for that, I must thank you."

"Mistress Burroughs, your affairs of the heart are not my business, unless they involve Sir Philip."

"And it is of my heart I speak. You knew I didn't care for Philip, and suddenly there you are at the theater with the unmarried Lord Cheddersby."

"You are forgetting he asked me to make the introduction."

"You are reputed to be a very clever man, Mr. Harding, and one does not have to be extremely perceptive to see that Philip is a childish man, likely given to fits of temper and jealous tantrums. I cannot believe you did not foresee this turn of events, although I hope you did not anticipate a duel."

"Mistress Burroughs, what are you implying?"

"That you have provided competition for my hand to either prevent my marriage, or make my uncle reconsider, or perhaps merely to buy me some time to find out more about Philip myself."

Mr. Harding looked horrified. "As Sir Philip's solicitor, it would be unethical of me to furnish an impediment to his plans."

She frowned, disappointed to think it might be merely coincidence after all. "I suppose one could argue you haven't done so. You have only made an introduction."

He nodded.

"I thought you were again acting out of generosity and kindness to a woman who has no one else to help her."

He flushed and looked away. Because he hadn't done so—or because he had? Despite all that had happened, she still could not reconcile the man she had met in Bankside with the apparently mercenary attorney before her. "Tell me, Mr. Harding, do you believe I deserve Sir Philip?"

"No," he replied quickly, and she felt a surge of triumph and excitement as he reddened to the tips of his ears.

He was not as impartial as he would have her believe. "Would you say I deserve better?"

"I have no opinion on that subject, except as befits my position as Sir Philip's solicitor."

"Ah, yes, your position as my intended's solicitor. Would you say Lord Cheddersby is a better marital prospect?"

"I have no opinion on that subject."

"None at all?"

"No. Please, Mistress Burroughs, go."

"Because you have many other clients—none of them as rich as my suitors. I understand that must be a powerful inducement to continue representing Philip, even if you would rather not."

"The reasons I do what I do are none of your business."

It was hopeless. Even if he did feel anything for her, he was not going to admit it.

And yet . . . and yet she could not leave without trying once more. If this was to be her last chance to comprehend him at all, she would make it count.

She faced him boldly and declared, "I think I would rather have Sir Philip's solicitor come between my suitors and me."

His eyes widened and he wet his alluring lips

with his tongue. "Mistress Burroughs, you are spouting nonsense, or harboring some sort of wild fancy."

"Call it what you will," she replied. "Perhaps there is even some Latin or legal term you would like to use. Whatever name you wish to put upon how I feel, I know that I believe I could admire and respect you more than I ever could Philip, and I begin to think more than I could any other man."

"You are being ridiculous."

"I understand that it must be hard for you to believe, in this day and age, that there is a woman who would rather marry for love than money or position, but you must believe me, Mr. Harding, when I swear to you that I am such a woman. I would rather live in poverty with the man I love than in a palace with a man I abhor. I want to marry a man worthy of my esteem and respect. I want to love and be loved."

To her dismay, his jaw clenched as he continued to regard her. "You know nothing about me, Mistress Burroughs."

"I know you are kind and chivalrous, or you would not have come to my aid on the riverbank."

Something scuttled along the wall nearby.

With a start, Vivienne glanced at the soiled plaster.

"It's a rat," Mr. Harding explained grimly. "This place is prone to them." His expression grew more intense, his scrutiny chilling, as if he were trying to see into her very soul. "I used to play with rats when I was a boy. If that is not enough to tell you that I am not worthy of your esteem and affection, ask yourself this question: How does a boy born in the gutter get to be a solicitor?"

Chapter 10

Vivienne Burroughs's steadfast gaze did not falter. "I assume through hard work and study."

"And?"

"And his own merit."

Rob took a deep breath. He understood the gulf between them, and he would make her see it, too, no matter how much it hurt.

"Listen to me, Mistress Burroughs, and understand why there can never be anything between us. I was found abandoned on a dung heap in an alley when I was but hours old. The man who found me was a beggar and a thief, and he saw an opportunity to make more begging and thieving by using an orphaned child. He took me to an old hag he knew who, by some miracle, did not kill me. When I was old enough, my guardian, such as he was, took me into his trade."

"It was not your fault if you broke the law when you were a child."

"Nevertheless, that was all I knew. Stealing, and mudlarking. Hours I spent moving through the disgusting tidal flats of the Thames, looking for anything I could sell. A nail. A piece of metal. A coin, if I was very lucky. Occasionally, I stumbled on a corpse."

Vivienne shivered, but he did not stop. She must hear everything. "And I picked pockets. Burgled houses. Robbed drunkards, striking them if they put up a fight."

Seeing the light of both pity and understanding in her luminous eyes, he ran his hand through his hair before he went inexorably on, steeling himself for the worst to come. "You need to know about the man who educated me, Mr. Godwin. I picked his pocket and he caught me, so I spun a false tale of woe for him. I claimed it was my first time, that I was desperate, that I had a mother and several siblings to feed. I made quite a show of crying, too.

"Mr. Godwin saw right through my deception and bluntly told me so. I confess I was never more frightened in my life. I was sure I was going to be imprisoned and either transported or hung."

"Obviously, you were neither."

"No. Mr. Godwin told me he had never heard

such a pack of lies in his life, not even from a lawyer. Then he asked me if I would like to put my gifts to better use.

"I had no idea what he was talking about. Did he want me to steal for him? I had done so before, for the man who had found me. Mr. Godwin thought that vastly amusing and assured me that was not exactly what he wanted of me.

"With my ability, I had the makings of a lawyer, he said, and he would be glad to educate me in that profession, take me as his clerk, and he would see that I became a solicitor, as he was, provided I would do all that he asked of me."

He studied her. "Do you understand, Mistress Burroughs? If I would do *whatever* he asked of me, I would have a great opportunity."

Her eyes widened, horrified, as the meaning of his words dawned on her and no doubt made him repulsive in her beautiful eyes. "He forced you to . . . ?"

Of course she couldn't say the words. "No, he didn't force me to do anything except study hard and work and do my best—but I did not know that when he first made his proposal. I *would* have done anything he asked."

He watched as the first jolt of horror gave way to disgust. He waited for her to flee in revulsion.

"Mr. Godwin would have been a disgusting, horrible man to make such a terrible, immoral offer to a poor and ignorant boy." Her expression softened. "There is no need to look ashamed, Mr. Harding. You were but a boy anxious to escape your poverty. I was desperate when I ran away from home, but I cannot even imagine the despair and suffering you endured every day, or the fate which awaited you if you had refused that solicitor's offer. How can I condemn you for that?"

Even though he thrilled to hear her words, there was more to make him ashamed. "*You* ran away rather than sell yourself in marriage to a man you did not want."

"Perhaps because I was not poor and starving in the streets," she replied gently. "If I had been, I surely would have welcomed Sir Philip, regardless of how I felt or exactly what he offered."

"Oh, God," Rob murmured incredulously, moving back until his heels hit the wall. Then he straightened. "There is more."

"More?" she asked, concern in every lovely, sympathetic feature.

"You must hear about Janet."

"Who is she?"

"Was."

"Who was she?"

"My common-law wife."

"Your . . . your wife?"

"We lived together and although we were little more than children playing house, we were lovers."

"How old were you?"

"About fourteen."

Her eyes widened, and he knew he must have shocked her.

Then, once again, her gaze grew compassionate. "Your hard life has made you mature beyond your years. I sensed that the first time I met you. And you both wanted to love and be loved, at least in some way. I cannot condemn you for that, especially when you obviously cared very much for Janet. What happened to her?"

Against mere curiosity or pity he could have found the means to sound cold and unfeeling, but not when faced with the sympathetic commiseration in her blue eyes. "She had the chance to become a rich man's mistress. She took it, as I took my chance. Then her lover cast her off and she threw herself in the Thames rather than come back to me."

"How terrible—and that is why you were so very determined to help another woman standing alone on the banks of the Thames."

"Yes." He took a deep breath. He had started on this course, and he must see it to the end. Vivienne Burroughs had to know all, or else whatever she felt for him was based upon the man he appeared to be, not the man he was. "I wouldn't have taken her back if she had, for by then I had tried to pick Mr. Godwin's pocket and was living in his chambers. Janet would not have been welcome there."

"But you would have helped her somehow,

just as you tried to help me," Vivienne said firmly.

He couldn't look her in the eye. "I honestly cannot say what I would have done."

She didn't speak for a long moment, and his heart sank. She wanted to think him some paragon of virtue, but he most certainly was not.

"Mr. Harding," she began, her voice sincere and steady, "knowing the outcome, we none of us can say what we might have done differently had we foreseen it, not for certain. We can suppose and we can guess, and I think it's a very honest man who admits that his response might not have been kind and generous. I won't condemn you for what might have been." She made a little smile. "But I can't believe you would not have helped her if you could. From all I have seen of you, Mr. Harding, that first night and here in your chambers, that is what you do. You help people."

Her words reached into his soul and for the first time since he had heard of Janet's fate, he felt the weight of his guilt lighten.

"You don't want to see other people in such a desperate situation," she continued. "I only wish I could be doing something half so wonderful," she murmured, looking down. "All I do is wear dresses."

He couldn't resist reaching out to place his hands lightly on her slender shoulders. "Because nobody lets you do otherwise. I know full well how society would consign us all to our places and keep us there."

"Yes, but a man can do something about it, more so than a woman. All a woman can hope to do is marry well."

"Yes," he said, letting go of her.

"If she is very lucky," she said slowly, "she might get to marry a man who is making a difference in the world by helping people less fortunate, and give him the home he deserves."

This was dangerous ground. She still had not learned all about his past, and she must.

"There is more to tell, I fear," he said. "That moment of choice with Mr. Godwin was not the end of it. People assumed I was his Ganymede. Why else would a man in that position suddenly take in a stray youth? It was the scandal of the law courts, and only his wealth and position prevented him from being brought before the court himself. For years I have had to live with the gossip and the rumors. You saw my clients— that is one reason I have so many poor and laboring. The better class do not want me."

"What care I for old rumors, when I know they are not true? Besides, I don't think that is the only reason you help those people. I saw your face when you spoke to that woman, as well as when you first spoke to me. You are pleased to help people. If you tell me otherwise, I shall know you are lying. Will you lie to me?"

He couldn't, not with her steadfast, resolute

eyes upon him. "I do like helping them, for they are uneducated people who suffer for their ignorance. I have known too many who have been destroyed by despair, and if I can offer hope—"

"As you did to me."

"If I can offer hope," he continued, nodding, "then that is some recompense for living with those rumors."

"Mr. Harding, you have nothing to be ashamed of, not your clients, or your work, or what people claim you have done. As for the better class, Lord Cheddersby came to you, did he not? And Philip."

"They are the exception."

"For now."

"Or perhaps forever."

"Perhaps." She came closer, her gaze searching his face. "For all the good work you do, I think you are lonely, Mr. Harding, as lonely as I am."

"You are not alone. You have your uncle, and your suitors."

"Oh, yes, my uncle who treats me as either a dressmaker's form to display his wares, or an article to be sold to the highest bidder.

"I assure you, I am lonely, too, and I will be lonelier and more miserable still if I marry Philip, or any other man I do not love."

"While I might agree that Sir Philip may not have the makings of a worthy husband for you, there are other men in London—rich, respectable men who will surely be only too happy to have a woman like you for a wife."

"There are not many men in London who are kind and generous and help others worse off than themselves. Or," she said, blushing and looking away, "who stir such a passion within me, I fear I shall melt with the heat of it. Or am I wrong to hope that you could come to care for me, when I have done so little with my life?"

This beautiful, intelligent woman who could have any man in London . . . *she* felt unworthy of *him*? Rob Harding, born of some whore and left to die? Pauper. Thief. Willing to do anything to save himself from poverty? "I am not worthy to touch the hem of your gown."

"This gown I have not earned?"

"Do you not know what an incredible woman you are, Vivienne?" he asked softly, drawn to her by feelings he could no longer restrain. "You are the bravest, strongest, most determined, wonderful woman I have ever met."

He gathered her in his arms. Gratitude, longing, hope and desire mingled within him at the touch of her soft lips as he kissed her. She shifted, her hands caressing his chest, her very touch firing his blood.

His kiss deepened as her embrace tightened. Burning desire kindled within him. How he wanted her, needed her! Loved and loving. No longer alone.

He caressed her back and her shoulders, the

soft satin of her gown a promise of the warm flesh beneath. His long, strong fingers traveled up her bodice and she shuddered when the tips brushed over the tops of her breasts. Pressing closer, she arched against his warm palm.

He should resist. She didn't truly know what the world was like, what it would do to those it deemed unworthy. He should order her to go, or flee his office if she would not.

But he couldn't. He simply couldn't, not when her lips moved over his with soft, yet firm, resolution.

With Janet, he thought he had known what love was, but now he doubted that. Now everything was different. He was different and Vivienne was like no other woman.

She wanted him passionately, as much as he wanted her.

With a low moan of desire, he kissed her fiercely, taking her mouth with fervent need. She yielded to his insistent kiss, parting her lips eagerly, her hands exploring his body as if she had never touched a man before and was anxious to know all.

His arousal growing, he pressed his body against hers, encountering damnable layers of skirt and petticoat. Yet he could touch the bare skin of her back, above the lacing.

With fumbling fingers, still kissing her, he feverishly attacked the knot and, when it was undone, thrust his hand into her loosened bodice to cup the soft, pliable flesh of her perfect breasts.

She gasped with surprised pleasure, breaking the kiss. "Oh, yes," she sighed as he leaned down to kiss her rosy, pebbled nipples. She grabbed his waist to steady herself.

He kissed her mouth again, hard and demanding, as primitive need intoxicated him. He wanted her, all of her. He wanted to possess her, to have her all for himself, forever.

She pushed apart his jacket and shirt and thrust her hand onto the bare flesh of his chest. The sensation was nearly enough to send him over the brink of ecstasy.

He almost didn't hear Dillsworth knocking on the door and softly calling his name.

But he did, so he broke the kiss and, breathless, called out, "What is it?"

"It's, um, Mistress Dimdoor, Mr. Harding. She's been waiting this half an hour."

"Yes, of course," he called out, still holding tight to Vivienne and aware that her breathing was as ragged as his own. "Another moment and I shall be finished with Mistress Burroughs."

Vivienne pulled away from him and, with trembling fingers, began to retie her bodice lacing.

"Mistress   Burroughs . . . Vivienne . . . I'm sorry."

She blushed. "I fear we were both carried away."

He sighed heavily and raked his hand through his hair. "Yes."

She cocked her head to regard him questioningly. "I am sorry we went so far, but I am not sorry you kissed me," she said as she smiled gloriously.

"I shall have to go to Sir Philip at once and tell him I cannot continue representing him."

Her brow furrowed with worry and she chewed her lip a moment. "Must you?"

"Vivienne, I've done more than I should as it is. I introduced Lord Cheddersby to you, and, I think, to once more be completely honest, with half a hope that he would indeed be a rival for your hand. To continue now, given how I feel about you . . ."

"What explanation would you give your client?"

"That I . . . that we . . ."

She took his hand and pressed a kiss upon it before looking up at him with determined resolution. "I think we can both guess what he might do then, for we can be sure he will not be pleased to hear what has happened. He will denounce you in the most vile terms possible."

"And you," Rob agreed, unhappily certain that she was right. Sir Philip would be a nasty enemy.

"You have worked so hard and come so far, I would hate to see your career destroyed because of me."

He stared at her, marveling that she would think of his reputation, already blemished, before her own.

"As much as I appreciate your concern for me," Rob replied, "it is your reputation that will suffer more."

"That doesn't concern me."

"You clearly don't know the damage and heartache gossip can cause."

"I am not totally naive—"

"But you are ignorant."

"I am not!"

He held his fingers to her lips. "I mean that as a statement of fact, not a criticism. Given that you are a carefully reared young woman, I would expect nothing else."

"I truly do not care what Uncle Elias will say," she insisted. "He doesn't care enough about me to even bother with my opinion in so important a matter as marriage, so why should his opinion about who I care for trouble me? As for other people, I value their opinion even less, except that they may criticize you. But for your sake, I think we must be cautious and patient. At the theater Philip provided ample proof that he has misrepresented himself. He is not nearly as friendly with the king as he led my uncle to believe. It could be that Uncle Elias will call off the marriage." She smiled with charming and unexpected shyness. "If so, I shall be free to be courted by another."

"That does not mean he will welcome me. He may prefer Lord Cheddersby."

"Yes," she agreed. "Except that he has reservations about Lord Cheddersby's associates."

"My past is well-known in legal circles, too," he pointed out.

"Yes, but," she said, another beautiful smile dawning on her face, "it could be that he will welcome a solicitor in the family, especially one also reputed to be clever." A twinkle of merriment appeared in her eyes. "Of course, you might be expected to do some legal work for nothing. . . ."

Hope sprang to life as he took her in his arms. "That is a bride-price I would certainly be willing to pay."

Once more they kissed, this time tenderly, hopefully.

"When can I see you again?" Vivienne asked. "There is still so much more I would like to know about you."

"And I, you," he said softly.

"Mr. Harding!" Dillsworth called out from the other side of the door.

"Yes, yes!" he answered, reluctantly moving away from her and going toward the door.

"Will you come to my uncle's tomorrow? You could say it is about the marriage settlement."

He frowned.

"I know this must seem dishonest to you, but—"

"But I will be there to discuss the marriage

settlement." He made a little smile. "There is no legal obligation for me to say I hope nothing comes of it."

"Tomorrow seems a long way away."

"For me, too," he whispered before he put his hand on the latch. "And I will see what I can do about keeping Lord Cheddersby safe. I am not without some means of offering protection without his being aware of it. He may seem a bit of a fool, but I am sure that, like most men, he has his pride."

"Oh, that's wonderful, Mr. Harding."

"Robert. Rob," he quickly amended.

"Rob," she whispered.

Then, as he opened the door for her and as quick as the blink of an eye, he was again the grimly formal solicitor. "Good day, Mistress Burroughs."

"Good day, Mr. Harding."

Chapter 11

That night, Rob stood with his back to the rough wooden wall of the building in Shoe Lane, the air fetid with sweat, blood and sawdust. He was not watching the cockpit, but looking at the entrance over the heads of the mob of men who cheered, moaned, roared or cursed, depending upon which of the bloodied roosters in the cockpit they had bet on.

Surely Jack would be here soon. He was here nearly every night, even when Rob had paid him to do something else. Jack didn't know he knew that, or that Rob forgave him the weakness that made him gamble. Gambling made Jack happy, even when he lost, and since Rob usually had some task for him, he wouldn't starve if he lost his last halfpenny.

A loud roar from one part of the crowd and

curses from the other told Rob the fight was over. He glanced at the ring. The winning bird, cradled and stroked by its owner, looked half dead; the loser appeared to be no more than a mass of blood and feathers.

If Jack didn't come soon . . .

At the moment, a familiar figure with a black patch over his eye sauntered through the door. He was greeted with merry shouts and salutations as if he were the prince of the cockpit.

"Hell, I'm nearly drowned," Jack cried jovially, shaking himself like a wet dog.

"Oy, Jack, have a care!" a man complained as drops of water flew off Jack's sodden hair.

Rob shouldered his way toward his friend and clapped his hand on Jack's shoulder before he started betting.

Jack looked as if he'd been caught with the crown jewels, while the men surrounding them exchanged puzzled glances.

"I need to speak with you," Rob said quietly.

"My attorney this is," Jack explained expansively when he realized who it was. "Little trouble with a woman."

He grinned, but Rob could see his dismay.

His cronies laughed, then all eyes except Rob's turned to the cockpit as a new pair of roosters were brought to the ring.

"Outside," Rob murmured.

Jack stopped looking at the birds. "It's bloody

raining." He nodded at the cockpit patrons. "We might as well be invisible, for all they care."

"I've got another job for you."

"Oh, is that why you're here?" Jack's eyes gleamed with interest. "Wouldn't be watchin' that neat little package of a female, would it? The one Martlebury's supposed to marry?"

"No."

"Damn."

"It's Lord Cheddersby."

"That fool of a fop? What's he been up to?"

"He was nearly involved in a duel with Sir Philip Martlebury." At the idea of anybody insulting Vivienne, Rob curled his fists so tightly, his short nails dug into his palm. It was easy to imagine the things he would like to do to the arrogant bastard who dared to insult her.

The things he could do, because violence had been as natural as breathing to him once.

But he was not that boy anymore, and he could not wield a sword like a gentleman. If he attacked Philip, he might kill him with his bare hands. And then he would be hung, as the man who had reared him always claimed he would be.

As that man had been when he had been caught with stolen property in his coat.

"A duel, eh? What's Cheddersby been up to? Dippin' his wick where he oughtn't?" Jack let out a low whistle. "Not samplin' Martlebury's bit of goods?"

"No. He was defending Mistress Burroughs's honor."

"He was, and not the other way around? I'll never understand the nobility. Still, couldn't blame a bloke for trying."

"Jack," Rob warned.

"Say, ain't you the touchy one. Just a question. No need to get your drawers in a bunch, although she doesn't look like the loyal kind to me."

"I didn't come here to talk about Sir Philip's bride," Rob said.

His friend's eyes widened, and Rob noted how bloodshot they were. Clearly Jack had been spending considerable time tonight in a tavern or alehouse.

"Damn it, man, you already got your heart broke by a whore," Jack muttered. "Ain't once enough?"

Rob grabbed Jack by his worn, wet lapels. "Don't you ever call Janet that again. Do you hear me?"

"Aye, I do!" Jack cried.

The men nearest them glanced over, so Rob let go. Their attention quickly returned to the squawking combatants.

"Damn me for a tinker, Rob," Jack muttered as he straightened his shoulders and tugged his jacket back into place. "She was my sister, after all. And there's no denying she done you wrong, takin' off with that nobleman. I just don't want to see you hurt again."

"Forgive me," Rob said, embarrassed by his lack of self-restraint.

"So, what is it you want me to do?"

"Keep watch on Lord Cheddersby. I fear Sir Philip may try to do him harm."

"Jealous sort, is he?"

"Very, and not wise," Rob added as he put a sovereign into Jack's grubby, outstretched hand. "Don't interfere unless he attacks Lord Cheddersby. I'm not a barrister, so if you're brought before the King's Bench, there's nothing I can do for you. The barristers aren't likely to come to the aid of a friend of mine, either."

"Then what am I to do if Cheddersby's in trouble?"

"Call an alarm and wait for the king's soldiers."

"If raisin' a hue and cry's all you want," Jack said genially, "I'm your man." He smacked himself on the chest, then coughed.

"Just keep watch over Lord Cheddersby."

Rob began to leave, but Jack's strong grip on his shoulder made him turn back. "I thought you was Martlebury's solicitor, not Cheddersby's."

"If Martlebury's in Newgate, how will I get paid?"

"Ah!" Jack nodded his approval and let go. "So Cheddersby doesn't know he's goin' to have a shadow?"

"No, and I don't want him to know."

"Martlebury wouldn't take kindly to your tender care for his rival, neither, would he?"

"It would not be in Sir Philip's best interest to harm Lord Cheddersby."

"Well, you know me, Rob. More of a shadow than a shadow ever was."

"Aye, Jack," Rob replied with a rueful grin. "I remember."

"Now how about a spot o' fun? Care t' make a little wager? I'll take Wiggy Jones's bird for a shilling."

"And then you'll no doubt take me for more," Rob answered with a low laugh. "I haven't been around the cockpit in years. I'd be a fool to bet against you."

Jack's eyes gleamed in the dim light, and when he spoke, his voice was full of good humor. "Aye, you would. How be three-to-one odds, eh?"

"Good night, Jack," Rob said with a wry smile as he turned to go. As he moved forward, his smile quickly disappeared, for he was anxious to get out into the cleaner night air, away from the pressing bodies and even more oppressive stench.

Nevertheless, he glanced back, intending to wave farewell to his friend. Jack, however, was already busy placing his bet.

* * *

At noon the next day, as the maids cleared the table and set out fruit for the final course, Uncle Elias smiled at Vivienne.

He had been smiling at her quite frequently during the meal, and she was beginning to feel nervous.

"You seem happy, Uncle," she finally ventured before the stress became unendurable.

"I am." Giving her another beatific smile, he leaned back in his chair. "I received an invitation this morning."

"Oh?"

"Lord Cheddersby has invited us to his fete."

Vivienne tried to look enthused. "Oh?"

"Yes. All the most important people in London will be there, I'm sure. Perhaps even the king."

"And the queen?"

Her uncle frowned. "Yes, and maybe the queen."

"Or Lady Castlemaine—certainly plenty of people who need fabric."

"Exactly. And he spoke of you in the highest terms. 'Your lovely niece' was the exact expression."

She smiled weakly. "Indeed?"

"Perhaps you will be more pleased with the honor he does you when you see his new house. It is a veritable palace, they say."

"I've heard Lettice describe it so."

"If the king is there, we must do our best to seek him out. Charles seemed most intrigued by you, my dear. You are a very pretty young woman, so that is perfectly understandable. And if he chooses you, you will be well rewarded."

"You persist in thinking there was something special about the attention he paid me?"

"I most certainly do."

"And thus you still believe I have the 'opportunity' to become yet another of the king's whores?"

Uncle Elias frowned. "That is a crude way to put it."

"It is the appropriate word. After all, by 'reward' you mean payment for services rendered, do you not?"

Her uncle's brows lowered in a scowl. "Vivienne, you claim you are not a child anymore, so don't think like one. If Martlebury or even Cheddersby suggested such a thing, naturally I would be upset. But we are talking of the king. If Charles likes you, you will be mistress of the most powerful man in the kingdom—and he is a very generous man. You will have a house, a title or two in all likelihood, and plenty of money."

"You would call that a fair exchange for my virtue?" she demanded.

Before he could answer, one of the maids appeared at the door. "If you please, Mr. Burroughs, that lawyer's here to see you. Mr. Harding."

Vivienne felt her face flush with excitement, and she quickly looked down at the linen table-cloth.

"Is he? Show him to the withdrawing room," Uncle Elias said as he rose. "He must have the preliminary draft of the settlement."

She likewise stood. "May I come with you, Uncle, and hear what it says?"

"I thought you didn't want to have anything to do with that document."

"I would rather be married than a man's mistress."

"I see. This is not the final version, not by a long ways," he replied warily, obviously not sure what to think about her sudden interest. "You won't be signing this."

"Nevertheless, I would like to understand something of what will happen to my dowry if we decide I should marry Sir Philip, after all. Don't you think I should?"

"Well," Uncle Elias mused as he strolled to the door, "perhaps you should. I will not live forever, and you should have some notion of what is legally yours according to the settle-ment—if you marry."

"Thank you, Uncle."

Together they went to the withdrawing room, and the moment she saw Rob standing so grave near the windows, happiness and heat combined within her.

Perhaps only she, of all the women in London, knew that a fiercely passionate man existed within that seemingly cool and reserved frame.

"Mr. Burroughs, Mistress Burroughs," Rob said evenly as he bowed.

"Good day, Harding, good day," her uncle cried, hurrying toward him. Vivienne hung back, determined not to betray to her uncle the emotions Rob invoked in her. "I gather you have brought the first draft of the settlement."

"Yes, sir, I have," Rob replied, pointing at the document already unrolled on the table beside him. There was a quill and ink at the ready, too.

"Excellent!" Uncle Elias glanced back at Vivienne. "I've decided to let my niece have a look at it and explain something of the terms."

"A very wise decision, Mr. Burroughs. I would more of my clients took the trouble to have their families informed of their legal matters."

Uncle Elias smiled and his chest swelled with pride. "I'faith, sir, I am not a fool, and neither is my niece. Besides, everybody knows how clever you legal fellows can be, eh?" He chortled and gestured for Vivienne to come closer.

She did so, acutely aware that Rob was looking at her, and that while his expression might not convey much to her uncle, she could see Rob's regard for her deep in his dark eyes.

Her uncle took a chair at the table, and she another.

"Won't you sit, Mr. Harding?"

"Thank you." He sat beside Vivienne, so close that if she put out her hand, she could touch him.

She struggled to calm her breathing—and not to touch him.

"Now, Vivienne," Uncle Elias began as if she were a simpleton, "we have it as follows: Your dowry goes to your husband, but remains in trust, so that neither you nor your husband can draw on the principle. You, and you alone, are free to specify who shall inherit the principle upon your death. During your life, the interest naturally goes to your husband."

"What if I have need of the principle?"

"What could you possibly need the principle for?" her uncle demanded. "Sir Philip is not a pauper."

"I can think of several things. My husband may gamble away the interest, and all the rest of his own money. If he has control of the interest and I no other income, how would I be able to live?"

Uncle Elias looked at Rob and raised an eyebrow.

"We could amend it that your niece could draw on the principle if she needs it, or receive a sum from the principle yearly."

"A yearly sum payable directly to me, or to my husband?"

"Directly to you," Rob replied, looking at her with a steadfast gaze.

"But that would erode the principle," Uncle Elias protested.

"What good will the principle do me if I and any children I may bear are reduced to living in poverty?"

"I must concede that is an excellent point, Mr. Burroughs," Robert said. "Your niece would make a fine attorney, I think."

Uncle Elias threw back his head and laughed. "Oh, yes, a woman attorney! What next—a woman physician? A female judge?"

"Who better than a woman to ensure that women and children are protected and considered?" Vivienne said.

"Again, your niece makes a fine point. And I must tell you, Mr. Burroughs, that I have seen this very situation. Indeed, I have gone to court to argue against such settlements, to allow a woman to get at money intended for her use, but not clearly stated as such."

"And won, too, eh?"

"After a long battle. In the meantime, the woman and her children suffered greatly."

"Vivienne could always come to me."

"If you are alive and able to help financially. I think I need hardly point out to a man of your business experience that the future is never secure. There could be a war or natural disaster that has a serious impact on your trade, or some other catastrophe. Indeed, Mr. Burroughs, from what I understand of your business, it is even dependent on such intangibles as ladies' tastes in fashion."

Uncle Elias frowned, but he didn't deny it.

"It would be in your best interest to think of every contingency. Or is it your intention to leave other money to your niece in your will?"

"What I put in my will is none of your business, or Martlebury's, either."

"Perhaps not. However, let me caution you that one should make one's wishes very clear in a will. Otherwise, it may be open to interpretation, and therefore languish in chancery for a very long time."

Uncle Elias looked at him suspiciously. "Harding, you are very free with your advice to a man who isn't your client."

"As I have said, Mr. Burroughs, I have seen cases drag on for years in the court. In those situations, no one really comes out the victor, for too much of the money is lost during the proceedings. I would prefer that your will be clear to save possible controversy that could very well involve your niece's husband. If that man is to be Sir Philip, it is my task to ensure that he does not become embroiled in chancery if at all possible."

"Ah," Uncle Elias said with a sigh. "So you think Vivienne should have access to the principle?"

"Perhaps in some manner."

"What if her husband forces her to give him the money?"

"We shall have to hope that does not occur, and I think, Mr. Burroughs, it would be safe to say from what I have seen of your niece," Rob replied, his voice altering ever so slightly, "that any man would have a very difficult time compelling her to do anything against her will."

"Yes, yes, I believe you're right," Uncle Elias acquiesced, while Vivienne hid her smile.

Philip wouldn't admire that sort of sovereignty, and it would probably throw Lord Cheddersby into nervous confusion. In fact, she could think of no other man of her acquaintance who would think her wish for even that much independence a thing to applaud.

"Uncle, where does it say how much you are giving me for my dowry?"

He pointed to a line on the parchment, and her jaw dropped with surprise. "Five thousand pounds?" she breathed. "So much? I had no idea."

"Naturally Mistress Burroughs herself is prize enough for any man," Rob said. His tone held no hint of his affection for her, but she felt it nonetheless. "However, Sir Philip is well aware of the value of his title."

"Mr. Burroughs, sir?"

They all looked at the door, to see the foreman from the business below standing there. "A word, if you please, about the bobbins, sir."

Uncle Elias got to his feet. "Excuse me a moment, will you? We've bought some new pieces for the machines and I fear we've been tricked by a clever talker. They keep breaking." He surveyed Rob with a measuring gaze. "I might need a solicitor to take the blackguard to court. Maybe you would be so kind, eh?"

It was all Vivienne could do to hide her happy smile. If her uncle suggested this, there was cause to hope he would not disapprove of Rob as a suitor for his niece.

There was the problem of Rob's current lack of wealth, but surely Uncle Elias could believe, as she did, that it was only a matter of time before he had more affluent clients.

When that happened, however, she didn't doubt he would continue to represent the poor, too. The importance of that work, and his passion for their plight, burned too brightly within him.

"If I am able to, I would be pleased to represent you," Rob replied, and she heard his genuine delight.

"Excellent! I shall return shortly."

"In the meantime, I will explain the entail of Sir Philip's estate to your niece."

Vivienne's hand crept slowly under the table. "There is no need to rush, Uncle," she said as she captured Rob's hand in hers. "Since I am a woman, no doubt it will take a while for me to comprehend."

Her uncle's expression told her he agreed before he turned and hurried off.

Leaving them alone.

Chapter 12

~~~~

"**F**inally I can touch you," Vivienne said quietly, delighting in the feel of Rob's strong hand in hers. "I have been wanting to ever since I came into the room."

He gave her one of his rare smiles.

"I told you he could very well find you acceptable," she noted.

"As a lawyer, perhaps," he replied. "I am less confident of my success if I were to announce myself hopeful of earning your love."

His fingers caressed her hand, and that alone was enough to make it difficult for her to breathe normally. "I do not think earning my love will be difficult for you."

His enticing lips curved slowly upward. "No?"

She shook her head. "No. In fact, Mr. Harding, I believe you captured my heart that night in Bankside."

He leaned closer and her heart thundered in her chest. "Rob," he reminded her.

"Rob," she whispered, lifting her face in anticipation of his kiss.

He put his powerful arms about her and she held her breath.

Below, a door slammed.

He started and moved back, breathing as hard as she. He ran his hand through his hair and cleared his throat. "About the entail—"

"I don't want to hear about any entails," she said softly. "If you are not going to kiss me, I would rather hear about you."

"Your uncle might ask you questions about Sir Philip's estate when he returns."

"In that case, he will believe that it was indeed too complicated for me to comprehend."

"I don't see how he could. It's quite obvious you're intelligent, and this entail is not very convoluted."

"Not everyone is as open-minded as you when it comes to the intelligence of women."

"Perhaps because I have encountered the same prejudice so often. Men born poor are generally assumed to be dullards."

"It must have been so hard for you, Rob."

He looked into her eyes and smiled. "Right now, I think everything I ever suffered was worth it. Otherwise, I would never have met you." He leaned closer, and she was sure he was going to kiss her.

Footsteps sounded in the hall. They drew back and let go of each other's hands as Owens shuffled past.

Although Owens didn't even look into the room, Vivienne realized Rob had grown even more tense. "I wish we could be somewhere else, where we could be alone."

"Perhaps this is safer," Robert murmured, his deep voice a low, incredibly arousing growl.

"Safer?"

"Have you any idea of how tempting you are, Vivienne? The moment I see you, it is as if I can scarcely remember my own name, let alone anything else. All I can think about is touching you, and kissing you."

"When you spoke to my uncle, you certainly sounded as if you were thinking about the marriage settlement more than me, except in a legal sense."

His grin charmed her. "Only with very great effort. In truth, I was nearly completely distracted by this little groove below your nose and above your lips." He placed a finger there. "Being this close to you is driving me mad," he whispered huskily.

"Rob?"

"Yes?"

"You burgled houses, did you not?"

He gave her a puzzled look. "Yes. Long ago."

"Could you still get into a house other than by the door?"

He frowned. "What are you suggesting?"

"My bedchamber window is the one a short distance above the stable roof in the mews behind here, and there is a very convenient drainpipe. That is how I was able to climb down the night I ran away. It should be easy for you to get in, especially if the window is unlocked."

"You want me to sneak into your bedchamber?" he asked incredulously.

"I can think of no other—"

She heard her uncle's heavy tread on the stairs and moved farther away from Rob.

"Forgive me for taking so long," Uncle Elias said as he strode into the room. "Did you manage all right without me?"

"Not really," Vivienne replied, keeping a straight face.

"I understand perfectly," Rob said evenly without so much as a glance at Vivienne.

Did that mean he would come to her bedchamber that night?

"Of course you do. You're a lawyer," Uncle Elias replied. "If you don't understand entails, what are the rest of us to do?"

"Yes, of course," Rob replied with a deferential cough. "Perhaps we should leave the matter of the entail, for the time being. If you look at this portion of the settlement, you will see that I made the change you requested."

Vivienne said very little as Rob continued to discuss the settlement with her uncle. She was too excited and anxious about the possibility of Rob coming to her, and too certain that Philip's cause was utterly hopeless, to pay much heed to the legality of a surely pointless document.

Instead she was content to listen as Rob went through the terms, and study the way the light played on the angles of his face or the curve of his jaw. Occasionally she found herself staring at his fingers as he pointed at a particular phrase or sentence, and had to subdue the urge to touch his hand.

After all, she would see him soon, and under more intimate circumstances.

Or so she hoped.

"I'm quite sure I don't need any help," Vivienne insisted later that night, a smile on her face but determination in her voice as she addressed Owens in her bedchamber.

Since Rob's visit she had spent the time in a fever of anticipation. Fortunately, her uncle believed it was the anticipation of Lord Cheddersby's fete that explained her lapses of attention and propensity to blush as the evening wore on, and she, of course, did not tell him otherwise.

"I'll help you put away your gown," the elderly maid said halfheartedly, leaning her head back a little to look at Vivienne with her crossed eye.

"No, no, I can manage, I assure you," Vivienne replied.

"Then I'll just latch this window," Owens muttered as she turned that way.

"No!" Vivienne blurted. The window had to be open for Rob to get in. The moment the word was out of her mouth, however, she realized she should have been more cautious. Owens regarded her as if she had just announced she intended to fly out into the night sky.

"I'll close it," Vivienne said, this time keeping her tone normal.

"Very well, mistress," Owens agreed with a shrug. "Just as long as you do. That night air will kill you. I remember a cousin of mine—"

Vivienne had to bite her tongue to keep silent. Owens might not be the swiftest of mortals, but even she would wonder why Vivienne was so anxious for her to be gone if she pressed her to hurry. That meant Vivienne had to endure Owens's description of her cousin's fatal, night-air-inspired illness as the maid slowly made her way toward the door.

"Good night, Owens," she said as the maid finally finished. "I promise I'll put everything away carefully."

Owens nodded and went out the door, leaving Vivienne alone.

After carefully hanging her gown in the armoire, she went to her dressing table and began to take down her hair, reminding herself that there was a chance Rob would not come tonight. Perhaps he would decide it was too risky.

As excited and hopeful as she was by the possibility of seeing him again, she had to admit it was dangerous. How would it look if her suitor's solicitor was discovered sneaking into the bedchamber of his client's intended bride?

If she were being practical, she would not have suggested this plan. She would have thought of another way.

Practicality, however, seemed to disappear when she thought of being alone with Rob.

As her hair tumbled about her shoulders, a soft rap sounded on the casement window. Turning swiftly, she spotted a face—Rob's face— peering in the window like a ghostly spirit.

She ran to the window. He stood on the sloping roof of the stable as comfortably as other men did a ballroom floor. Despite the chill night air, he wasn't wearing his jacket, but only a shirt and breeches. Shockingly, his feet were bare.

"Open the window full, then stand back," he said quietly.

She did so and he swung himself up and over the sill. He jumped down into her room as lightly as if he had been sired by a cat.

"I've never seen anything like that," Vivienne murmured with awe.

Rob glanced around the unfamiliar room and, with the instincts of a thief, noted the thick red and white damask bedcurtains and spread, the bronze candle stand bearing several beeswax candles, the small feminine items on the dressing table, and the armoire near the door where she probably kept a cask of jewelry, the contents easy to carry off or throw to the ground and take from there to be pawned.

"It is simple enough when you've had practice," he said, his dishonest observations slipping away as he looked at Vivienne.

She was like a heavenly vision, with her thick hair curling loose about her shoulders, her white nightgown ethereal. If she had sported a halo, it wouldn't have struck him as surprising.

Even if the feelings she inspired were all too earthbound. He wanted to sweep her into his arms, carry her to the bed and make love with her until morning.

In order to calm himself, he fastened on the subject of his past experience. "This was very easy. Finnigan used to lower me down from the roofs holding on to my ankles," he explained. "It was my job to get into the house and sneak down to open the door for him."

"Good God!" she cried softly, clasping her hands before her. "You must have been terrified."

"The first few times," he admitted.

Going to the window to close it, she passed him, and he caught the subtle, enticing scent of her rose perfume. She leaned over the sill and looked out the window. "Where are your other clothes?"

He moved farther into the room, away from her. "I left them on the stable roof. Leather soles and wool stockings are too slick for climbing on slate. I found that out the hard way. It slowed me down, and Finnigan didn't like that."

She turned to face him, her expression full of sympathy. "Oh, Rob, I'm sorry."

He shrugged. "I am just glad I was never caught. It would have been the noose for me, or transportation, I suppose. Given what I have heard of what happened to some of the boys I knew, I think I would have preferred hanging."

"But you were a child."

"In the eyes of the law, I would have been nothing but a thief."

She moved toward him, her silk gown softly swishing against the floor. "I suppose I should be counting my blessings."

In his rational mind, he knew he should back away. Better yet, if he were being truly rational, he would never have come here. Indeed, he had spent the better part of the day trying to convince himself to stay away. Not only did he find Vivienne too passionately tempting—although that should be enough to dissuade him—it would be disastrous if he were caught with her.

Her reputation would be destroyed.

Yet when night fell, all he could think about

was being with Vivienne and that he had never been caught housebreaking.

When she came toward him and put her arms around him, he couldn't tell her to stop. He couldn't even move, because he loved the feel of her in his arms, the scent of her perfume, the way the candles made her skin like gold.

Then she raised herself on tip toe and kissed him, the movements of her lips as soft and light as the brush of a moth's wing.

Now, at this moment, he could dare to hope that a future with Vivienne was not impossible. As his embrace tightened around her, he could believe that anything was feasible.

She stopped kissing him and splayed her hands on his chest, looking up into his face. "I fear, Mr. Heartless Harding, that I am clay in your hands. There is no other man I would allow to sneak into my bedchamber."

The warmth of her hands penetrated his clothing, and as her touch sent the blood thrumming through his body, he thought he might always feel their imprint. "There is no other woman I would take that risk for."

He ran his hands up her slender arms in a slow caress, over the soft silk of her sleeves to her shoulders shrouded with her unbound hair.

She had the most marvelous hair, and he wanted to run his fingers through it, to feel it slip over and around his hands.

He heard a sound and glanced sharply at the door. "I should go—"

"No, not yet. The floorboards creak in this house, but that doesn't mean somebody is right outside my door. Still . . ." She took his hand and led him toward the bed.

"Vivienne, what are you doing?"

She gave him an enticing smile. "Please sit."

"Where?"

"On the bed."

He looked at that massive piece of furniture, covered in a fine damask coverlet that matched the curtains. The headboard was ornately carved with vines and grapes, like the posts. He guessed that he would sink six inches if he got upon the featherbed.

In his chambers, he slept on a bed slung with ropes and a mattress stuffed with straw, and considered himself lucky.

But the expensive nature of the bedding was not what made him hesitate. "Vivienne, this might not be wise."

"If I were wise, I would not have invited you here," she replied with a charming smile. "If I were wise, I would never have kissed you when we stood in the street. Indeed, if I were wise, I would have fled from you the moment you spoke to me in Bankside. Fortunately, while I am not a fool, I am apparently not at all wise."

"Are you not afraid to be alone with me and

on your bed?" he persisted. "You know I was not raised a gentleman."

"You are more of a gentleman than most supposed gentlemen I have met. Now please sit down." When he still hesitated, she suddenly put her hands on his chest and shoved. Caught unawares, he fell back—and landed on the featherbed, sinking six inches into the down.

His heart beating like a musician's drum, he struggled to sit up. As he did so, she lifted a single candle from the stand, put it in a smaller holder and blew out the rest of the candles.

By the time he had succeeded in sitting up, but before he could get to his feet, she was beside the bed, the glow from the candle lighting her lovely face. "Please, Rob, I want to be alone with you, without fear of interruption."

"But Vivienne, I am in your room. On your bed. If anybody were to enter—"

"They will not see you." With another smile, she slowly began to draw the curtains around the bed. "And I trust you are an honorable man."

Simple words simply spoken, but they meant the world to him.

He would stay, at least a little while yet.

Just before she closed the curtains completely, and still gripping the candleholder, she got upon the bed, then reached behind her and tugged the curtains together so that there was no opening.

This was like some beautiful, glorious dream. With the dim light glowing upon her beautiful face, enclosed in such intimacy, the luxurious surroundings and the delicate scent of her perfume, he might have been in a fairy tale, or some fantasy upon the stage, or a potentate's tent in an Oriental land. She even sat cross-legged, her silk gown billowing out around her. "There. Nobody will see if they open the door," she said softly as she settled into place.

This was too private, he thought with something akin to panic. He didn't know if he had the strength to keep away from her.

A lustful assignation was not what he wanted. He wanted everything to be as honorable as possible, and he should not put himself in the way of such enticement.

She shifted closer.

"Vivienne," he said with a hint of desperation in his voice, "we should not be here like this."

"I'm not afraid of you."

"You should be."

"Why?"

"Because I am but a mortal man, and you are a very tempting woman."

"Yet you always manage to be so restrained."

"I am not normally sitting on a bed with a desirable woman."

"I am holding a candle," she noted. "You must be careful, or you will set the bed on fire."

"I could always blow it out."

"Yes."

She still wasn't afraid, or even anxious. She looked excited, even aroused, and she was breathing as hard as he.

Her obvious desire inflamed his passion. "What would you do if I did blow it out?" he whispered, his voice low and husky with yearning.

"I don't know," she confessed.

Intending to take her in his arms, he moved forward, until the flicker of the candle brought him to a halt. *God in heaven*, his rational mind shouted, *what are you doing? You were a Bankside thief and you have no more right to be here than to proclaim yourself king.* "This is wrong, Vivienne." He raked his hand through his hair. "Being in your bedchamber is wrong, and being on your bed is worse."

"You are here by my invitation."

"That does not make it right."

She cocked her head. "Will you presume to make my decisions for me, too?"

"I care about you, Vivienne, and it is because I do that I should go. I am only a man, and you entice me beyond all reason."

"Are you a beast, Mr. Harding? Are you trying to tell me you have no more self-control than a dumb animal?"

"I hope I have more morality than an animal."

"I believe you do, and therefore I see no reason we cannot conduct ourselves with propriety."

"Vivienne, we are sitting on your bed with the curtains drawn."

"For privacy. The king conducts state business in his bed. Why can we not have a conversation under similar circumstances?"

"The king does not conduct state business with a beautiful woman in his bed."

"How do you know? Maybe he does. I gather Lady Castlemaine is forever interfering in the affairs of state." Vivienne's expression grew both serious and pleading. "Please, Rob, don't run away. I am very tempted by you, too, you know, yet I am determined to know more about you. I want to talk to you without fear of interruption, and I can think of no other way to go about it." She put her hand on the bed and pushed herself back. "I promise I shall sit over here, as long as you won't leave."

In truth, he didn't want to go. He wanted to stay. But she was so very alluring, looking at him with her luminous blue eyes, her full lips parted, her low round bodice exposing the tops of her lovely creamy breasts.

He should go. Now. At once.

And yet . . . "Very well, I will stay, but I would rather we talked about you," he said. "Your family, and how you came to live with your uncle, for instance."

With a nod of her head, she agreed. "That is a simple enough tale," she replied. "My parents died at nearly the same time, of the same fever. I lived, and was sent here as a temporary measure, I suppose, until a school or other place could be found for me. Then one day my uncle realized that he received more orders for his goods if I was seen in them and he let me stay."

Although she spoke matter-of-factly, he heard the undercurrent of pain and sorrow beneath. She had been as lonely and unloved as he, and had known the bitter anguish of loss.

She gave him a wistful smile. "I realize that compared to your life, my past is not so bad. Mind you, my parents and I were not nearly so well off as my uncle. I once heard him say that his brother, my father, had no head for business, and I daresay he was right. Still, it could have been much worse, and I promise you, Rob, that I will never look at an urchin in the streets the same way again."

"Your past is not as wonderful as I thought it must have been," he admitted. "And mine was not all deprivation and sorrow. As you had your parents, I had Jack and Janet."

"Who is Jack?"

"Janet's brother. You saw him with me at the theater, I believe. He was the man with the patch I was speaking to."

"Yes, I did see him. I confess, I tried not to

look at you and couldn't help myself. What happened to his eye?"

"Nothing. He doesn't wear the patch because he has to. He claims women think it's attractive."

Vivienne giggled, and the lighthearted sound in the intimacy of their "tent" delighted him. "Attractive? Only if one has an affinity for pirates, I think."

"Well, whatever you or I think, I must confess it does seem effective." He sobered again. "I have sent Jack to watch Lord Cheddersby. If Sir Philip tries to harm him, Jack will call an alarm. I suspect that despite my warning, he would even interfere. Jack enjoys a good fight."

"Did he ever fight you?"

"Often."

"You won, didn't you?"

He made a wry grin. "Not always. Jack can be very fierce."

"Did you ever wear an eye patch to attract the ladies?"

"No. Women liked me well enough without it."

He saw the merriment leave her eyes, and although he regretted that, a part of him insisted she must know this about him, too. "I have not lived a celibate life, Vivienne."

"I didn't suppose you had."

Forgetting his resolution not to touch her, he reached out and took her warm hand in his as he looked into her eyes. "But after Janet left me, there has never been another woman I cared about in my life, not until I met you."

Her expression serious, but her eyes dancing with delight, she waggled her finger in a warning gesture. "Have a care what you say, sir. I am trying to keep away from you."

He nodded, for she was right. He should watch where his thoughts and words tended.

"So tell me, what else did you do when you were a boy? You could not have been stealing all the time."

"Jack and Janet and I would spend hours sometimes floating twigs down the gutter, pretending they were ships sailing out to sea. Jack's were always pirate vessels."

"Perhaps that is why he has such an affinity for an eye patch," Vivienne observed.

"That might very well explain it," he replied with a low chuckle. "Janet's was always a merchant vessel carrying rich fabrics and jewels."

"And your ships, Rob? What were your ships carrying?"

He looked down at the damask coverlet. "Mine were passenger vessels, taking people to far-off lands to begin a new life."

"I wish I could have seen you as a boy, Rob."

"I am very glad you did not," he replied with a rueful grin. "I was thin as any twig we set sail, and my nose ran all the time. Also, I was filthy. It took Mr. Godwin's housekeeper an hour of scrubbing to get me clean, and it was weeks before we got all the dirt out from under my fingernails."

Shifting forward, Vivienne lifted his hand and examined it, holding the candle close to her face. "I don't see any dirt there now, just ink on your fingers."

She turned his hand over so that she was looking at his palm. "You have nice hands, Rob."

He couldn't move. He couldn't even pull his hand away, not then and not when she pressed a delicate kiss upon his palm.

"Vivienne," he moaned softly, tearing his eyes away from her lips on his hand to look at the top of her head. "Vivienne, stop."

She raised her questioning eyes.

Then she blew out the candle.

Chapter 13

Rob gasped.

"If the candle is burned too low," Vivienne explained, "Owens will be suspicious."

That was partly true. It was more true, though, that she found it difficult to see the pain flash across his face as he told her of his past, and keep away from him. Every ounce of her wanted to take him in her arms and hold him tight. She feared he might bolt like a startled horse if she did, and since she wanted him to stay, she wouldn't risk it.

"I should not stay."

"Rob—"

"Vivienne." The featherbed shifted as he moved closer. "If I don't leave you now," he whispered huskily, "I will have to touch you. And if I touch you, I will want to kiss you, and if

I kiss you, I won't want to stop until I make love with you."

She swallowed hard, feeling how close he was to her. "Perhaps I would not want you to stop," she confessed in a small, small voice.

"Vivienne, you don't understand what you are saying."

She stiffened. "Yes, I do."

"No, you don't," he insisted. "I cannot deny that I want you with a passion I have never felt before, and I'm sure you think you feel the same for me. But passion can be fleeting. And . . ."

"And?" she prompted, wishing she had not blown out the candle, Owens or no Owens, so that she could see his expression.

"And I don't want to take advantage of you."

"You would protect me from myself?"

"Yes."

It was on the tip of her tongue to chide him for treating her like a child—until she realized that she would be criticizing him for the very thing she had admired him for earlier. He helped and protected people. Wouldn't it be wise to listen to him, especially when she wanted him not for a night, but for the rest of her life?

Nevertheless, she wasn't about to surrender completely, not in this. "I'll agree on one condition."

"A condition?" he said, obviously surprised.

"That you will come back tomorrow night."

She inched forward, until their knees touched. "I want to know you, Rob, and I want you to know me. Please tell me you'll come back tomorrow. I promise I shall not kiss you if you do."

"Oh, Vivienne," he said with a sigh.

"Rob, I am a very stubborn woman, and I suppose you should know that about me, too, unattractive though it may be. I will acquiesce to your concern about my lack of willpower—"

"I meant no criticism."

"What else was it? But I do not blame you. I confess that I may not be thinking with a clear head where you are concerned. Therefore, to prove to you that I am not a fool, I will let you leave without so much as a kiss—but only if you promise me you will come back tomorrow. How else can we discover if there is more between us than lust, and since I can see no other way to be alone, what else can we do?"

"You argue like a lawyer," he muttered.

"Thank you."

"Vivienne, you said you were clay in my hands. I fear I am clay in yours, because I cannot refuse."

"Good."

She rose and parted the curtains, and as she did so, a shaft of pale moonlight illuminated him.

Sitting on her bed, his open shirt white against his skin, his long legs tucked beneath him, his gaze focused on her and her alone, his mouth parted as if in hopes of her kiss, he looked like some kind of specter from another world sent in answer to her prayers for the perfect man to love.

She exhaled slowly as he stood and came toward her, his gaze so intense, she felt as if they were the only two people in London, or perhaps even the world.

Then, as if reading her mind and her heart, and despite his own words, he cradled her head in his lean, strong fingers and pulled her to him. His mouth captured hers in a long, luxurious kiss as if they had all the time in the world.

She clung to him, wrapping her arms about him, demanding with her lips and her hands that he stay and never, ever go.

He broke away. "Oh, God save me, Vivienne, I cannot help myself. I dare not come here again. The temptation is too great."

"I don't think—"

He put his finger against her lips. "You must. We are both in the throes of a passion that I fear is stronger than either of us, and so risky and dangerous. We must try to be reasonable."

"I don't want to be reasonable. I'faith, I fear I cannot be reasonable where you are concerned. My heart demands otherwise."

He cocked his head and regarded her as studiously as he might a complicated will. "You judge in haste, Mistress Burroughs, for you have not heard what I consider reasonable at this point in time."

"You are not going to try to tell me we mustn't see each other ever again?" she asked hopefully, for there was a hint of amusement in his deep voice.

"In view of the present circumstances, and," he continued, his voice lowering to an intimate whisper, "the feelings I cannot master, no matter how hard I try, I think it would be unreasonable to attempt to deny myself the pleasure of your company. I doubt I would be able to maintain that resolution."

"I am glad you're being sensible."

"Well, sensible about my irrationality, I suppose," he agreed.

"When and how can I see you?"

He frowned. "That I do not know." And then, to her great joy, his wonderful lips curved up into a smile. "But I do know this: If there is a way, I will find it."

"Or perhaps I can think of something."

"That is a distinct possibility, my clever Vivienne."

No compliment on her form or beauty had ever delighted her as much as him calling her clever.

"So, I will not bid you good-bye," he continued as he sat upon her windowsill and swung his legs outside. "But only adieu."

"Adieu, my love," she whispered, wrapping her arms about her as he smiled once more before dropping down onto the stable roof.

She hurried to the window and watched as he cautiously, with a catlike stealth, crept across the roof, then dropped from sight.

"So there I was, nearly falling out of the box, and if Neville hadn't grabbed the back of my jacket, I would have plunged to my death—right at the climax, too," Lord Cheddersby declared as he walked beside Vivienne in St. James's Park three days later.

He had come to visit and asked Uncle Elias if he could escort her for a walk about the park. Uncle Elias had readily agreed, not asking Vivienne how she felt about it. However, even if he had, she didn't think she could have refused on the grounds that she was hoping Mr. Harding might stop by.

So now here she was, ambling about St. James's Park supposedly listening to Lord Cheddersby talk about his friends, Owens dutifully trailing behind, yet all the while wondering if Rob had come to her uncle's, only to find her absent. Perhaps he would use the marriage negotiations as an excuse. It would not be the best way to meet, as experience had shown, but it had been three days, and she was beginning to fear he might not be able to find another way.

She did not doubt that he wanted to see her. He had made that very clear when they parted before. She only feared that he would try to ensure as little risk as possible. Although she could not fault him for that, it was likely that there must be some risk—not that she feared taking a risk, if being with him was the prize.

If he didn't contrive a way to see her soon, she would slip away from Owens and go to his office. Or, she mused as she glanced at Owens walking slowly behind them, maybe she could think of a way to get away from both her maid and Lord Cheddersby this very day.

As she continued to survey the park, she also looked for Rob's friend who was supposed to be watching out for Lord Cheddersby. She had seen no sign of him, but he was probably an expert at keeping his presence a secret. The only people near to them at present were a couple—a tall, roguish-looking fellow in a bright yellow coat and a very pretty young woman who hung on his arm and whispered in his ear.

"Surely your friend would have been upset if you had fallen," Vivienne said, realizing that she should, perhaps, comment on what her companion had just said.

"Oh, yes, of course, he would have been concerned for the state of my pate, but he would have been furious just the same."

Vivienne subdued an urge to smile. She was sure Lord Cheddersby, who was looking very serious, had not meant to make a rhyme.

"As it was, my new jacket was ripped from collar to hem," Lord Cheddersby concluded with a sigh.

"You sound as if you miss Lord Farrington and Sir Richard," Vivienne noted.

"I do! I have nobody left."

"You must have some friends in London if you are having a fete."

"Oh yes, a few. A hundred or so. And the king, of course."

"The king will be there?"

"I cannot say for certain. It all depends on his mood. He may, or he may not."

"I think I had better not tell my uncle about that. He would be so disappointed if the king did not come, after all."

"Well, I must say I don't mind if Charles doesn't trouble himself. He's rather . . . over-whelming."

"He struck me as a very pleasant man, for a king."

"Oh, I assure you, Mistress Burroughs, that I meant no criticism. He is a pleasant man, especially to his good friends and his mistresses. Lord, I don't know where he finds the patience to put up with half of Lady Castlemaine's tantrums."

Vivienne cleared her throat delicately. "I understand she has her ways of compensating him."

"Indeed, yes," Lord Cheddersby replied matter-of-factly, "if you think that's sufficient. I would rather have more peace."

"I think you are a very wise man in that regard, my lord."

"Do you really?" he cried, looked at her with unabashed delight.

"Yes." She hesitated a moment. "And you have Mr. Harding for a friend."

"Yes, I do, I suppose, but he's rather forbiddingly grim. Still, I've invited him to my fete, too."

This pleased Vivienne much more than the possibility of the king's presence.

"To be honest—and although I am pleased he accepted—I really thought he would decline," Lord Cheddersby confessed. "He doesn't seem the sort to go to fetes. I mean, have you ever seen anybody so frighteningly solemn? I swear he makes me feel guilty even when I haven't done anything more serious than curse my tailor."

"Have you known him long?"

"Oh, yes, he's been making my clothes since I was five."

"I meant Mr. Harding."

"No, not really. Lady Dovercourt knew him and recommended him quite highly. Her father hired him, and I gather he was pretty sharp about such things. I was very glad to have him in the matter of . . . well, in the matter I needed him for."

"Really?" Vivienne prompted, halting for a moment.

She didn't notice that the couple nearby had also come to a stop, or that the young woman was studying her with great interest.

"It was a minor piece of business, but he did it very well, I must say."

"What sort of business?" she prodded.

Lord Cheddersby's flush deepened. "Nothing important."

He had not made such an abrupt response to anything else she said, so Vivienne did not press him further. "He seems a very competent lawyer."

"I was quite desperate for company when I asked him along to the theater," Lord Cheddersby admitted with a genial smile as they continued walking toward the canal. "I am very glad I did, because he allowed me to meet you."

"Yes, he did."

"Would you care to stop at a coffeehouse? I would be happy to buy you some chocolate."

Vivienne shivered at the thought. She had tasted that bitter brew once, and it was horrid. "No, thank you, Lord Cheddersby. Perhaps it is time we headed home. My uncle may be wondering where we are."

"Oh, yes, indeed." As they turned back, Lord Cheddersby came to a halt so suddenly, he nearly fell over. "Good Lord! That's Nell Gwynn," he cried, staring at the young woman clinging to the young man. "Oh, odd's bodikins, it's her. Here. In the flesh. She's even more beautiful than on the stage. Oh dear, I feel faint."

"Here, my lord, hold on to me," Vivienne offered as she struggled to put her shoulder beneath his arm, for the young man had truly gone deathly pale.

Then she realized the couple were approaching.

"Do you need any help?" the young woman asked.

She really was quite pretty, with rich chestnut hair and bright hazel eyes, and now Vivienne could see that Lord Cheddersby had been quite correct. It was the same woman she had seen upon the stage of the King's Theatre.

As for the man beside her . . . it was Rob's friend. Up close, he looked more frightening than he had at the theater, lack of an eye patch notwithstanding, and as his gaze raked her body, he seemed an insolent rogue. Yet Rob called him a friend. Given their upbringing, perhaps she was being too quick to pass judgment.

Lord Cheddersby staggered to a more upright position, then bowed. "M-mistress Gwynn, this is delightful," he stammered like a peasant facing a royal princess. "I cannot tell you how much I enjoyed you in *The Happy Troubadour*. You were a revelation!"

"Well, parts of me were revealed right enough," she replied with a hearty laugh. "And who might you be, sir?"

"Me? Oh, I am . . . I am . . . Foz . . . Fozbury . . . I think."

Vivienne thought she had better come to her

companion's aid. "This is Lord Cheddersby," she said. "And I am Vivienne Burroughs."

"Ah!" The actress nodded knowingly as she glanced at the man beside her. "This is Mistress Burroughs, Jack. Mistress Burroughs, Lord Cheddersby, this is Jack Leesom."

Lord Cheddersby's brow furrowed. "Do I know you, Mr. Leesom? Have we met at the races at Newmarket, perhaps?"

"I don't think so."

"Maybe you saw him at the theater?" Nell suggested. "He's there nearly as often as you."

"Oh, yes, I believe I did," Lord Cheddersby said, clearly relieved to have that mystery solved. "You were talking to Mr. Harding."

"You know Heartless Harding?" Nell asked.

"He never told me he knew you!" Lord Cheddersby cried.

"He never told me he knew you, neither," she replied with rather surprising coyness, given her bold manner and brazen comment moments before. "I'll take him to task for that, I will. Imagine him knowing a fine young lord like you and not telling me. Why, it's selfish, that is. Very selfish."

Lord Cheddersby blushed bright red from his collar to his wig. Meanwhile, Vivienne glanced at Jack Leesom.

Who winked at her.

That was not at all pleasant. He made her feel

as if he thought she belonged on the stage. Or in a brothel.

"Why, here he is. I'll give him what-for right now," the actress declared, looking past Vivienne.

She glanced over her shoulder, and sure enough, beyond a clearly stunned Owens, Rob came striding toward them, his visage as grim as usual.

"Well, Rob Harding, aren't you the fine one?" Nell demanded as he drew closer. "Fancy you knowing Lord Cheddersby here and not telling me about him."

"Mistress Gwynn, I have several acquaintances that I don't mention to you," he replied gravely as he made a polite bow.

Vivienne feared she was blushing more than Lord Cheddersby had, and didn't know where to look. Nevertheless, she couldn't help but steal a glance at Rob.

He looked wonderful, if serious, his bearing more regal in his plain black woolen clothes than Lord Cheddersby's or even, she decided, King Charles's.

"Good day, my lord, Mistress Burroughs, Mistress Gwynn, Mr. Leesom." He looked at Vivienne. "I have just come from your uncle's." His gaze continued toward Lord Cheddersby. "He tells me he has just received a shipment of some particularly fine silk from Italy, and he thought you might be interested, my lord, so I offered to bring you the news. He fears it will not be long before it is sold."

"Italian silk?"

"The silk itself is from Cathay. He bought it from an Italian merchant."

An obviously conflicted Lord Cheddersby looked at Nell Gwynn, then back to Rob. "Silk from Cathay?" he repeated in a whisper.

"Cathay," Robert confirmed. "He implied there was no time to be lost. Allow me to suggest that you get a hackney coach back to Mr. Burroughs's." He glanced at Owens. "I also suggest you take the maid with you. She's looking very fatigued."

With a pang of remorse, Vivienne noted that he was quite right. Owens looked exhausted.

"Oh, dear me . . . I don't know . . ."

"Please, Lord Cheddersby, I don't mind," Vivienne said, "and the day is so fine, I would like to walk a little more. I shall be quite safe with Mr. Harding, I'm sure, out here in the park. I promise you we shall head straight back to my uncle's."

"I've always wanted to see silk from so far away," Nell Gwynn murmured.

"Have you? Have you really?" Lord Cheddersby asked eagerly. "Why don't you come along with me, then? I shall be delighted to purchase some for you. A very small recompense for the pleasure you gave me at the theater."

Nell smiled like a cat with a bowl full of

cream in front of her. "Well, I'd be a fool to say no to that, wouldn't I? And there'll be plenty of room for that old deary in a coach, won't there? She reminds me of me mother, except the maid is sober," she added with another laugh as she slipped her arm through Lord Cheddersby's. "That'd be all right, wouldn't it, my lord?"

Lord Cheddersby suddenly looked as torn as Paris trying to decide between the goddesses. "I don't think I should leave Mistress Burroughs like this."

"Mr. Harding is most trustworthy, I'm sure," Vivienne said, careful not to sound too keen.

"Real silk," Nell said with a sigh. "All the way from where Marco Polo went. And a piece for me? I'll have to be sure to thank you proper, my lord."

Whatever objections Lord Cheddersby had, they obviously withered away at that. "Come along, then, Mistress Gwynn, Owens," he said, offering the maid his other arm. "I'll tell your uncle to expect you shortly, Mistress Burroughs."

"Please do," she replied with a nod that he didn't see, for he was already heading off with Nell and Owens.

Very aware that Jack Leesom was still with them, Vivienne faced Rob, who gave Jack a pointed look. "Don't you have something to do?"

"Nell'll watch him like a hawk if there's a present in it."

"Jack," Rob chided softly.

"Oh, all right. I'm off after His Lordship who's so delighted about fabric." He gave Vivienne a jaunty bow. "Farewell to you, Mistress Burroughs. You keep your wits about you, now, and don't let Rob take liberties."

A slightly sheepish expression appeared on Rob's face and a blush colored his cheeks, making her feel curiously lighthearted. "I'm sure I have nothing to fear from Mr. Harding."

"Oh, I don't know about that," Jack mused. "He's done some pretty naughty things in his day."

"I know."

"You do?"

"Jack," Rob growled in warning.

Jack grinned. "Right. I've got a job to do, so off I go. Until another time, Mistress Burroughs." He reached out and took her gloved hand, then, before she could pull it away, lifted it to his lips and kissed the back of it.

She was very glad she had gloves on.

Before he sauntered off in the same direction as Lord Cheddersby, Mistress Gwynn and Owens, he made a sly, smug little smile that didn't cause her to feel any more disposed to like him, even though he was Rob's friend.

"And thus we are alone," Rob murmured, his lips slowly curving up in a smile.

"Did you plan this, Mr. Harding?" Vivienne demanded with mock indignation.

"I wish I could say that I did," he confessed with a smile, "but in truth, it is pure serendipity. I could think of no better excuse to see you than the marriage settlement. It truly was your uncle's idea to summon Lord Cheddersby. I believe he sees a large profit from the man.

"As for Nell and Jack, I know Jack sometimes invites his female friends along on such jobs. He claims it makes him less noticeable."

"Nell Gwynn strikes me as a very noticeable woman," Vivienne observed.

Rob grinned, an expression so delightful, she had to laugh. "I will have to mention that to Jack. Somehow, though, I don't think he will listen to me."

Vivienne realized that there were a few other people nearby, several of them eyeing them curiously. "As happy as I am to see you, I think it might have been better for us to meet at my uncle's."

Again he grinned, and this time, there was a hint of mischief in his dark eyes. "Then let us leave this public place."

She flushed hotly even as she put her hand on his arm.

"And go where?"

"Why, to your uncle's, as promised." He looked

down into her eyes. "I grew up in the streets of the city, so I know them very well. You will be amazed at the different ways one can take to the same destination. I intend to take you by my secret route."

Chapter 14

As Vivienne and Rob made their way through the back lanes and alleys that lay within the populous city, there were still more people about than Rob would have liked.

He wanted to be alone with Vivienne.

However, he could take some comfort in the fact that none of the people they encountered were ever likely to have anything to do with a merchant of Mr. Burroughs's affluence, so they would not know who Vivienne was, or tell him about seeing her with Rob.

Occasionally, someone who knew him, either an acquaintance or former client, would call out to him, and they would stop and converse for a little while. No matter what reason they assigned for Vivienne's silent presence beside him, the people were inevitably respectful and polite.

Nevertheless, every time they were stopped in this way, he gave Vivienne a sidelong glance, half afraid that he would detect some sign of dismay or disgust in her expression for the lower-class people with whom he regularly associated.

He never did. In fact, she seemed quite fascinated.

And then, finally, when they were within a half mile of the mercer's buildings, they turned into a lane that ended in a brick wall at one end and twisted abruptly at the other. No windows looked out upon it, and it wasn't malodorous with trash or offal.

"There is nobody here. And this seems so out of the way, there is not likely to be, I would guess," Vivienne remarked as she stopped and turned to him with a pleased smile. "I knew you were an admirable man and worthy of respect, Robert Harding, but I had no notion you were so well liked."

He blinked. "I don't think I am liked. Appreciated, perhaps, for the work I do, but . . ." He shrugged.

"I saw it in the smiles of all those people when they greeted you, Rob. They like you as well as respect you, and I can understand why when I see you with them."

She smoothed the front of his plain wool jacket. Even that simple caress was enough to make his heart race. "You are different then, or more like you were the night we met. I thought the second time I met you I must have been mistaken to believe you a kind man, but I know now that the man I met in Bankside is far more the real Robert Harding that the cold solicitor who came to my uncle's house with Sir Philip."

His heart seemed unsure how to beat, even as a part of him wondered if this was why he had brought her this way home, to see how she reacted. And perhaps to prove that he was admired and respected.

As for the apparent affection of people, he had always hoped it was so, but this was the first time anybody had given credence to those hopes, and that it should be Vivienne pleased him greatly.

Nevertheless, he felt honor-bound to take her by her slender shoulders, look down into her questioning blue eyes and say, "This is my world, Vivienne, and I have shown you the best of it, not the worst."

She smiled. "Do you think to frighten me off with this demonstration? If so, I must tell you that you have failed miserably. I know that I have lived a somewhat coddled life, Rob, but anyone who lives in London has to comprehend that there are parts of it and lives being lived that are nearly beyond our ability to imagine." She slipped her arms about his waist as she continued to regard him steadily. "With your education, you could have left London and gone to York or Salisbury or any other city in the country and started to practice law. You chose to stay. Why?"

"Because . . . because I thought I was needed, because I could understand the plight of the poor."

Again she smiled, her expression lighting him as if from within. "Can you not see, Rob, that all you show and tell me only proves that you are an even better man than I suspected? Do you expect your noble generosity, your heartfelt wish to help people, to dissuade me? It will not."

Her expression changed to one both questioning and worried. "Do you fear that one day I will grow disgusted with your life and desert you, too?"

In truth, he had not consciously thought that; yet, as he stared down into her sympathetic face, he knew that she had seen even deeper into his heart than he had. "Perhaps I do," he admitted.

"Have no fear then, Rob," she whispered softly. Tenderly. Affectionately. "Seeing you with those people only makes me love you more."

Was it possible for the heart to swell, to feel as if it could joyfully burst the confines of your chest? At this moment, Robert believed that such a thing was indeed possible.

And then, in the next instant, he was kissing her, not with the passion that she always stirred within him, but with responding tenderness. Affection.

Love.

A more complete, total love than he had ever known.

His lips slipped along her soft cheek as he held her close, and he whispered in her ear, "Vivienne, my darling, my love, of all the things I had hoped for in my life, I had never foreseen how happy I could be, perhaps because there could have been no way of knowing that such a woman as you would cross my path, let alone come to care for me, and so quickly. . . ."

As he said that, a dark shadow fell across his hopeful path. "Vivienne, although I don't doubt the strength of my feelings for you, or the sincerity of yours, this has happened so quickly."

Her gaze faltered, and again his heart seemed to lose track of its natural rhythm. He was not sorry that he said what he had, for he believed it to be true.

Yet he wished it were not so.

Then she lifted her head and looked at him with firm conviction. "Rob, things happen quickly all the time. We both know that life can change in the seeming blink of an eye. One day, I had a mother and father who loved me, and each other. Three days later, I was an orphan. One day, you were a pickpocket, the next you had been given a wonderful opportunity to better your lot. One night, I was alone and desperate, and then a wonderful man appeared out of the fog to offer me hope."

"Vivienne—"

She put her hand on his cheek. "Rob, you are wise to be cautious, I know, but please don't let the speed with which our feelings have grown convince you that they will be any weaker for all that."

"I just can't believe that I should be so lucky in my life."

"Lucky is not how I would describe your life."

"Whatever I have endured has been rewarded by your love," he murmured as he bent his head to kiss her once more, intending it to be as tender and gentle as before.

Yet how could it be, after hearing her determined, confident, heartfelt words? This time, as the passion flared within him, he could not subdue it.

With a low moan of surrender, he pressed her closer, reveling in the sensation of her curvaceous body against his. He slid his hand beneath her soft velvet cloak to the even softer silk of her bodice beneath. She relaxed against him, and he could feel her giving herself up to her desire, just as he was. His kiss deepened, and his tongue slipped easily through her parted lips to intertwine and taste.

Panting, he broke the kiss to trail his hungry lips along her throat as she arched back, as supple as a willow bending in the breeze.

He wanted her so much! He wanted to make love with her, possess her body as she possessed his heart and mind, take her at once, here . . .

In a back alley as if she were a Bankside whore?

Breathing heavily, fighting the powerful, natural urge singing in his veins, he forced himself to stop.

Her lips swollen, her eyes dark with desire, Vivienne looked at him with confusion.

"This isn't what I want," he said hoarsely. "Not like this."

Understanding dawned, and Vivienne softly said, "Then come to me tonight, in my bedchamber, as you did before."

He shook his head. "No, Vivienne. As tempting as that is, I don't want to sneak about as if I am still some kind of thief, stealing your virtue dishonorably.

"I think we must not see one another alone again until Sir Philip's suit is dispensed with. Then I will be able to court you honorably. And then, whatever happens, we know we tried to conduct ourselves as an honest man and woman who are unashamed of their feelings should."

"When you put it in such terms, how can I disagree?" she replied. "But," she continued, toying with the button of his jacket, "I will not like it."

He covered her hand with his. "Nor will I. Indeed, I think it will be torture. Nevertheless, I believe it must be so. There must be no cause for scandal or shame, beyond that which we cannot avoid because of who I am."

"Then I hope Sir Philip gives up very soon."
She smiled. "I do think my uncle is much less
keen on him than before, thanks to Lord Cheddersby. And the king."

"The king?" Robert said, his eyes widening.

"Yes. Have you ever heard anything so ridiculous? One meeting, and my uncle already has me
ensconced in a house of the king's providing,
with servants and jewels and who knows what
else." She laughed softly. "There is no need to
look so grave. I promise you, this is my uncle's
wishful thinking, and nothing more."

She was so certain, he had to believe her, even
though a part of him could easily accept that any
man who set eyes on her would want her.

She slipped her arm through his and gave
him a disarming smile. "As loath as I am to part
with you, I fear we have lingered here long
enough, especially if we do not want to give my
uncle any hint about our feelings."

"Good God, yes," Rob cried, aghast that he
had not thought of this himself. He started to
walk quickly, Vivienne at his side.

"And it is not as if we will never see one another," Vivienne remarked, slightly out of breath
as she tried to keep up with him. "You will still
come to my uncle's house occasionally, I trust.
And you will go to Lord Cheddersby's fete,
won't you?"

She halted and forced him to stop, too.

"Robert, I am not a racehorse. I cannot keep up with you if you go so quickly."

"Forgive me."

They started walking again, this time at a more reasonable pace as they entered another lane.

"You will come to Lord Cheddersby's fete?" she asked.

He smiled down at her. "Yes, I'll be there, torturing myself because I cannot touch you, but feasting on the sight of my love's sweet face."

"Speak to me in that manner any more today, Mr. Harding," she warned him in a manner that was both teasing and serious, "and I will drag you to my bedchamber regardless of who might see us."

"Here you are at last," Uncle Elias declared as Vivienne entered the withdrawing room the evening of Lord Cheddersby's fete. As usual, his first act was to survey her gown, in this case a truly delightful creation of pale blue damask silk, the outer skirt drawn back and held with satin ribbons to reveal an ornately embroidered silk petticoat. It was, Vivienne thought, one of the prettiest dresses he had ever had made for her. Her only concern was the scooped neckline, which was too low. Surely some of the fabric used for the full, puffed sleeves could have been spared for the bodice.

"Lovely, my dear," Uncle Elias said approvingly. "And I see you're wearing your hair in the fashion of the ladies of the court. It becomes you."

Loose ringlets fell about her bare shoulders as current fashion decreed. Such a style was, perhaps, a bit daring, but considering that the ladies of the court had adopted it, and most especially since her hair had been loose that night when Rob had come to her bedchamber, she had decided to try it.

Uncle Elias's brow furrowed as he continued to regard her. "You look quite flushed. Are you unwell?"

"No," she blurted. She took a deep, calming breath and thought of an explanation her uncle would like. "I am so pleased to be going to Lord Cheddersby's house. Lettice has told me it's quite magnificent."

"It is," Uncle Elias confirmed. "As large as a palace, and quite on the edge of the city. Parts of it actually look out onto Hampstead Heath, so he's spared all the noise and coal smoke." He cocked his head. "Does this mean you would look favorably on him if he expressed an interest in marrying you?"

She lowered her eyelids as if bashful. "Well, he hasn't done so yet."

Uncle Elias smiled broadly as he sat on the sofa. "No, not yet. And with that in mind, I thought it wise to invite Sir Philip to accompany us in our coach tonight."

"Sir Philip?" she asked, not hiding her surprise. "I didn't realize Lord Cheddersby had invited him."

She had been dreading another confrontation between Philip and Lord Cheddersby. Fortunately, she had seen neither one of them the past few days. Lord Cheddersby was no doubt busy with the preparations for his fete. As for her erstwhile suitor, she was beginning to hope he was starting to realize that his chances of securing her hand were fading.

Until, regrettably, this moment.

"He invited him," Uncle Elias replied.

"And Sir Philip accepted?"

"Obviously. When he told me, I extended an invitation to share our coach, to which he eagerly agreed."

"You have seen him recently?"

"Yesterday, at the coffeehouse."

"But Uncle," Vivienne protested, "if we arrive with Philip, what is Lord Cheddersby to think?"

"I hope he thinks he had better make his intentions more plain, and quickly, too."

So, even if her uncle didn't want Philip for a nephew by marriage, he would use him to prod another suitor into action.

Just as he used her as a dressmaker's form.

"Mr. Burroughs, Sir Philip has arrived," a footman announced from the door, and in the next moment, the young nobleman marched into the room. He nodded at Uncle Elias, who rose, bowed and returned to his seat.

Then Philip looked at Vivienne. Lust flared in his eyes, and she wished the bodice extended right up to her neck. She gave her uncle a side-long glance, but apparently he saw nothing amiss in Philip's behavior.

"You look splendid, Mistress Burroughs," he declared, bowing low. "I shall be the envy of every man at Lord Cheddersby's tonight, even the king."

Uncle Elias sat bolt upright. "The king?"

"Yes. Haven't you heard?" Philip replied, sauntering toward Vivienne. "He will be at Cheddersby's fete."

"I had no idea!" Uncle Elias replied, his eyes glowing with delight.

As upset as she was by Philip's arrival, she was happy to have the king's attendance confirmed. Charles's appearance might distract Uncle Elias enough that she could slip away and meet Rob alone for a few too-brief moments.

"Did you know anything of this?" Uncle Elias asked her.

"Lord Cheddersby told me he had invited King Charles, but was not overly hopeful of his attendance, so I thought it wiser to say nothing."

"Didn't Lettice Jerningham say anything?"

"I haven't seen Lettice in several days."

"What of Lady Castlemaine?" Uncle Elias demanded of Philip. "Will she be there? Or the queen?"

"The queen is still recovering from her illness, so she will not be there, and as for my Lady Castlemaine, who knows? She may accompany the king, or she may be in a temper."

Uncle Elias glanced at Vivienne again, and she could see that he was torn between his ambitious hopes for her and his own desire to see the king's beautiful paramour.

It occurred to Vivienne that if Philip and her uncle thought the king Philip's rival, that would spare Lord Cheddersby from both Philip's wrath and her uncle's machinations.

She sank down onto the edge of the chair and gave Philip a seriously questioning look. "Do you know, Sir Philip, if what I have heard about the queen's illness is true? Was she really so delirious she thought she had borne him a son and asked his forgiveness that the child was so ugly?"

Philip's eyes narrowed. "So they say."

"Is it also true that Charles wept and, fearing that she was dying, said that if his son be like her, he would be a fine child?"

"I have heard that, yes. I trust you have also heard that he still spent much of his time with other women while the queen was on her sickbed?" Philip added, obviously annoyed.

Uncle Elias rose and strode to the door before Vivienne could respond. "Where the devil is the coach?" he demanded as he went out into the corridor. "We don't want to be late to Lord Cheddersby's."

"No, we don't," Philip murmured as he offered Vivienne his hand to help her rise. "I am very much looking forward to making an entrance with you."

His expression was so proprietary, she wanted to slap him. Instead, she said, "Perhaps because it may be the last time you do so."

His smug smile made a shiver of fear run down her back, and his grip on her hand tightened. "Oh, I don't think so, my dear. You and your uncle are playing a very risky game, but it is one I intend to win."

She didn't know what he was implying, but she knew it meant danger. "I thought you must be the one playing games," she replied warily. "Or should I say, that you had given up the chase."

Despite the unfavorable opinion she had always had of Philip, she was not prepared for the gleam of both hunger and hatred that suddenly flared in his eyes as he raked her body with his gaze. Or his fierce strength as he tugged her closer. "Do you think you and that fat uncle of yours can make sport of me, Vivienne?" he growled. "Do you think to play me for a fool, with either that dolt Cheddersby or our lascivious sovereign? If I haven't been to see you, it's because there was no need."

"Philip, let go. You're hurting me," she said firmly, willing herself not to be afraid of him. "And don't think you can threaten me, or my uncle."

"Oh, I won't—as long as you understand that I will not be dismissed like an unwanted servant. There are things I can do, steps I can take, to ensure that we are married. And I will, my fair, stubborn bride, never doubt but that I will."

"The coach is ready at last," Uncle Elias declared from somewhere in the corridor. "Come along, you two."

Tearing her hand from Philip's, Vivienne marched from the room, all her pleasure at the thought of seeing Rob again thoroughly doused, replaced by the sudden terrible dread that she had underestimated Sir Philip Martlebury and the extent of his rancor.

Chapter 15

⟨◦◦◦⟩

Uncle Elias was so preoccupied by the possibility of seeing the king, he didn't notice that neither Vivienne nor Philip said a word the whole way to Lord Cheddersby's enormous house.

Vivienne sat opposite her male companions and stared out the window as the coach rattled over the cobblestone streets toward the west end of London, out of the city into what was nearly the countryside. She wouldn't look at Philip, didn't want to meet his gaze or see him regard her as if she were a toothsome morsel to sate his appetite.

Why was he so secure in his determination that they could not refuse him? He couldn't know about her feelings for Rob or, she didn't doubt, he would have said so, at least to her. He had had time enough for that—yet he had given no specific reason for his self-assurance.

If her uncle withdrew his support from her marriage to Philip, what could Philip do? What steps could he take to make her marry him?

Perhaps, she mused as they passed out of the city, this was merely a ruse, with nothing substantial to back it up. Maybe this was nothing but an idle threat, the same way he had threatened Lord Cheddersby at the theater, only to back down when the nobleman drew his sword.

She glanced at Philip, silent and scowling, his gaze on the passing buildings.

Yes, she thought, her happiness reasserting itself. He was the kind to make threats, but if it came to a confrontation with her uncle, and her uncle was determined she would not marry him, she was certain Uncle Elias would triumph.

By the time their coach rolled into the courtyard of Lord Cheddersby's magnificent house, as large as any estate in the country, Vivienne was more excited by the possibility of seeing Rob than she was afraid of Philip.

Her uncle disembarked, followed by Philip. Confident in her assessment of the situation, she allowed Philip to help her out of the coach and escort her into the house after her uncle.

Once inside the magnificent double doors, she gasped. The building was astonishing, from the entrance hall with its floor and walls of marble, to the grand staircase leading upward to the principal rooms, presided over by a ceiling painted with a host of allegorical figures. Vivienne had never been to Whitehall or Hampton Court, but she doubted even those royal homes could be so luxurious and fine.

Her uncle stared as if he found himself in faroff Cathay, while Philip seemed momentarily stunned by the obvious wealth of their host.

A footman took their cloaks, and they went up the wide staircase, arriving in a long room which was already filled with a crowd of people, the air heavy with the scents of perfumes and powders.

She couldn't see Rob among the throng.

Or Lord Cheddersby, or the king, for that matter. And she was acutely aware that Philip was standing too close beside her. On the other hand, he was close enough that she could give him a hard nudge with her elbow—

"Oh, my dear, here you are!" Lettice Jerningham screeched from somewhere close by.

Vivienne momentarily forgot about Philip as she saw Lettice, wearing a sumptuous gown of violet satin and velvet, bearing down on her.

And then, behind the approaching Lettice, Vivienne spotted Rob. He stood near the wall all by himself, beneath a portrait of what must have been one of Lord Cheddersby's Elizabethan ancestors.

If she felt out of place in the grand house among the mob of courtiers and wealthy people,

Rob looked it, with his simple black woolen clothing and stern demeanor. Indeed, he looked like an angry schoolmaster with a class full of mischief-makers.

Her uncle, meanwhile, seemed to be as happy as she had ever seen him. No doubt he was mentally calculating how many bolts of fabric it would take to clothe everybody here, and the profit he would have if they would only see the wisdom of buying their silks from him. In another moment, though, he looked like a hound on the scent as he moved toward the distant sound of music. Apparently he had forgotten Vivienne or Sir Philip existed.

"My dear, how delightful!" Lettice said as she finally reached Vivienne. "What a wonderful gown! Sir Philip, I am charmed to see you again. I will not gamble with you again, though, you naughty boy," she said with a coy simper. "You took my last guinea the last time we did."

Philip inclined his head, making a very minimal bow. "Your servant, madam."

"Oh, and there is Mr. Burroughs over there. I see he has discovered that the king and Lady Castlemaine are with Lord Cheddersby in the adjoining room dancing. Sir Philip, I am going to insist that you dance, for I know you are quite excellent at it," Lettice said, practically dragging Philip away. "Come along, now, Vivienne. He may dance with you next."

Vivienne could hardly believe her luck. Her

uncle had gone off, no doubt in search of Lady Castlemaine, and Lettice had taken Philip away through the crowd, all of whom, having glanced at Vivienne once, now paid her no heed whatsoever.

She might as well be invisible.

Hoping she could stay virtually invisible, she sidled backward, glancing over her shoulder. Rob was standing just where he had been before.

Nearly imperceptibly, he shook his head and frowned. Then he glanced pointedly at the doorway on his left.

He was right to be so cautious. So far, nobody was paying any attention, but that could change.

Determined to be gone before anybody noticed her or her uncle returned, she darted quickly through the door.

Now where?

She went through the rooms that led into one another, each one luxuriously appointed, scarcely noticing exactly how they were decorated. She was more intent on finding somewhere relatively private.

Finally, near the end, there was a room of a type she had heard of. It must be a state bedroom, intended for the lord of the house. It was a large room with an open area for His Lordship to entertain his friends and associates. The huge curtained bed was in an alcove, set apart from the rest of the room by a balustrade. Only the lord's closest friends would get behind the balustrade, and only his best friends would be allowed into the small room, called a closet, which was beyond that.

It all seemed very grand and formal for Lord Cheddersby.

Someone standing not five feet behind her cleared his throat, making her start and quickly turn.

It was Rob.

She ran into his arms. "Oh, how I've missed you," she murmured, her cheek against the rough fabric of his jacket.

"And I, you," he replied, holding her just as close for a moment before drawing back and glancing around. "Unfortunately, I fear that while we are alone for the time being, this is even less private than that alley. I was hoping to have a chance to speak with you alone."

Vivienne looked around. Since all the rooms led into one another, anybody could wander through, just she had.

She took Rob's hand. "I think there is a place we can be more private," she said, leading him to the balustrade, then around it.

"I feel like I'm housebreaking again," Rob confessed warily. "Where are you taking me?"

"This door should lead to—ah, I'm right!" Vivienne cried in a whisper as she opened the ornate door that led into a small room illuminated by the moonlight and the torches standing in the courtyard to light the drive. Unlike the formal room outside, this was quite charming, with lovely, simple furnishings, including a cupboard bed. There was a door leading out of it on the opposite wall, and Vivienne guessed it was the back stairs. Even Lord Cheddersby might wish a clandestine meeting now and then.

"I suspect this is where Lord Cheddersby actually sleeps," she said. She gave Rob a rueful glance. "I feel like a housebreaker, too."

He let go of her hand. "Then perhaps we shouldn't stay."

"No," she protested with a wry smile. "Who can say when I may have another chance to be with you? It was too long from the last time until this, so I will happily risk being caught here."

"With me?" he whispered as he pulled her close.

"Yes," she said with a sigh as she reached up to kiss him.

He tilted his head away from her, and although she was disappointed not to kiss him, she was delighted by the merriment in his dark eyes. "I thought you wanted to talk to me."

"So I do, but you should recall that I am something of a wanton. Did I not kiss you when our acquaintance was but an hour old?"

"You certainly did—most thoroughly, as I recall—and I enjoyed it very much."

"Then why should I not kiss you again?"

"Because, my lady love, as I have said, I fear

once we start, I will not want to stop, and until I can claim that right legally, I do not think it wise to tempt myself."

"So," she observed, her sense of delight and excitement growing, "you would claim me legally?"

"Yes."

"How?"

"I would ask you to be my wife."

"Wife?" Her heart thundered in her chest as she repeated that word.

"Wife," he confirmed. "If you could ever consider me worthy enough for a husband."

She frowned darkly, lowering her brows in her most fierce expression. "Robert Harding, are you *never* going to believe that I think you the most worthy of men? What more can I say or do to convince you?"

"You make me feel more important and respectable than anyone in my life, and I do believe that I am somewhat better than a dog," he said wryly, "but I was years a pauper and thief, Vivienne. It may take years to convince me I am not still destined to end my days in a noose. In fact," he mused with a hint of a smile, "it may take daily reminders."

Vivienne sat on a low sofa near the back-stairs door. "Oh, and you think that your wife will have nothing else to do, perhaps?"

He sat beside her and took her hand in his, once again grave. "Vivienne, any wife of mine will have a great deal to do, because I will not be able to afford servants. One maidservant, perhaps, but not much more."

"I am not afraid of work, Rob, any more than you are. My mother only ever had a maidservant, plus me to help her as best I could."

"I daresay you were a delightful helper."

Vivienne shook her head. "I was more hindrance than help. I would forget what I was doing and fall to daydreaming. Or I would get distracted by something outside. I would wander off in the marketplace, especially if there were jugglers or tumblers performing. She would get quite angry with me."

"And then forgive you when you cried."

Vivienne's eyes widened. "How do you know?"

He caressed her hand. "Because I love you, too, and that is what I would do."

She raised his fingers to her lips and gently kissed them. "You should not have said that, Rob, for you may regret telling me how to get my own way with you."

His eyes darkened in the moonlight. "Do you think to have your way with me, Vivienne?"

Her blood fired at the look of desire on his face. "If I can, as often as I can," she whispered.

Passion flared, and like two shivering travelers finding a fire in the wilderness, they were helpless to ignore it when Rob pulled her into his strong embrace.

In his arms, she felt light and strong and free, as liberated as a bird on the wing. No more fears or dread, no more worry. No more loneliness.

She loved him, and he loved her. They would be together. She would be his wife. She knew it as well as she knew her name.

His kiss deepened, his tongue teasing hers as they intertwined like dancers. Her arms tightened about him, holding him closer, as if she were trying to meld their bodies into one being formed of love and desire.

Her hands stroked his back and ran over the coarse cloth, feeling the taunt muscles beneath.

No pampered nobleman he, but a man who had labored and struggled and risen above his terrible beginnings to claim her heart.

If she thought him worthy, he had said.

If he thought *her* worthy—as he apparently did, judging by the ardor of his embrace.

Panting, she drew back and searched his features before her gaze locked onto his desire-darkened eyes. "I love you," she whispered.

He smiled, a wonderful smile that was both triumphant and yet modest, too. "I have never been happier, Vivienne. My love. My sweet, sweet love."

Again he kissed her, and once more the heat of passion exploded between hem. She inched forward, then slipped.

"This sofa is too narrow," Rob murmured, his lips against her cheeks.

"Yes," she agreed.

"Perhaps we should go—"

"No, not yet. Please, Rob, not yet."

She eased herself to the floor and reached up to take his hands. Taller than she, he loomed above her in the dim light like Hades claiming Persephone, the dark lord of her heart.

Her heart pounding, her body demanding, her skin aching for his touch, she drew him down to her.

Primitive desire banished all thoughts and took control of them both as his lips meandered along the slope of her chin. She had never known such burning need, such incredible desire.

She wanted him. More of him. All of him. The man she loved. The man she needed.

When he teased the taunt peaks of her breasts through the satin of her bodice and the linen of her shift with his fingers, her knees trembled and her limbs grew heavy.

He sat back on his ankles and tore off his jacket, then laid it under her head.

"Always thinking of others," she whispered.

He lay beside her. Raised on one elbow, he played with one of her ringlets with his free hand. "I adore your hair," he said, bending to kiss the lock.

She laughed softly, a tremulous sound, combined as it was of excitement and pleasure. "I like your hair, too. I am very glad you do not wear a wig."

"I cannot afford one."

"I hope you will always find a better use for your money than that." She reached up and tugged at his cravat until it was loose about his neck. "I noticed your linen is always very clean."

"You were studying my linen?"

"I confess I have been studying you at every opportunity," she replied. "You are a very handsome man."

"Am I?"

"Oh, yes. No doubt that is why I have such an urge to see you without your shirt on." She began to undo his shirt.

"In view of your startling confession, Mistress Burroughs, I admit to a secret desire to see you naked."

Her breath caught in her throat, and not because she was ashamed. "Naked?"

"Completely," he said with a slow, roguish smile. "Or if not completely, I would settle for parts."

His hand lightly cupped her breast, then gently kneaded it.

She gasped and closed her eyes, delighted by the sensations he aroused. "Don't stop," she moaned softly.

"I won't," he whispered.

Then he knelt between her legs and his mouth crushed hers possessively while she insinuated her hand into his shirt, feeling his chest and the rapid rhythm of his heartbeat that matched the exciting throbbing of her own blood.

"Make me yours, Rob," she pleaded softly, tugging open his shirt and pressing heated kisses against his bare flesh. She wanted him now, with every particle of her being, the need fiercely physical, as if without him inside her, she would die. "I want to be yours, Rob," she pleaded.

"No, Vivienne," he murmured hoarsely. "I am yours."

With a low growl of savage desire, he shoved up her skirts and petticoat, then freed himself. She made a small cry at the brief pain as, with a long, slow groan of conquest, he pushed inside her moist and waiting body.

In the next instant, she forgot the pain. She gasped, arched and nearly swooned as he began to thrust. Leisurely at first, his movements deliciously, tormentingly slow as her body accommodated itself to him.

Her mind swirling with new sensations, she clutched the hard curve of his arm muscles and felt more than heard the rasp of his breathing, hot on her ear.

The hard, virile thrusts quickened, taking her to a new realm of sensual pleasure. Of womanhood.

Within her, it was as if something burst, like a dam trying to hold back the raging waters of a flood, and as she cried out, a low rumble began deep in his throat. It burst free as he collapsed against her.

She lay still while the throbbing subsided, and she could feel him still inside her, a part of her.

He was perfect, and being in his arms was perfect. Perfectly wonderful, perfectly natural.

She cared for a man who had been honest with her. Who thought of her welfare before his own. Who was so good and generous to those less fortunate.

And whose hands and lips and body made her feel so alive.

This was not how she had imagined losing her virginity. She had imagined a large bed with white sheets and a handsome, loving husband gently persuading her.

She did not bemoan the lack of a bed, or the gentle persuasion. "I love you, Rob," she sighed.

He raised his head to look at her, perspiration on his brow. "Vivienne?"

"Yes?"

"I love you more than I have ever loved anyone in my miserable life."

Tears of both joy and sympathy filled her eyes as she tucked a stray piece of hair behind his ear. "I am going to do my best to see that you're never miserable again."

Then suddenly they heard a man's disgruntled voice outside the door.

Chapter 16

⌒◝◜⌒

The lovers froze.

"Do you know who that is?" Rob asked in a whisper as he withdrew and stood, hurriedly straightening his clothing.

"No, I have no idea," she murmured as she shakily got to her feet, too, looking down at her wrinkled and disheveled gown in dismay. She glanced in the mirror on the dressing table and saw that her hair was equally untidy. "I can't be seen like this!" she hissed in a panic.

Rob grabbed his jacket from the floor. "We'll go down the back stairs and say you got lost. This house is so enormous—"

The door to the closet opened.

"Odd's fish! What have we here?" King Charles declared, his brown eyes bright with surprise, and not a little humor, as he took in the scene before him.

"Your Majesty," Rob gasped, bowing and trying to push Vivienne out of sight behind him.

What kind of nightmare was he in? Had he gone mad? He had just made love with Vivienne on the floor of another man's bedchamber.

As if that were not shameful enough, being discovered by the king was a disaster.

If Mr. Burroughs heard what they had done—and why would he not?—he would be furious with Vivienne, punish her who could say how and never allow them to marry. He would likely denounce Rob for seducing his niece, but that was minor compared to what might happen to Vivienne if her reputation was destroyed.

Charles glanced over his shoulder and said to someone they couldn't see, "Keep watch, Buckingham. If that Jerningham creature comes this way, tell her we have returned to Whitehall."

He sauntered into the closet and closed the door behind him.

This was indeed a nightmare, Rob thought desperately, looking over his shoulder to see Vivienne pale and apparently immobile by the back-stairs door.

How could he have let this happen, he who prided himself on his self-control?

"Some women can be a damned nuisance," Charles remarked as he ran his gaze over Vivienne and her wrinkled gown and disheveled hair. "While other women we cannot get enough of."

He suddenly transfixed Rob with a look. "A loving woman is a wonderful creature, wouldn't you agree?"

"Yes, Your Majesty," he replied as a feeling of helplessness washed over him.

"Good evening to you, my dear," Charles said, finally addressing Vivienne. "You are the charming young lady we met the other day after that *other* performance, are you not?"

Rob moved back and took her cold hand in his. Whatever happened, he must take the blame for this.

Then she squeezed his hand and gave him a reassuring smile.

"I was introduced to you at the theater, Your Majesty," Vivienne boldly replied. "And this is Mr. Robert Harding, a solicitor."

Was there a more dauntless woman in London? Or one more deserving of his admiration and respect as well as his love?

The king chuckled and winked at Rob as one man of the world to another. "We hope you will excuse our untimely interruption."

"Majesty, I fear you are making a mistake. Mistress Burroughs lost her way and I—"

"And you were assisting her? Well, well," Charles said, and Rob realized the king did not believe him. "Her gown seems rather ruined, and her face quite flushed in a way we recognize, but if you wish to maintain that story, very well. We know you attorneys are all excellent liars and it is foolish to contradict you."

"Sire," Rob began, wanting to protest that he was an honest man—but he had just lied to the king of England.

"I love Mr. Harding and he loves me," Vivienne declared.

She was marvelous. Utterly, completely marvelous.

But this was still a disaster.

"We envy you, Harding," the king said as he ran another slow, measuring, and obviously approving gaze over Vivienne.

Another emotion arose in Rob at the proprietary gleam in the king's eye.

"Yes, we certainly do envy you," Charles announced. He leaned forward and spoke to Vivienne in a conspiratorial whisper. "We realize Harding is a handsome fellow, but we don't suppose you would consider gracing the royal bed?"

While Rob fought to subdue his rage, he realized that Vivienne seemed in firm control of her emotions.

"No, thank you, sire," she calmly replied to the king's lascivious request.

Charles chortled. "We feared you would say that."

He found this situation amusing? He expected them to share his sense of humor?

Rob had met arrogant men before, but this was beyond anything he had experienced.

The king ran his impertinent gaze over Vivienne again. "I daresay Martlebury will have apoplexy when he finds out what has been going on here. You needn't look so shocked, my dear. Surely it is not so surprising that we hear all the rumors and gossip. So many courtiers seem to have nothing to do but gossip. We understand Martlebury's been bragging about the young lady with the rich uncle he plans to marry. Apparently, he has been counting his proverbial chickens too soon—or do you intend to marry Martlebury anyway?"

"Sire," Vivienne said firmly, "I *never* intended to marry him. That was all my uncle's plan."

"Martlebury is a nobleman and a courtier," Charles pointed out.

"Yes, Your Majesty, but I could never love him."

"You love this attorney?"

"Yes, Your Majesty," she affirmed, looking at Rob again.

"Majesty," Rob said, letting go of Vivienne's hand and stepping forward. "While I fear I acted without due regard for Mistress Burroughs's honor, I assure you nothing would make me happier than to marry her."

"A noble sacrifice."

"Majesty!" Rob cried in protest, no longer caring that the man before him was his sovereign.

"It would be no sacrifice—unless it be on her part, for I have little to offer her."

"Except yourself," Vivienne hastened to add.

"As happy as this outcome would apparently render the both of you," the king noted, "we do not think Mr. Burroughs would agree to such a match. The good man strikes us as the kind to put profit before pleasure, except where Lady Castlemaine is concerned, apparently."

Rob slid a glance at Vivienne's face, which grew even more pale. "Lady Castlemaine?" she murmured.

"Odd's fish, yes!" Charles cried. "Your uncle has sent her so many presents, we have quite lost count. And we are worldly enough to know he does not send them purely out of the goodness of a generous heart."

Vivienne clasped her hands together. "Majesty, my uncle is a good man, if somewhat stubborn in his ideas and—"

"With exquisite taste in women," Charles placidly interrupted. "He also sees Lady Castlemaine for the beautiful, greedy creature she is. If he persists in his pursuit with such exquisite gifts, she is likely to repay him with what he so ardently desires."

Vivienne and Rob exchanged astounded looks.

"She has never been loyal, and never will be," Charles explained. "But since there is but one king of England, she will always come back, and because she possesses talents no man should be quick to dismiss, we accept her as she is—as she accepts her king. However, that does not mean that we intend to encourage any man with sufficient means to tempt her. Therefore, we would very much enjoy—how shall we put this?— exacting a measure of retribution for his efforts to enjoy our *grand amore*'s favors."

"I don't understand, Majesty."

"Nor I, sire," Rob added.

"Then we must say you are both surprisingly slow—and you, Mr. Harding, are reckoned a very clever fellow," the king replied with another chuckle. "However, given what you have been doing, we will excuse you.

"Now, since we understand your uncle has great plans for you, Mistress Burroughs, your infatuation—"

"Sire, I *love* Mr. Harding."

"Vivienne," Rob warned, thinking it unwise to interrupt the king.

"Well, I do!"

The king grinned and nodded. "You must forgive us, my dear. Love, as you mean it, is not something we encounter every day.

"To resume, your love for this man would, we believe, not be met with favor by your ambitious relative."

"Sadly, I fear you are probably right, Your Majesty," Vivienne agreed.

"While you, Mr. Harding, would likely stand

a better chance to claim this lady's"—his grin widened—"hand if the field were clear of obstacles like Martlebury and the rich, but perpetually befuddled, Cheddersby."

"Perhaps, Your Majesty," he answered warily.

"Oh, come, come, Mr. Harding! You are reckoned a very clever and dutiful solicitor, and Mr. Burroughs is merely a silk merchant, no matter how many airs he puts on. We think you would stand an excellent chance, especially if his niece already loves you. Therefore, we shall be delighted to help you."

"Help us, Your Majesty?"

"There is no need to look so shocked, Mr. Harding. We would be delighted to assist you young lovers—and incidentally put a bump in the ambitious road to Lady Castlemaine's bed Mr. Burroughs seems so busy a-building."

The last part of Charles's declaration convinced Rob that Charles meant what he said: He wanted to help them—to cause problems for a man who was attempting to gain his mistress's notice, and more besides.

"Now, then, we have just thought of a plan which we shall be delighted to put into effect. It shall mislead a few people, but we have misled people before. We well recall hiding in that tree to escape Cromwell's men and disguises and all sorts of subterfuge. We promise this will be nothing so dangerous and will undoubtedly prove much more amusing, with a happy outcome." He looked at Rob. "Go down the back stairs and fetch Mr. Burroughs."

Rob hesitated. The man ordering him was the king of England; nevertheless, Rob was loath to leave Vivienne alone with him. He had heard too many stories of the king's decadent ways.

Charles's brows lowered ominously. "You did hear us, Mr. Harding?"

"Your Majesty, I fear I cannot."

He braced himself for the regal wrath, only to see the king's gaze soften. Charles approached and clapped a friendly hand on Rob's shoulder. "We give you our word as the king of England that she will be safe. Odd's fish, man, it's not as if we are desperate for women, you know. We had to take refuge from one of them here, after all." His expression changed, to something more serious and stern. "Or we could always send Buckingham to fetch him and you can explain what you were doing here with his niece that has left her in such a state of dishabille."

Ignoring the king, Vivienne went to Rob, took his hands and looked up into his flushed face. "Do as he commands, Rob. Please."

Rob's glance flicked to the impatient, toe-tapping monarch.

She dropped her voice to a low, nearly inaudible whisper. "You must do as he orders you, Rob. He is the king." Her hands squeezed his. "But hurry back to me."

Finally Rob nodded. "Very well," he murmured. Then, and still with obvious reluctance, he made a brief bow to the king and departed.

Vivienne turned toward Charles and clasped her hands to still their trembling. Although what the king had said was true—there were no stories of Charles forcing himself on an unwilling woman—she still did not want to be alone with him.

But they had no choice. If the king sent the duke of Buckingham to fetch her uncle and forced them to explain what they were doing alone together, it would be terrible for Rob. She could hear her uncle's enraged denunciations, and Philip's, too. She didn't doubt that they would both do their best to see that Rob's career as a solicitor was destroyed because he had ruined their plans.

"Please, sit down," Charles said genially as he gestured at the sofa.

When he smiled with what seemed genuine benevolence, she started to believe he meant what he said about helping them, although she wished she had some idea of exactly what the king planned to do.

She sat on the sofa and watched him stroll over to Lord Cheddersby's dressing table, where he examined the items spread upon the top.

"And thus we shall await your lover's return and the others' arrival," he remarked.

"Yes." Another thought occurred to Vivienne. "Sire?"

"Yes?"

"Will you not be missed?"

He looked at her in the mirror. "We suppose we already are, but people will realize Buckingham is gone as well, and put their own interpretation on the situation."

"I see." Lettice always claimed that Buckingham was the king's procurer. Vivienne hadn't quite believed her; now she did.

"We only hope that Jerningham woman thinks we are far away, preferably in another woman's bed. A more persistent woman we have yet to encounter, thank God."

"She admires you greatly, Your Majesty."

Charles made a very skeptical face as he turned toward Vivienne. "If we were not the king, she wouldn't look at us twice."

"You are a most attractive man, sire," Vivienne replied, sensing that this would be a wise thing to say.

And it wasn't exactly untrue. When he smiled and his eyes lit up with laughter, he was not unattractive. He was not Rob, of course, but not unattractive.

"What of Lord Cheddersby? He strikes us he would make a doting husband, and he seems most intrigued by you. A clever wife could be the making of the fellow."

"I love Mr. Harding, Your Majesty."

"We understand that, but the fellow, for all his personal attributes, is poor, and Foz is very rich."

"I would rather be poor and *happy*, sire."

"Odd's fish, really?" He shook his head and his expression became very serious. "We have been poor, you know, Mistress Burroughs, and indebted, too, when we were in exile. It is a most unpleasant condition."

"I will not mind it, as long as I am Mr. Harding's wife."

The king grinned. "Very resolutely said, my dear. We believe you mean it."

"I assure you, I do, sire."

"Bad luck for Foz, then."

"Perhaps, but I don't think he loves me. He has never said or done anything that suggests that he does."

"If so, this is a most peculiar situation. Lord Cheddersby falls in love as easily as some men breathe."

"Then he will not break his heart over me."

"An excellent point. We are glad to agree. Indeed, upon further consideration, it strikes us that it would be a pity to see the fellow married. He amuses us greatly falling in and out of love."

Vivienne thought this was not a particularly nice way to refer to a person and his emotional attachments, as if they existed solely for one's own amusement.

"We do not mean to imply that you are not beautiful and desirable, Mistress Burroughs," Charles observed. "You are very beautiful and very desirable."

It only took him three steps to cross the room. He took her hand in his, and she had no choice but to rise when he gently tugged.

"Majesty?" she queried, trying not to sound as full as dread as she felt.

"A king can order people to do whatever he wills." He stared into her eyes, and there was no mistaking the lust in his. She had seen that selfish desire often enough in Philip's.

"Your Majesty," Vivienne replied, desperately wondering if there was any way she could pull her hand from his without making him angry.

Charles abruptly turned his head, and she heard the voices, too: her querulous uncle, Sir Philip's annoyed response and Rob's low murmur.

Just as abruptly, the king pulled her toward the sofa, shoved her down, dove atop her and kissed her, his wet lips covering her mouth.

Struggling, she managed to turn her head and gasp, "Majesty!"

"Quiet," he commanded in a whisper. "Do you want to spoil the performance?"

What kind of plan was this?

"Good God! What is the meaning of this?" Uncle Elias thundered from the doorway. "Unhand my niece, you varlet!"

Red-faced, he grabbed the back of the king's jacket and hauled him to his feet. "You disgusting scoundrel! I'll kill you!"

Frowning mightily, the king adjusted his garments. "It is Mr. Burroughs, is it not?"

Blanching, Uncle Elias fell to his knees, regardless of his new silk breeches. "Your Majesty! A thousand pardons, Your Majesty! I didn't know—didn't recognize . . . forgive me!"

Aghast at what was happening, Vivienne wiped her lips with the back of her hand and sat up. Philip stood scowling behind her uncle, Lord Cheddersby was behind *him* looking horrified and Rob was behind them both. He glared with murderous rage at the king.

This was disastrous! What had the king done?

Horrified, she looked at Charles again—and realized Charles was enjoying watching her uncle grovel with terror.

But what of her and Rob? Were they merely secondary players in his performance, too?

Lord Cheddersby turned and, although this was his private room in his own house, left them.

The full impact of Charles's action struck Vivienne. If Charles never persisted with an unwilling woman, people would think she must have been willing, perhaps even eager, for his embrace. She would be regarded as another of his conquests. Before the next day was out, it would be taken as fact that she and Charles had made love in Lord Cheddersby's closet, probably for several hours.

She wanted to cry out in anger and dismay—until she realized something else.

Philip would surely not want her anymore, not if she were another man's paramour. Neither, obviously, would Lord Cheddersby. The "obstacles," as the king had called them, were gone. Indeed, if she were now considered devalued goods, her uncle would probably be happy to be rid of her, to anyone who would take her.

Happiness immediately replaced her anguish, and she could only hope Rob would guess this, too—or at least control himself enough not to strike the king. Otherwise, he would be taken to prison, losing his liberty when she had just achieved her own.

"Majesty, truly, I didn't recognize you in that . . . that position," her uncle whimpered.

"Stop whining and get up," Charles commanded. "Who do you think you are to lay hands upon your sovereign? Men have been sent to the Tower for less."

As much as she chafed under her uncle's imperious decisions, Vivienne was truly distressed to see him so afraid.

"Sire," she said, "as my guardian, he is bound to protect my honor. Given what you were . . . well, he couldn't see your face."

The king's lips curved up into a smile. "My dear," he said with a melodramatic sigh, "we fear it is our fate to be as soft as butter in a woman's hands. Very well, we forgive him."

"Thank you, sire."

The king smiled slyly. "We hope to provide many more opportunities for you to be grateful."

Chapter 17

⌒⌒⌒⌒⌒

This was something Vivienne was *not* happy to hear, especially when she saw that expression on King Charles's face.

Swallowing hard, she darted another look at Rob, who glared at the king as if he were the worst brigand in England.

"Martlebury?" the king said to Philip.

"Sire?"

"We understand you wish to marry this lady."

"It is my dearest desire, Majesty," he answered with more humility than she would have believed him capable of.

While Vivienne wondered what to make of this, Charles made a noise in his throat that sounded suspiciously like a disapproving grunt.

Philip must have thought so, too, for he colored—as well he should. What kind of man could see his apparently wanted bride in another man's arms and react in such a sniveling manner?

Another glance at Rob told her that Philip's attitude was very different from his. He was equally angry at her persistent, unwelcome suitor and the king.

"And who is this behind? Ah, Mr. Harding. No need to look so shocked, Mr. Burroughs. We have heard of Heartless Harding and his amazing marriage settlements."

Vivienne stared. He had?

The regal brow wrinkled. "Since when does being a solicitor also require one to carry cloaks like a footman?"

Her annoyance and dismay at the king's behavior began to lessen.

Uncle Elias turned and snatched Vivienne's cloak out of Rob's hands. "I meant no disrespect. Mr. Harding gave me to understand Vivienne wished to leave. Th-that she was unwell," he stammered, clutching the garment tightly, regardless of what his grip might be doing to the fabric.

"She seems exceptionally healthy to us."

"Yes, Your Majesty."

"Sire, Uncle, I confess I am feeling somewhat unwell," she said, and that was certainly no lie. More, she wanted to be gone from this place, and all these people except Rob.

Charles suddenly grabbed her hand and

lifted it to his lips. All her former dread and dismay returned full force as his smoldering, questioning gaze held hers. "Until another time," he murmured, "which we hope will be sooner rather than later."

Sweet merciful heaven! What was happening here? Was his passionate embrace not merely a ruse?

The king straightened. "Mr. Harding, would you be so good as to go to Lady Castlemaine and tell her we have been delayed? And then perhaps you would be kind enough to call the coach for Mistress Burroughs and her party?"

Apparently, while it was rude of Uncle Elias to treat Rob like a servant, it was perfectly all right for Charles to treat him like a lackey. Indignation burned within her, fierce and protective, her pride wounded for his sake.

His jaw clenched nearly imperceptibly, Rob bowed. "Good evening, Your Majesty. Mistress Burroughs. Sir Philip. Mr. Burroughs." He turned on his heel and left without so much as a backward glance.

Not even at her.

She couldn't help what the king had done. He had surprised her, too. Was Rob annoyed, or merely obeying his king's command with the same reluctance as before, when he had been forced to leave her alone with Charles? What else could he do, especially with Philip and her uncle present?

"Where has Lord Cheddersby got to?" the king demanded.

"I . . . I don't know," Uncle Elias said immediately, as if he feared Charles suspected he had murdered him.

"Ah, well, I'm sure he'll turn up eventually." He faced Philip. "Martlebury, we need a partner for tennis in the morning."

Sir Philip's eyes widened as if he had just been made a duke. "I would be honored, Your Majesty."

Vivienne's lip curled with scorn. What a horrid toady he was!

"Just as long as you can hit the ball," the king said with a deep chuckle. "You must come to Whitehall very soon, Mr. Burroughs," Charles said to Uncle Elias, "and your charming and beautiful niece, too, of course."

"I fear I may be indisposed," Vivienne said sternly.

Uncle Elias gasped, while the king's lips curved up into a shrewd smile. "We don't think that would be very wise, my dear. Not wise at all. It is your king who requests your presence, and we would dislike having to explain exactly why we think you should comply. So, we shall see you soon, will we not?"

Feeling trapped by his veiled threat, she mumbled, "Yes, Your Majesty."

"Excellent. Now you all may leave us."

* * *

"Good God, I could have been sent to the Tower!" Uncle Elias muttered as the coach rattled over the cobblestones. Beside her, Philip said nothing.

Uncle Elias wiped his sweating brow. "You should have told me you had an assignation with the king."

"I didn't have an *assignation*," Vivienne replied through clenched teeth. She never felt more upset, confused and angry in her life, and she was utterly unsure of the final outcome of this horrendous situation.

Then, mindful that this terrible business might be turned to good account if it rid her of Philip forever, she truthfully said, "It simply happened."

Uncle Elias regarded her studiously. "He pursued you?"

She didn't reply.

"Well!" Uncle Elias declared, slumping back against the wall of the coach, momentarily stunned. "I thought Charles was taken with you, but I had no idea how much."

Vivienne slid a glance at Philip and saw, to her shock, that he not only wasn't disturbed by this observation, he actually looked pleased. "You are not upset, Sir Philip?"

"Not at all," he replied, turning to her with a smile that instantly chilled her blood.

"You still wish to marry me, even though you yourself saw me in the king's arms?"

"So what of that?" Philip replied with cold calm. "Be his mistress. That is even more reason for us to marry. My Lord Castlemaine owes his earldom to his wife, after all, and I'm sure to be just as amply rewarded for sharing."

Vivienne could not, unfortunately, refute that, but that didn't lessen her disgust. "What of your honor?"

"What of it? It is yours that will be sullied more than mine, and I assure you, I can overlook that with suitable remuneration."

"He has a point, Vivienne."

She ignored her uncle. "You would sell your wife to the king?"

"If the price was appropriate, of course, just as you must have leapt into his arms expecting some compensation. You know full well he is already married, so what can you hope for but the material rewards of being a royal mistress?" Philip's lips jerked into another smirking smile. "Or will you claim to be in love with him?"

Merciful God, had she endured the king's horrible embrace for nothing?

It was all Vivienne could do to shout that she most certainly did not love Charles. She loved Rob—but because she loved him, she held her tongue.

"I should think you would be glad I still want you."

"You *don't* want me. You want money or a title, or anything else legally possessing my body will get you!"

Desperate to have some good come from the king's unwanted lustful act, even more anxious to be rid of Philip once and for all so she would be free to marry Rob, she regarded her uncle with fierce determination. "While this man may have a financial reason to want to marry me, I do not necessarily need him to get a title if I become the king's *amore*," she pointed out. "Charles will give me one if I ask, will he not?"

"That's true," her uncle said, his eyes widening with that realization.

Philip grabbed her arm. "Without a husband, you'll be nothing more than a whore."

She yanked her arm away. "And if I agreed to this disgusting proposition, what would you be but my pander?" She faced Uncle Elias. "Why should we tie our family to this impoverished noble if we don't have to?"

"You do have a point," he mused aloud, regarding Philip as he might an overpriced commodity. "And he does not have nearly the influence he led me to believe."

"Think again, Burroughs," Philip growled, reminding Vivienne of his earlier implied threat. "We have an agreement."

"Do we?" Uncle Elias retorted. "I know I have not signed anything, nor has my niece. Have you, Vivienne?"

Was that it? Was the promise of marriage all he had to claim? "No, Uncle."

"You old buzzard!" Philip snarled, his face feral in the dim confines of the coach as he turned to glare at Vivienne. "What kind of greedy harlot are you, to play such games with me? I'm a nobleman willing to tie myself to you and this fat *tradesman* when you are nothing." He shoved his face close to Uncle Elias's. "I will marry your niece and get that dowry, by God, or I shall take you to court for breach of promise."

"What?" Uncle Elias cried, while Vivienne could only stare incredulously—and wish Rob were here.

"You heard me. I shall sue you for breach of promise, *per verbe de futuro*." Philip's smile grew with smug satisfaction. "You think only lawyers know Latin and the law?"

Now more than ever Vivienne wished Rob were here, to give them the benefit of his legal expertise.

"That is ridiculous," Uncle Elias retorted, his jowls quivering with angry indignation. "I have never heard of a man bringing such an action. You'll be laughed out of the courts."

"I think not. Have I not been led to believe the marriage would take place? I most certainly have, and I have the draft of the marriage settlement to prove it."

Her uncle flushed and looked away.

His silence further unnerved her. Could

Philip indeed take them to court if she didn't marry him? Lawsuits could be costly. What would her uncle consider the least expensive: fighting Sir Philip, or giving in to his demands? He might try to force her to marry the odious man after all.

If only Rob were here!

Philip looked at her with his cold, cruel eyes. "So prepare yourself, my dear. You are either going to marry me or your rich uncle can damn well compensate me. I should at least get the full amount of the proffered dowry, if not more."

Desperate, Vivienne grasped at one thing that might dissuade the man. "I am no longer a virgin."

Both of them stared at her, but she didn't care what they thought of her. She must and would rid herself—and her uncle—of Philip.

Philip stuck out his chin. "So what if Charles has had you? We can both enjoy your considerable charms—as long as I receive sufficient remuneration. Then I shall be able to buy all the virgins I want."

"You are disgusting!" Vivienne hissed.

"And what are you except a slut?" he demanded. "You gave yourself to a man not your husband."

"Does it not trouble you in the least that you will be famous as a cuckold?" her uncle said, finally speaking.

"You really are an ignorant upstart, Burroughs," he sneered. "Chances are I would be cuckolded sooner or later anyway. It is the way of the world. At least if I marry a mistress of the king, I get something out of it. I should think you, being a tradesman, would understand the nature of trading."

"I do indeed," he retorted. "So I appreciate when someone tries to trick me into overpaying."

He rapped on the roof of the coach and it rocked to a halt, nearly sending Vivienne tumbling onto the floor. "Get out, Sir Philip," her uncle commanded, opening the door. "As my niece has pointed out, she has a royal protector now, so there will be no wedding between you and this *fat tradesman's* niece."

"How dare you—"

"I dare because I am her guardian, and I decide who she will wed," Uncle Elias snapped as the coachman put down the step.

"You'll regret this, the pair of you!" Sir Philip declared as he disembarked, stepping down into the stinking gutter. He cursed as he looked at the sole of his soiled boot.

"Close the door," Uncle Elias commanded the gaping driver, who hurriedly obeyed. In another moment, the coach was again making its way down the street.

"I fear we have made an enemy, Uncle," Vivienne said quietly after a long moment.

"Perhaps, but the king is much more important."

That observation brought Vivienne no comfort.

She chewed her bottom lip. Despite the results so far—dissuading Lord Cheddersby and ridding her of Philip—the king's scheme seemed to be more and more wrong-headed with each passing moment.

What might her uncle do when he discovered that the king had no real interest in her and was only pretending in an effort to help her?

At least, she hoped the king had been pretending—that the lust she saw in his eyes was merely habit and nothing more than a part he was playing to get back at her uncle.

What if it wasn't? What if his motives were not entirely unselfish? He had certainly kissed and fondled her with more enthusiasm than the situation warranted.

And underneath all these ruminations ran another thread, of more importance than anything else: Where was Rob, and would he come to see her tonight? She desperately needed to see him, and talk to him, to discuss the possible repercussions of tonight's events—and to be held in his arms, where she felt safe and secure in his love.

"I wonder when Charles will invite you to live at the palace," Uncle Elias reflected. "If he does, you should ask for your own house instead. On the river, of course, so he can come and go as he pleases. I can think of two or three available. And be sure to ask for jewelry whenever you can, Vivienne. Smaller pieces are generally easier to sell later. Diamonds are best. And make sure he supplies plenty of servants and clothing. Oh, and a coach-and-four, as well."

As the coach continued on, Vivienne paid no heed to her uncle's mercenary observations and thought only of Rob.

Rob shivered as he waited on the cold slate tiles of the stable roof outside Vivienne's window. A chill drizzle dampened him, making his shirt cling to his back.

As a coach rattled into the mews, he moved closer to the wall, both for shelter and to be more in the shadows. Listening carefully, he heard voices. Vivienne and her uncle had finally returned, thank God.

After what had happened tonight, he was so anxious to see her alone that he could not even bear to wait until the morning.

He had had no idea that the king intended to make it look as if he had been with Vivienne, not him. Neither had she, he was sure. When he had returned with her uncle and the others, she had looked as upset, angry and distressed as he felt.

Since leaving Lord Cheddersby's, however, he had decided that he and Vivienne were surely wrong to be so upset, that what had happened had been the king's only means to help them. It was quite obvious from the look on Lord Cheddersby's face as he passed Rob that he was no longer interested in Vivienne, and surely Sir Philip would not be, either.

Unfortunately, the price for that freedom was going to be Vivienne's reputation.

He should have acted with more restraint, not made love with her. Then they would not have been at the mercy of the king and his impromptu plan.

A light was kindled inside Vivienne's bedchamber. Peering inside, he waited until the slow-moving, elderly maidservant finally left the room. Then he tapped on the window. Vivienne ran to the window and unlatched it.

"Oh, Rob," she cried, throwing her arms about him after he climbed inside.

He held her gently. "Vivienne, if I had known what he was going to do—"

"If *I* had," she interjected.

"I wish I had behaved better. Then we would not have found ourselves desperate for any aid, and so at the mercy of whatever Charles proposed. I should have guessed he would do something like that."

"You may be a very good lawyer, Rob, but you're not a seer. I didn't know what he was going to do until he did it."

"This has gotten much more complicated than I ever thought it could," Rob replied. "We have been too hasty."

"Blame my impetuous nature, then. It was I who kissed you first."

"It was I who made love to you."

"*With* me, Rob, and I do not regret that."

"Truly, Vivienne?"

"Truly," she replied, meaning it.

He sighed and stroked her hair. "What happened after he ordered me to go?"

She raised her eyes. "My uncle and I are probably going to Whitehall."

"What for?"

"I don't know."

One reason came to Rob's mind, but she looked so worried, he sought to reassure her. "I daresay it's part of the ruse, to make them believe his feelings for you are genuine."

Vivienne pulled away and went to the window, looking out over the stable roof, away from him. "I fear they may be."

Rob had tried not to think that, but he could not disagree. He could, however, hate the man. "I dreaded that, too, but I hoped I was wrong."

"After you left, he implied that if I didn't come to Whitehall, he would tell Uncle Elias what he saw."

"Oh, God, Vivienne!" he cried softly, going to her.

She tried to smile, and her effort touched his heart.

"What have I done?" he said remorsefully. "I have ruined your reputation, and now—"

"I don't care about that."

"Are you sure about your feelings, Vivienne?" he asked, voicing the question that had been haunting him ever since he had left her with the king. "You have already lost much, and I think only of your honor."

"Although I regret losing Lord Cheddersby's good opinion, I am grateful for the outcome," she assured him. She backed away a bit. "You're wet. You will catch a chill."

He shook his head. "It's not raining hard. I have been wetter than this many times, and I am rarely ill, or I would have died long ago, given the less than tender care I received."

He saw the sympathy in her eyes and looked away, toward the fine furnishings that cost more than he had ever made in his life. "I wonder if you really understand what you give up for me," he mused aloud.

"And I wonder if you can understand what I would suffer without you—a loveless marriage to a greedy, grasping man who thinks of me only as an item he has purchased. You will save me from a terrible fate, Robert, if you marry me."

"Gossip doesn't trouble you at all?"

She shook her head. "Not if the reward for my

endurance of it is you." Then her expression clouded.

"What is it?" he asked, the look on her face filling him with new dread.

"Lord Cheddersby is out of this, and out of danger from Philip, too," she replied.

"That is good, is it not?"

"Yes, but I fear we have not seen the last of Philip."

Chapter 18

❦

"**W**hat do you mean?" Rob asked, puzzled.

"He says that if I do not marry him, he will sue my uncle for breach of promise."

Rob's mind worked as fast as it ever had.

Sir Philip had a case, possibly a good one. Mr. Burroughs had agreed to preliminary terms; Rob had the notes to prove it. He also had the tentative draft of the marriage settlement, finished and sitting in the drawer of his desk.

To be sure, the contract itself was unsigned, but there was enough to establish a case for Sir Philip, and women had won judgments with less evidence.

"You think he could do it?" she asked anxiously. "You think he has a case?"

"Unfortunately, he may. Your uncle did make

verbal assurance in my hearing that the wedding would take place."

"Nothing was signed, was it?" Vivienne asked, worried that things had happened of which she was ignorant.

"No, not yet—but I have the preliminary documentation of the wedding agreement, proof of both parties' belief that the marriage was forthcoming."

"This is bad, isn't it, Rob?"

"Yes." He raked his hand through his damp hair. "I confess this never occurred to me. I fear Sir Philip is a smarter man than I took him for— and it is always a mistake to underestimate your adversary."

"But surely he won't win."

"He might, if he has a good lawyer."

"Not you?"

Rob had to smile. "No, my love, most certainly not I."

"You could— No, you must not."

"What?"

"I was going to suggest you represent my uncle and me."

"I could not, for I would have to testify on Sir Philip's behalf as to the documentation and your uncle's remarks." He sighed heavily. "Which will not endear me to your uncle."

"No—but he has only himself to blame should this lawsuit come to pass. He will be paying for his haste to accept Philip at his word, and for his refusal to listen to my protests when this marriage was first proposed." A hopeful look blossomed on her face. "Perhaps when Philip realizes my uncle will be like a fighting dog with his opponent's ear in his teeth, he will think better of his plan."

"I hope so," Rob said with a sigh. "Your reputation has already been forfeit, and I fear that will not be the end of it, especially if Sir Philip does what he threatens. There will be more scandal."

"I truly don't care about that. You have already endured more prejudice and innuendo than I ever will, and for no good reason, so I think I can endure some whispers."

"When we marry, there will be more whispers and rumors."

"Yes, I suppose so. Therefore, while I would quite happily wed you tomorrow, I believe we must be patient and wait for a few months, even if Philip does reconsider suing my uncle."

She sounded so confident, and yet he had thought of something else that obviously she had not. "Vivienne, it could be that we may not be able to wait."

"I am as anxious as you, my love, but—"

"But what if we have made a child?"

Her glorious smile reached into his heart and lightened it anew. "If it is so, we shall have to reconsider our plans. But let us look at the good side. If I am with child, my uncle will surely want to marry me off as quickly as possible. There is no way on earth Philip will have me if I bear another man's child, unless it is the king's, so there are worse fates that could befall me than bearing your baby. Indeed," she concluded in a loving whisper, "I would welcome that more than I can say."

He laughed quietly, but joyously. Wondrously. In a way he had never really laughed in his life as he gathered her into his arms. "Gad, Vivienne, whatever comes, I will face it, and gladly, if you are by my side!"

"And once we are man and wife, I will never leave you, Rob. Not as long as I live."

The old sense of unworthiness came back to him, and before he could conquer it, he said, "Not even for the king?"

"Certainly not," she replied without hesitation. "If our sovereign does harbor any lascivious notions, I will make sure he knows I do not reciprocate."

"He is the king, Vivienne."

"He is a man, Rob, and one who has plenty of women eager to be in his bed. As he said, he has never had to take a woman by force." Her embrace tightened. "Let us think of other things now, when we are together and alone."

"Very well," he agreed as her hands began to stroke him and the light scent of her perfume entranced his senses.

"Let us think of our future together," she

whispered, shifting closer and sliding her hand down his chest, "when I will have you in the house every day, and every night."

Rob grabbed her hand and pressed a hot kiss to her palm. "You are a temptress, Vivienne."

"Determined," she corrected, running her other hand up his muscular thigh.

"Passionate," he sighed as his lips stole along her cheek.

"Stubborn," she moaned as his hand stroked her breast and he kissed her with all the fire she roused within him. She arched toward him, her mouth moving over his with unspoken desire and invitation.

Slowly, slowly, her hands moved up his arms, her touch inflaming him even more.

"Oh, Vivienne," he sighed, reveling in her embrace. "I love you more than I have words to express. I will love you till the day I die."

"Then love me tonight, in my bed," she said, her voice a low, enticing whisper.

He drew back, uncertain. "Tonight?"

She smiled, her eyes both understanding and teasing in a way that smote him to the heart. "Now you need not have any concern for my honor, sir, if we are found together. I have none, remember? I gave it away for love." Her eyes sparkled with captivating mischief. "And I love you too much to send you back out into the rain."

Rob tugged Vivienne back into his arms. "I

didn't think I could ever be this happy," he said softly before he kissed her.

With equal fervor, she returned the kiss, passion meeting passion and exploding into burning desire.

He swiftly untied the lacing of her bodice. Sighing, she twisted so that it was loose enough for him to slide his hand into it and caress her warm, soft breast.

Excitement swept over and into them. Rob shucked off his shirt and let it fall to the ground, regardless of his usual care of the few things he possessed.

Vivienne wriggled out of her gown and it puddled in a heap of silk and satin on the floor.

Rob bent down to pull off his stockings and when he straightened, Vivienne wore only her thin chemise, made of fabric so fine it was nearly transparent. Her breasts rose and fell with her quick breaths and the aroused peaks of her nipples pressed against the thin material.

"Oh, sweet heaven," he muttered thickly, his voice weighty with desire as he swept her up into his arms and carried her to her bed. She sank deep into the featherbed, on the clean white sheets and silk damask spread.

Nearby, beeswax candles flickered, sending shadows of the bedcurtains and his body dancing on the tester. The polished wood smelled of wax and wealth.

"What is it?" she whispered, watching him.

"I have never been in a bed like this."

"Only *on* one."

"Nor with such a wonderful, desirable woman," he murmured, forgetting the furnishings as he gazed at her questioning face. "I feel like a pauper in a princess's chamber."

She reached up to caress his cheek. "Rob, I was the poor one until I met you," she whispered. "I was alone, with nothing and no one. You have saved me from that. You are my knight, my champion, my dearest, dearest love."

Her hand moved lower, to the buttons of his breeches, which were strained against the evidence of his arousal. "We are equals here, Rob. Equal in love and equal in need."

"My darling, my love," he murmured, feeling the weight of his past slipping from his shoulders. He would be tender and gentle, not as he had been before.

He would be the lover she deserved. "I am going to pleasure you, my love. I want you to feel as you have never felt before," he vowed as he pulled off his breeches and lay back down beside her.

How can that be? she wondered vaguely as his lips swept down upon hers. *What more could there possibly be?*

She soon found out as he stroked and caressed her as if they had all the time in the world together. Then his lips moved, trailing his marvelous fingers.

It was as if her body were a new country, more foreign to her in its responses than to the man exploring it. He seemed to know every small, secret place where a touch of fingertip or lip would send her into dizzying new realms of pleasure and sensation, until she lost track of all the places he touched.

Then her breath caught in her throat as his palm came to rest between her legs. Arching, she pressed against him, the feeling that engendered both wonderful and yet lacking.

He kissed her collarbone and she clutched the hard curve of his shoulders, oblivious to almost everything except the constant pressure of his hand. Slowly, he began to move his hand, increasing the pressure ever so slightly, while his mouth teased her nipples through the thin fabric of her chemise.

The movement of his hand quickened, and she could think no more. All she could do was surrender to the sensations.

Incredible sensations, of fullness and fire and tension building. Building.

She knew what she wanted, needed, had to have—what he had done before. As marvelous as she felt now, she would still feel incomplete until he was inside her.

When he was ready. When she had made him ready, as ready and anxious as she was.

He groaned softly as her tongue flicked across his naked chest, the hairs tickling her nose.

His chin nuzzled her chemise lower and lower, until he captured her nipple between his lips. His tongue flicked over her as she squirmed, held prisoner by that never-ending pressure of his hand moving in slow, deliberate circles.

Then his finger slipped inside her—and she was over the brink, carried away on waves of such incredible feeling and relief that she cried out, unthinking of who might hear, until his mouth swooped down upon hers and silenced her with an ardent kiss.

Still arching, still throbbing, she thrust her tongue into his mouth. A low moan escaped his throat as he moved over her and between her parted knees.

She took hold of his shoulders and raised herself to meet him. Her hand guided him eagerly.

He pushed inside her—and again a cry of pleasure rose in her throat. She pressed her mouth to the bare skin of his neck to stifle it.

He thrust inside her again and again, powerfully virile, making her his. Possessing her as she was possessing him, taking all that he offered and giving all of herself.

With a fierce, savage, guttural growl, he stiffened and new waves of sensation rocked her, leaving her spent and weak as he laid his head on her chest, her damp chemise against his cheek.

"I wanted . . ." he began, panting softly, "I wanted to be slower this time."

Enveloped in the bliss of love, she laughed softly. "You were. Any slower, and you would have murdered me."

"I did not think I was so fine a lover that I could kill you with desire."

She was even more delighted to hear the hint of laughter in his voice. "I assure you, you could."

He withdrew and moved to lie beside her, insinuating one muscular arm beneath her so that she lay nestled in his arms, her head against his chest.

He lightly ran his finger over her cheek.

"What are you thinking?" she asked, seeing a small wrinkle between his brows.

"Of the first time I felt velvet," he said. "It was so soft, like something from another world. But it was not as soft as your skin."

"Where was it? How old were you?"

"I was . . . perhaps seven, give or take a year." He sighed. "I confess I don't really know how old I am. Finnigan stole a child's velvet coat. He put it on me and said what a fine gentleman I looked. He thought that very funny."

"If he could see you as Heartless Harding the solicitor, he would not laugh."

"No, I suppose not."

"It must have been so terrible, Rob."

"I daresay it was, but I thought everybody lived like that. Some days, I honestly believed I lived well because Finnigan didn't beat me very often. Jack and Janet were beaten nearly daily by their father, until he fell beneath a wagon one night when he was drunk and was crushed to death."

She winced and he hugged her a moment. "Forgive me, Vivienne. Parts of my life are so sordid and terrible."

"If I am to be your wife, please don't try to shield me." She sighed. "I wish we could marry tomorrow," she murmured as she caressed his naked chest.

"So do I," he replied. He kissed the top of her head. "I confess a part of me doubts what is happening, as if this were all but a blissful dream."

"I only hope our love can make up for what you've endured. If there is anyone undeserving here, it is I. I have done nothing—"

"Except love me. And be the most brave, determined, unprejudiced person I have ever known. Most women of your class would flee in horror from marriage to a man who grew up as I did."

"Which would only prove them stupid fools, and I am very glad not to be counted among them," she replied pertly.

He chuckled, the sound a low rumble in her

ear as he embraced her. "Gad, Vivienne, you make me happy."

"You make me happy and, I fear, wicked," she said in a low seductive whisper as she began to pull off her chemise. "What else would explain this sudden desire to be as naked as you, my love?"

"A need to be loved again, perhaps?" he suggested hoarsely.

"Is it too soon?"

"If it is, we shall find a way to spend the time until I am able," he promised with a rueful—and incredibly seductive—chuckle.

A watchman called out the hour.

"Lord, is it that late?" Rob cried softly, regrettably letting go of her. "I had better leave."

"Must you?"

"Yes. I truly don't think I should be discovered in your bed," he said as he rose and retrieved his discarded breeches.

"I wish you could stay all night."

"As do I, my love," he said. He went to the candle stand and blew out the spluttering candles, leaving them in the dark, which didn't seem to hamper his movements at all. "I'm sure my dreams would all be sweet if I were with you, but I dare not linger. The streets are busy early, and I must not be seen leaving here—certainly not climbing down the stable roof, or all your concern for my reputation will be for naught."

"I wish there was a moon. It is so dark."

"Have no fear. I see quite well in the dark, and as I said, I learned well how to climb at night."

"I wasn't thinking of that. I want to see you."

He turned to look at her over his shoulder as he pulled on his shirt. "Soon, as I shall be able to admire your lovely body for as long as I like, too."

"When we are married, I won't let you leave me so easily."

"I shall have to work."

"I suppose."

"Vivienne, I will have to work, or we shall have to take to begging in the streets," he said, sitting beside her on the bed and taking her face between his palms to kiss her lightly. "I have done quite enough of that."

She put her hands over his. "I was but jesting, Rob. Of course you must work. I daresay I shall be busy, too, managing our house."

"You are sure it will not be too much?"

"Not when it is our household, our family." She put her arms about him and laid her head on his chest. "We will survive, even if my uncle throws me out of his house with only the clothes on my back."

Rob rose with obvious reluctance. "Stay in the bed where it's warm until I'm gone, then close the window tight."

She nodded, watching him as he pushed open the casement window.

Despite his words, she scrambled from the bed to kiss him farewell one more time.

His passionate response told her he was glad she had. "Farewell, Vivienne," he said as he pulled away and began to climb out the window.

"Farewell, Rob, my love," she whispered.

Wrapping her arms about herself for warmth, she watched his athletic body creep along the stable roof as if he were no more than a shadow from the moon.

When she could see him no longer, she hurried to her armoire, found a nightdress and put it on. Then she spotted her discarded dress and quickly picked it up.

It was a wrinkled mess, much like the sheets of her bed. She shook out the dress and leaned it over the back of a chair before she jumped back into the warm bed.

Which smelled of Rob.

Unless Owens was as stupid as she was old, she would realize Vivienne had not been alone in her bed.

She could "accidentally" spill perfume on her sheets. That would take care of that.

These were small problems, easily remedied.

The king's possibly lascivious intentions and Philip's lawsuit were much more troubling.

Nevertheless, she silently vowed, together she and Rob would find a way through this swamp.

They must.

* * *

As Robert hurried away, a man stepped out of the shadows of the stable and watched him disappear around a corner.

"Well, well, well, Rob, old son," Jack Leesom muttered. "Not done thievin' yet, after all, or aimin' high."

Chapter 19

Rob looked up when Sir Philip strode into his chambers the next morning and threw himself, uninvited, into the chair across from his desk.

Rob half rose and bowed, then sat and regarded his client impassively. He had been anticipating Sir Philip's arrival and had asked Bertie to show him in the moment he arrived.

"It's all over the city," the nobleman declared. "You should have heard them buzzing about Vivienne and Charles at the tennis court, and with him not ten feet away. He heard them, of course, and the old lecher couldn't have looked more pleased about the gossip than if somebody had handed him a thousand pounds."

"To what 'old lecher' do you refer?"

"Why, Charles, of course."

"I would have a care how you speak of the king," Rob remarked, "and he is only thirty-four."

"As for Mistress Burroughs, she is the most brazen hussy I've ever met. She would hardly let me touch the tips of her fingers, but she let him slaver all over her like a dog."

Beneath his desk, Rob's hands curled into fists as he waited for Sir Philip to get to the point: the legal action he intended to take against Mr. Burroughs. "He is the king, and you are not."

"I know that! I'faith, I was delighted she had caught his eye. The king hasn't invited me to play tennis with him for months, and suddenly there I am, in the royal tennis court. I daresay the Burroughses have seen the last of that fool Cheddersby, too. I swear that fellow is a Puritan in fancy dress. So all was quite well in hand— until her old buzzard of an uncle had the effrontery to call off the marriage."

"You do not wish to end the negotiations, even though we all saw Mistress Burroughs in the king's arms?"

Sir Philip chuckled his nasty chuckle. "The king's gratitude for sharing one's wife is worth a great deal."

"Enough to give him your bride?"

Sir Philip's lip curled with scorn. "You sound like a Puritan—or Vivienne. It's only her body he will have."

"While you will have . . . ?"

Sir Philip smiled. "Her dowry and a better title, at the very least, I don't doubt."

"What if she were to bear the king a bastard?"

"Even better, for the rewards will be that much greater."

"I see you have reasoned this out."

"Absolutely, so I will not allow Burroughs to dismiss me as if I were nobody. I was led to believe that the wedding was as good as done, and it had better be done, or Burroughs will be sorry. We'll sue him for breach of promise."

"*Assumpsit?* That is usually a suit brought about by women."

"I know that, man. But I will have that dowry, or by God, that tradesman will compensate me."

"You will be free to wed another," Rob pointed out.

Philip looked smug. "I know that, too—but why should I be denied my rights just because I am a man? There is nothing in the law that says such a suit can only be brought about by a woman, is there? I would expect a man of your"—his disgusting grin grew—"breeding to be more open-minded."

"I did not say your case was without merit, Sir Philip. I simply indicated it was highly unusual."

"And that's why I need you to argue it, for you are reckoned the cleverest solicitor in London. There should be a hefty fee in it for you, too."

"No, Sir Philip, there will not be."

"What?"

"I must decline to represent you in this matter."

"I have a good case—you know I do. That man gave me plenty of cause to believe his niece and her dowry were as good as mine. We've got the draft of the marriage settlement for proof."

It had crossed Rob's mind to burn that document this morning, but that would have been unethical, so he had not. Mr. Burroughs would have to take his chances in a court of law if Sir Philip pursued this. "Perhaps he did imply a certain sequence of events. Nevertheless, I shall not represent you in this matter."

"Why the devil not?"

"Because it is my prerogative to decide which cases I take and which I decline. In this particular instance, I decline."

"You arrogant bastard!"

"Your epithet only hardens my resolve, Sir Philip," Rob noted with a dispassion that hid his fierce anger. "You may, of course, find another solicitor to take the case, although that may be somewhat difficult once it becomes known that clever Heartless Harding has refused it."

Sir Philip jumped to his feet. "You rogue! You base, disgusting sodomite! How dare you—"

Rob likewise rose, his gaze boring into the irate man before him. "My clerk will be happy to give you all the documents pertaining to the case. Good day, Sir Philip."

Sir Philip looked about to speak, took another look at Rob's resolute face, turned on his heel and marched from the room.

Rob slowly returned to his seat and let out his breath.

Then he smiled. He did have his reputation, after all—the good as well as the bad.

Her eyes full of sympathy, Vivienne regarded the woeful Lord Cheddersby seated in her uncle's withdrawing room. He looked utterly miserable, his shoulders slumped, his eyes downcast, his every breath a sigh.

When she had been told a gentleman was waiting for her, she had eagerly anticipated Rob. Instead, she found the despondent nobleman.

The dark circles beneath Lord Cheddersby's eyes indicated he might have had as sleepless a night as she.

As for what might have kept Lord Cheddersby awake, she hoped it had nothing to do with her. Unfortunately, his attitude and his presence there told her it might.

Had she been wrong about his feelings? Did he care for her? If he did, and if he said so to Uncle Elias . . . No, that must not happen. She had endured the king's disgusting kisses to be free; she must be free.

"I am happy to see you, my lord," she began

in as bright a tone as she could muster. "I never got the chance to compliment you on your new house."

He raised his sad eyes to gaze at her. "My very big house with all those rooms."

"Why, yes," she agreed warily.

He rose and walked toward the window, then spoke softly, without looking at her. "I don't think I've ever been so shocked in my life. In my own private closet, too."

She didn't have to ask to what he was referring. "I'm sorry, my lord," she said, genuinely regretting that the events of last night had happened in the hapless nobleman's home—or anywhere.

She wasn't referring to making love with Rob. She could not be sorry for something so wonderful. It was the unforeseen aftermath that filled her with remorse.

Lord Cheddersby turned toward her. "I was so upset, I didn't know what to say or do. I ran off like a . . . like a coward."

"You had done nothing to be ashamed of."

He straightened, and she was reminded of how he had been in the theater that night, when he had so courageously risen to her defense. "I suppose you're wondering why I'm here."

"Yes, I am, my lord."

"Although this gives me very great pain," he said, "I felt it necessary to come to you and tell you . . ." His voice trailed off, and he flushed.

"What is it, my lord?" she prompted gently.

"I fear there are some nasty rumors going about concerning you and the king."

Vivienne sighed. "Not unexpected, under the circumstances, are they, my lord?"

His gaze grew a little more severe. "Lettice Jerningham is implying that she has known of a liaison between you for some time, and that the reason you are not already engaged to Sir Philip is that you have been the king's lover. She claims that Philip offered to marry you at the king's behest, to squelch gossip."

"That is the most ridiculous thing I have ever heard," Vivienne replied, truly horrified. "Philip wants to marry me for my uncle's money. You saw him last night—he was as shocked as anybody to discover me with the king."

"Yes, I thought he was as taken aback as I, and I told Lettice I didn't think there was a word of truth in her tales. I also told her she shouldn't spread unfounded rumors."

Vivienne rose and went to him, taking his gloved hand in hers. "Lord Cheddersby, I thank you from the bottom of my heart for championing me."

Lord Cheddersby managed a hopeful smile. "After all, Charles kisses women all the time," he said with something like his usual cheerful tone. "That doesn't give people the right to say that you were . . ."—he frowned—"that he and you . . . that you're not a virgin anymore!" he finally spit out.

As she faced the kindhearted man, she wanted to tell him the truth—that her lover was not the king, but Robert Harding, and that she was going to marry him.

But she couldn't, not if there was the slightest chance Lord Cheddersby still cared for her. "Lord Cheddersby, if you hear anyone else say that, do not contradict them."

He stared at her, obviously confused.

"They are right. I am no longer a virgin."

As she saw respect for her dwindle and disappear from his honest eyes, to be replaced by shocked disappointment, she suddenly realized exactly what she had lost along with her reputation.

It would have been nearly unbearable if she had not had a good cause, and she could sympathize with the pain Rob had suffered because of the lies told about him.

"I thought . . . I thought you were different from most of the women I've met at court, Mistress Burroughs," Lord Cheddersby stammered as he tugged his hand away. "I am more sorry than I can say to discover I was wrong. I . . . I have to go. Good day, Mistress Burroughs."

He went to the door as if he could not leave her fast enough, then glanced back at her over his shoulder, his expression both sad and disappointed. "If, after the king is done with you, you need any help or assistance, I will be glad to do what I can."

"That is most generous of you, my lord."

"Yes, well, I've seen what has happened to some of his other lovers, and I wouldn't want it to happen to anybody else. Farewell, Mistress Burroughs, and good luck."

"Farewell, my lord."

After he left, she sank down upon the sofa and told herself there had been nothing else she could do.

She straightened abruptly as Uncle Elias strode into the room, a letter sealed with a huge blob of red wax in his plump hand. "Ah, Vivienne, my dear, here you are. A messenger has come from Whitehall!"

He thrust the letter at her and she saw the royal seal. The king or one of his advisors must have sent it.

"Open it!" Uncle Elias demanded impatiently.

She did, and when she saw the signature at the bottom, her stomach lurched with dread.

My dear Mistress Burroughs,

Thank you for a most enjoyable evening. Given that it was mutually beneficial, your presence is requested at Whitehall this evening. Sincerely,

Charles R.

She thought of the lustful gleam in his eyes when the king lay atop her and the way he boldly caressed her, and her doubts as to his true intent began to multiply.

"Well?" Uncle Elias asked. "What does it say?"

"It is from the king," she murmured.

"I supposed as much. What more?"

"He requests my presence at Whitehall this evening." There and then she could explain to Charles that there was no need to continue the ruse, she decided.

If his actions had been only feigned.

Uncle Elias's eyes lit up like torches. "Tonight?"

"Yes."

"Excellent!"

He was all but rubbing his hands together with glee.

"Lord Cheddersby has just called. I fear we have seen the last of him."

Uncle Elias shrugged.

"He told me that I am being talked about, and it is not flattering."

"By jealous women, I don't doubt," Uncle Elias replied, rocking back and forth on his heels as if his excitement and delight must take physical form. "All the ones the king has not bestowed his attention upon, I'm quite sure. Don't trouble yourself about it. That's the price you must pay for the royal favor."

The price she must pay. Yes, he would put it that way, and apparently he thought she was going to be getting her money's worth.

This would all be worth it only if she could be Rob's wife.

Slouched in a wing chair, Sir Philip Martlebury glared at his footman over the rim of his brandy glass. "Didn't I tell you I wasn't to be disturbed?" he demanded, his words slightly slurred as he put his drink down on the table beside him.

"Yes, Sir Philip," the trembling servant replied. "He said it was important. Very important."

"Who said?"

A man shoved his way past the footman and walked to the center of Sir Philip's library. "I did."

He was about Philip's age, with greasy dark hair that hung about his broad shoulders and clothes that had clearly seen better days. He also sported a patch over his left eye.

"Who the devil are you?"

The man removed his patch. "Don't recognize me, eh, Martlebury?"

Sir Philip straightened, then glanced at the gawking footman. "Leave us."

The servant obeyed, closing the door softly.

"Well, well, well," Philip drawled, reaching again for his brandy. "I thought we'd seen the last of you. Or have you got another sister to sell? My father's been dead these five years, though, and I have different tastes."

A muscle in Jack's jaw tensed. "Maybe you don't want Vivienne Burroughs, after all."

The glass of brandy halted its progress to Philip's mouth.

"Ah, now you're interested." Without waiting for an answer, Jack strolled over to the decanter on the side table and lifted it to his lips. He drank down several large gulps, then set it beside Martlebury with a bang. "She doesn't want you because she's got a lover, and I know who it is."

Philip scowled. "The whole city knows who it is, you oaf. The king."

Jack grinned. "Think so, do ya?"

"I do. So if you thought to sell me that information, you can go now."

"Oh, I've got plenty to sell, 'cause it ain't the king."

"What, some brother of yours?"

"A friend, as a matter o' fact."

"What friend of yours could be the lover of a woman like Vivienne Burroughs?"

"Cost you them rings you're wearin' to find out."

"You're lying." Philip took another drink. "Why would I do that?"

"For my rings, which are worth considerably more than you asked of my father for the pleasure of your sister's company."

"I was just a boy then. I come up in the world since."

"To where you would sell friends?"

"A man has needs."

Sir Philip eyed him speculatively. "I won't argue with that," he remarked. "But if Vivienne Burroughs has a lover, he's a royal one, and more power to her—and so to me," he finished.

He opened his mouth to call for the footman, but in the next instant, Jack was behind the chair, his hand clamped over it.

"Listen to me, you pompous ass," he hissed in the nobleman's ear. "I can stick you quick as a wink and be out that window before your servants get here. It ain't the king who's had her, and there ain't goin' to be no reward for you being cuckolded. If you want her uncle's money, what I know will mean that you get it. Now, are you goin' to pay me for what I have to say, or do I rob ya and slit your throat?"

His eyes full of panic, Philip nodded.

"I wouldn't make any loud noises if I were you." With his other hand, Jack drew out his long, sharp knife. "The rings, Martlebury."

The nobleman quickly took them off and held them out.

Jack came around the chair and snatched up the jewelry.

Philip wiped his lips. "I could have you thrown in prison for robbery."

"Aye, ya could, but then you won't find out who's been plowing Vivienne Burroughs's furrow."

Philip reached for his brandy. His hand shaking, he raised the glass to his lips and drank before speaking again. "Well, who is it—Cheddersby?"

"Rob Harding."

"That's ludicrous. Heartless Harding?"

"The very same."

"He's representing me."

"He's representing you, all right—in her bed."

Philip's eyes narrowed with suspicion and disgust. "I've heard stories about Harding and Godwin. He's a sodomite."

Jack's lips curled scornfully. "Then I'm the king's long-lost brother. Stories, they are. I tell ya, he's already made love to her at least once, so if you want Vivienne Burroughs, you've got her. Her uncle'll be glad to be rid of her—unless you think he'll let her marry a solicitor, and one with scarcely a penny to his name."

"You're a scoundrel and a liar. When have they had a chance?"

"He was with her t'other night. Climbed in her bedchamber window like the thief he used to be. I seen him meself."

Philip rubbed his naked fingers. "If that's true, I'll have him thrown in prison, the lying rogue."

Jack grinned. "Worth a few baubles, ain't it?"

"I believe it is, yes," Philip agreed slowly. "If you're not lying."

"I can prove it."

"How?"

"He'll be climbing in her window tonight, like as not. You could wait in the mews and see for yourself. He'll go in to her very bedchamber and there won't be a peep out of the house because he's welcome."

"She would hardly let me touch her, that whore," Philip muttered as his hands balled into fists.

"We're all whores, ain't we, in one way or another?" Jack noted dispassionately. "Dog eat dog. Every man for himself. That's the way of the world."

"I daresay that's how you justified selling your sister to my father."

Jack's jaw clenched again. "You're selling your title for money, ain't ya? You gave me them rings in exchange for what I had to tell ya. I sell what I have, no different."

"I think peddling your sister to a disgusting old lecher is quite different. She fought him, you know," Philip continued coldly. "Bit and scratched. He had to beat her senseless the first time. She was better after that. Never made a sound, not even when he was done with her and cast her out."

"Because she was havin' his bastard."

"So what of that?" Philip asked rhetorically with an airy wave of his hand.

Jack regarded him studiously. "On second thought, maybe I oughta kill you."

Philip straightened. "You wouldn't dare. My servant saw you."

"Thievin,' murder, I swing either way."

"You didn't rob me," Philip said desperately. "I gave you the jewels."

Jack smiled. "So you did, and don't you forget that, in case it comes before the courts. What are ya going to do to Rob?" His eyes gleamed eagerly. "Kill him?"

"Sully my sword with the likes of him? Oh, no, Mr. Leesom, nothing so crude as that. I will ruin him. I will send him back to the gutter where he belongs."

"Fair enough," Jack said. His gaze roving over the many portable, valuable items so carelessly displayed, he sauntered to the door.

"How much did my father pay you to kill Janet?"

Jack slowly turned back. "I never killed her."

"It doesn't matter to me. I am just curious."

"She done herself in. Too ashamed to go back to Rob, too afraid he'd turn her away. Even then he had a high and mighty opinion of himself."

"How much will it cost for you to cripple him?"

"What, hamstring 'im?"

"No. I want him castrated."

Jack's eyes narrowed. "Like a bull?"

"He has enjoyed what should have been mine," Philip said. "He has aspired far beyond his place. I want him alive to contemplate that, and all that he has lost. How much?"

"Two hundred pounds and passage to the New World," Jack replied after a moment's thought.

"Very well."

"When?"

"We'll go to Burroughs's house tonight. If he comes there as you say he will, you can do it then. You *are* capable of overpowering him?"

"O' course."

"Especially since he will not be expecting an attack by his friend."

Jack ignored Philip's remark. "What'll you be doing?"

"If you are such a clever fellow, I'm sure you can help me climb in a bedchamber window."

Jack ran his measuring gaze over the man and looked doubtful. "Won't it be enough to watch 'im climbin' in?"

"What, and miss the opportunity of calling Vivienne a whore to her face? I think not." An evil, rapacious smile grew upon Philip's face. "And when I make her pay for cheating me, I will enjoy it all the more if Harding has to watch."

Chapter 20

Vivienne and Uncle Elias stood uncertainly in a corner of the Banqueting House of Whitehall Palace. Around them, the women were attired in fine silks and satins, but had painted their faces and exposed so much naked skin, they might have been actresses. Or whores.

The men were no better, for the majority of them seemed drunk. And as for the language . . . Vivienne was shocked by the obscene words and suggestive nature of most of the conversations she overheard.

She glanced up at the ceiling, where she understood one of the scenes depicted represented Temperance subduing Wantonness. Apparently Wantonness had gotten the upper hand during this reign.

Even Uncle Elias, who had so yearned for this

invitation, appeared to be dismayed by what he was seeing and hearing.

"I don't see her anywhere," he muttered more to himself than to Vivienne.

"Lady Castlemaine?" Vivienne proposed, realizing his dismay had sprung from another source.

Uncle Elias started as if he had forgotten she was there. "Yes, and the king isn't here, either."

"Then perhaps we should leave," she suggested. "Maybe he's changed his mind about me."

Or it could be that she and Rob had been worried about the king's motive for nothing. Perhaps he had simply seen a way to help them, albeit one that allowed him liberties she would never permit otherwise.

Somebody tapped her on the shoulder. "Yes?" she said, turning swiftly to discover a man dressed in livery behind her.

"Mistress Burroughs?" he asked, bowing and giving her such a knowing look, she thought he must be the most insolent servant she had ever encountered. "Yes."

"I am Chaffinch, the king's page. Will you please step this way?"

She had heard of him; he was the servant most in the king's confidence.

"Go, Vivienne," Uncle Elias growled under his breath, "and remember what an opportunity this is. Don't throw it away."

A swift look at the faces of those nearby confirmed that they were also making assumptions as to Charles's reasons for summoning Vivienne. What else *would* they think, given who had come to fetch her, Charles's reputation and what had happened at Lord Cheddersby's?

"I would not keep the king waiting, Mistress Burroughs," Chaffinch murmured.

Vivienne glanced at her uncle. "Will you wait for me?"

Uncle Elias glared at her. "Who can say how long you may be?" he replied. "You must stay with the king for as long as he wants you."

Why she had expected him to say otherwise, she didn't know. "Very well, don't wait," she snapped before turning on her heel. "Come along, Mr. Chaffinch. To the king."

She held her head high and ignored the speculative looks, sly smiles and excited whispers as the man led her through the crowd to a door that led to a corridor.

Then they turned another way, and another, until she was quite lost. With a shiver of dread, she wondered if that was the intention.

Finally, Chaffinch halted before a large double door. "The king's private apartments," he informed her as he opened them.

Vivienne stepped into a room full of scarlet and gold, ornately decorated with scarlet wallpaper and gilded trim. Fine, delicate baroque furnishings filled it, and it was illuminated by what could have been a thousand candles. Perfume and the scent of burning wax filled the air, and she found it difficult to breathe—especially when the man seated with his back to the door rose and faced her.

King Charles wore what appeared to be a dressing gown over his untied, lace-trimmed shirt and dark breeches. He was so casually attired, it was as if he were nearly naked.

"Majesty," she murmured, her heart pounding as she curtsied.

The doors closed behind her with a dull thud.

They were alone.

"Ah, Mistress Burroughs. Vivienne," he said, coming to her and taking her hand to raise her. He stood eye to eye with her, smiling. "We are so delighted to see you."

"You invited me to Whitehall, Your Majesty, so naturally I came," she replied, barely resisting the urge to pull her hand from his warm grasp.

"Of course we did. We have an appreciation for beauty, and so we enjoy having it to hand."

"I am not a painting or a sculpture, sire."

"No, you most certainly are not." He finally let go of her and strolled toward a table covered with a white, gold-embroidered cloth that reached to the polished parquet floor. A crystal decanter and glasses were on it. "Would you care for some wine?"

"No, thank you, Your Majesty."

He turned to her, his mustache moving up

with a grin. "There is no need to be so cold and unfriendly, Mistress Burroughs. This is necessary, is it not? People must believe you care for us, not your true *amore*."

So, this *was* only a ruse. Her breath rushed out in a sigh of relief. "Yes, Your Majesty."

"The rumors are going about that we have seduced you," he noted with amusement. "We understand there is already a wager among our friends on how long you will keep our royal favor."

Anger began to replace her dread. Her situation was born out of desperation, not a desire to amuse him. "Majesty, I didn't know exactly what you had planned, and since you are my king, I did not question you. But I assure you, I have no great liking for the tales being spread. I accepted them as the price I must pay to rid me of my unwanted suitors so that I can marry the man I love. You must forgive me if I do not find our dilemma a source of amusement."

The king's brow lowered ominously. "Not that we have the greatest of respect for the legal profession, given that their whining and chastising gives us more headaches than we care to experience, but it strikes us that you and your lover are hardly in a position to be so high-minded. It is not the finest of professional conduct for Robert Harding to be seducing his client's intended bride."

"He didn't seduce me, and the only people

who believed I was Sir Philip's intended bride were Sir Philip and my uncle. *I* never did."

"Very bravely and boldly said, my dear." The king's gaze intensified as he put down his glass and sauntered toward her. "Yet we fear you have lost your good name in this business."

"Yes, sire."

"Quite a price to pay, and for a solicitor, too. We noticed his honor is not suffering."

"Robert Harding is a kind, generous man who has suffered much and strived and worked and endured more rumor and gossip in his life than I can imagine. My moral reputation is a small sacrifice compared to the price he has paid to rise in the world."

"We judged you an unusual woman," Charles noted with another smile, and another look in his eyes that made her shiver.

"Majesty, I love Rob, and he loves me. We are, of course, very grateful for your help."

"Philip is bringing a lawsuit, we hear, for breach of promise."

Was there anything in London this man didn't know? "Yes."

"Your lover still represents him?"

"No."

"Ah. How very convenient. It would not do, of course, for him to represent the man whose bride he covets."

"Majesty, I have explained. I did not want

Philip." She doubted King Charles understood love at all.

The king got a speculative look in his eyes. "Since you seem to care so much for this lawyer, you might do well to remember that you are in the presence of your king. We have influence and power that can be used for good. Or ill."

"Majesty?"

"You think that we are not really attracted to you? That we kissed you *merely* to aid another man? You underestimate your charms, Mistress Burroughs."

"Your Majesty, please!" she said, backing away.

"Please what?" he replied, coming closer as if she were his prey. "Kiss you again?"

"No!" She glanced anxiously at the door. Was it locked? Could she run? Did she dare?

He smiled. "Did you not enjoy it before? Come, think of all that we could offer you. A place at court. A house. A title or two. Would you not be well compensated for giving up a mere solicitor?"

He could not have said anything else that would have emboldened her as much as this. She straightened her shoulders defiantly and said, "When you offered to help us, I believed you were doing so because of my uncle's pursuit of Lady Castlemaine, and because we had no choice. You are, after all, the king. Now I discover you are indeed seeking to assuage your lust. You may be my sovereign, but at this moment you are acting no better than any knave in the worst part of this city."

A scowl darkened his features. "Have a care to whom you speak, Mistress Burroughs. There is a charge that has been leveled at your lover which we have overlooked, because we assumed his accusers were jealous of his success."

"What charge?"

"That he is a disgrace to the courts."

"Because of his low birth?"

The king shook his head.

"Because of some of the things he may have done?"

"Yes."

"He stole out of ignorance and desperation."

"It is not of theft we speak. It is something else entirely, of a particularly disgusting nature, concerning the man for whom he clerked."

She met Charles's gaze boldly. "He is innocent of such behavior."

"You would have us believe you, and not these other legal men?"

"Yes."

Charles strolled around her. She could feel him surveying her body, which trembled now not with fear, but righteous indignation. "You sound quite fierce."

"Because those men don't know the truth."

"We have a certain influence in the courts,

Mistress Burroughs. We wonder what you would do to raise your lover even higher in the world. After all, you are not noble, or titled, or rich. You are but the niece of a merchant."

Her eyes narrowed, for she knew this tone of voice, this contemplative expression. She had seen it when her uncle's customers and suppliers were in a mood to bargain.

"What are you suggesting, sire?" she asked, although she knew full well.

"We are suggesting, my dear, that you should not be too hasty to dismiss royal favor. People already assume we are lovers. We fail to see why it should not be so."

"Because, Your Majesty, I love another, and because such an immoral bargain should be beneath a king."

Charles's face turned as red as the velvet upholstery on one of his ornate chairs. Then he marched to the door and threw it open. "Chaffinch!"

The page appeared instantly, as if he had been waiting beside the door the entire time.

"Take her back to her uncle and tell him to take her home," Charles commanded. "We shall not be seeing them at Whitehall again." He glared at her. "Farewell, Mistress Burroughs, and consider yourself fortunate that you are not being escorted to the Tower. Go!"

She hurried out of the door, then hesitated, forcing herself to turn back to the king. "Your

Majesty, what do you intend to do to Mr. Harding?"

"Perhaps you should have thought of that before you treated your king like dung beneath your heel," Charles snapped. "Go away, Mistress Burroughs. We do not care to look at you, and if you do not leave, we shall call the guards."

Chaffinch grabbed her arm. "Come away," he muttered harshly as he tugged her out of the room. "Can't you see you've upset him?"

"But—"

"You stupid wench," the page growled as he pulled her along the corridor. "You have no notion of what the king has to deal with every day. The Dutch, the Spanish, the French, his queen, Lady Castlemaine."

"You are right, I don't," she replied, yanking her arm from the page's grasp. "But that doesn't give him the right to treat me like a harlot."

Chaffinch halted and regarded her sternly. "Look you, mistress, everybody he meets wants something of him. Given all he's endured before finally being restored to his rightful place, did he ask so much from you, his subject?"

"I would gladly give him the duty a subject owes a king. He wanted more than that."

"He'll likely gamble or dance all night after this," Chaffinch concluded in an annoyed mutter, ignoring her comment as he once again pulled her along. Vivienne tried to tell herself that perhaps the worst was over. Charles was not reputed to be a vindictive man. Maybe once his first burst of anger ended, he would not trouble himself with them at all, for as Chaffinch had said, he had other, surely much more important, things to consider.

With such optimistic thoughts trying to overcome her fear, she followed Chaffinch through the maze of hallways. Soon enough she heard the buzz of a number of voices and recognized the way into the Banqueting House.

Chaffinch opened the door and gestured for her to enter.

She did—and the room fell silent as every head turned to look at her.

Blushing to be the center of speculative attention, she surveyed the room, searching for her uncle. After what seemed an eternity, while more brows rose questioningly and people exchanged significant glances, she spotted him with a group of courtiers.

Ignoring everybody, she made her way toward her uncle, whose expression grew more aggravated as she approached. "What are you doing here?" he demanded, regardless of his company.

"We have to leave."

"Why? What have you done?"

"It is what I would not do," she replied. "If you are not willing to leave, Uncle, I will depart without you."

He must have seen the determination in her eyes, or heard it in her voice, because he nodded his head, took hold of her arm and led her from the room.

Chapter 21

As the coach rumbled away from Whitehall, Uncle Elias glared at Vivienne as if she had single-handedly ruined him. "You little fool! How could you refuse him? He's the king, by God!"

He continued to berate her, but Vivienne kept her gaze on the buildings they passed and ignored him. Fog had come up from the river, making everything gray and damp. She thought of Rob, waiting barefoot on the stable roof to be with her.

How she hoped he would come to her tonight! She had to tell him what had happened. More importantly, she had to be with him, to feel his love surround and strengthen her.

To remind herself that whatever came, she still had him.

"It may not be too late. We could go back—"

"No!" She turned toward her uncle. "You didn't see his face, Uncle. I assure you, it is too late. He will not have me now."

"You cannot be certain—"

"I am."

He cursed harshly. "To be so close, to have an entry into the court itself . . ."

"Yes, Uncle, I fear there has been a business opportunity lost," she said flatly.

"Not just that. You've lost a chance for a title, estates, a noble husband after—"

"After the king is done with me?"

"Yes, by God. It's happened before. I don't see why it should be any different for you."

"Take heart, Uncle," she said, determined to silence him. "Perhaps all may yet turn out well. As a woman who refused the king of England, have I not increased my worth in some circles?"

His eyes widened and a smile dawned on his plump face. "Gad, I had not thought of that."

"No," she murmured, going back to watching the damp buildings pass by and worrying about the consequences of her refusal, "I did not think you had."

" 'Allo, Rob, nice night for a walk, ain't it?"

Rob spun around and peered into the darkness. Above him rose the Burroughses' living quarters; around him were the smells and small noises of the mews. "Jack? What are you doing here?"

His friend sauntered out of the shadows. He gestured toward Vivienne's window. "That's hers, ain't it?"

"Are you drunk?"

"No, Rob. Perfectly sober," his friend replied as he came closer.

"What are you doing prowling about here? You're not . . ." He dropped his voice. "You're not up to no good, are you?"

"That's good, comin' from you, at this time o' night and in this place."

Rob again glanced at the window.

"Oh, yes, mustn't stand here flappin' my gums when you've got the beautiful Vivienne waitin' on ya. Except she ain't there. Spreadin' her legs for the king, I hear. Gone to Whitehall, the pair o' them, so the stableboy says. Very talkative chap, he is, especially when somebody else pays for his nip at the tavern 'round the corner."

"Jack, you must be drunk. Go home."

"Why should I, when you ain't? You're sliding between the sheets with a woman you ain't married to, and don't think you can lie and tell me no. Remember I watch people, old son. That's what you pay me for, isn't it? But sometimes I watch without bein' paid." He smiled as he continued with unmistakable sarcasm, "Very fine and very noble, I must say, with Martlebury

your client, too. O' course, you've lots of experience stealin'. First my sister, now Sir Philip's intended bride."

"I never stole your sister."

"Yes, ya did. You took her away from me."

Rob stared at his friend, who had given no
sign, no hint of his bitterness. "We took you in
when we could."

"Oh, aye, like a stray dog. I was her brother,
her family, tied by blood. But she give all that
over for you."

"And she left me, Jack. Are you forgetting
that?"

"No," he growled. "I was glad when she did.
And now so are you, I daresay. Left you free to
taste that Burroughs wench, and maybe more,
eh? Marriage, maybe? You'd be set for life with
that old man's money."

Struggling to come to terms with what he was
hearing, Rob stepped away from Jack. "We're in
love."

"You was never goin' to marry Janet, were
you?"

"This is hardly the time or place to discuss
this—"

"Why not? Why not here in the streets?
Many's the talk we used to have, sittin' in the
gutter. All forgotten now, eh? And the nights we
used to count ourselves lucky if we got to sleep
in straw, in a place that didn't stink too much."

"I haven't forgotten."

"I thought maybe you had, now that you've come so high up in the world, high enough to think you can marry Vivienne Burroughs. You always did aim high. You made no bones about that."

"Jack, we both used to talk about making something of ourselves."

"But you meant it. Really meant it. Believed you was cut out for better things. That you was better than the rest o' us, even Janet. Don't think Janet didn't know that, neither. She knew you'd succeed, too, somehow, and that you'd leave her. She used to cry about it sometimes."

"I didn't know. She never told me."

"That's why she left ya, before you left her. She knew you'd never take her back when the man was done with her. She drowned herself rather than be turned away by the high and mighty Rob Harding."

"Is that . . . is that really true?" Rob asked, despair and guilt weighing on him like a pile of stones.

"Would I lie about it?"

Rob's eyes narrowed as he regarded the man he had thought his friend for so long. A man who had kept bitter anger and envy hidden, and hidden well. "I don't know, Jack. I begin to think I don't know *you.*"

"And here you were so sure you did. Sure you knew all about me—poor, pauper Jack with his whores and his gambling. What are you but poor pauper Rob with his harlot, taking her without vows?" Jack laughed scornfully. "Always so sure, Robbie, always so certain you knew everything."

"I was your friend—"

"Friend? Oh, yes, your friend you use like an errand boy or spy. Here, Jack, keep an eye on this one. Find out what you can about that one. Oh, by the by, here's a few coins for yer trouble from your friend the solicitor."

"Jack, this is ridiculous. If you don't want to do the jobs I hire you for, don't."

"Oh, you *are* the very soul of charity! I could spit!"

Rob watched Jack warily, uncertain what he might do. "I loved Janet, but she didn't tell me her fears. She broke my heart when she left me. And what was I supposed to do when I was given the opportunity to better my lot? Say no, thank you?"

"You might a put in a word for me, your friend!" Jack cried, his voice full of the anger, envy and frustration that had festered for years. "You might have said, what about Jack? Any place for my friend in your house? Good God, Rob, I woulda been happy to be the lowest servant in that man's house. Instead, you left me behind in the gutter to rot."

Guilt and remorse consumed Rob as he listened.

For it was as Jack said. He had done nothing,

said nothing, to help his friend. He had been too afraid he would lose his own chance. Too selfish.

"You left me just like you woulda left Janet, so I—"

Rob's head shot up. "You what? What did you do?" His eyes widened. "It was her choice to leave me, wasn't it, Jack?"

Jack shook his head. "Oh, no, you don't. You're the sinner here, not me. I tried to help her—and meself, too, I don't deny."

Rob was across the distance between them in an instant. He grabbed Jack's collar. "What the devil did you do?" he snarled.

Jack twisted out of his grasp. "She went up in the world, same as you. She just needed a push."

Rob stared at him with naked disgust in his eyes. "How did you push her, Jack? Did you sell her off as if you were her pander? Your own sister? You did, didn't you?"

"She'd have been all right if she hadn't been so besotted with ya. She could have screwed that old aristocrat out of lots of money being his mistress and bearing his brat—"

"She was with child?"

"What's that to you? If she hadn't been so stupid, she would have been all right. But no, she has to take it into her head to try to fight 'im off. Then after, she still couldn't see that she should be happy with what I'd done fer her. She even has to drown herself because she thought you'd be too proud to take her back. She was right, too. I know it, and so do you."

"I don't know it," he cried. "I don't know what I would have done."

"I do! You would have thrown her back into the streets, the same as that wench you're bedding will be when her uncle finds out about her. And he will. Sir Philip already knows." Jack smiled triumphantly. "Ah, now you understand. Now you're not so damned sure of yourself. When your whore gets back from Whitehall, who do you think will be waiting in her bed?"

Had Vivienne really gone to Whitehall, then?

If so, why?

The king must have invited her.

For what reason?

The memory of Charles on top of her, running his lascivious hands over her body, burst into his mind.

"Do you think she'll be waitin' for you, all warm and willin'?" Jack scoffed. "Think again, old son."

Rob forced himself to concentrate on the danger at hand. "Who else would it be?" he demanded harshly. "You?"

"Wrong again, my clever fellow. Sir Philip was right interested about your little rendezvous and he don't climb too bad, for a bawcock. O' course, he had some help."

Rob stared at him incredulously. "What have you done?"

"Earned a way to get out o' this stinkin' country," Jack snarled. "Away from the jackanapes and away from *you*."

A stable door opened and the tousled head of a groom appeared. "Go in," Rob commanded. "This is none of your concern."

The groom disappeared at once.

"We've roused the mews," Jack said, backing away. "Damn you, you coward."

"I don't give a damn who hears us. By God, I could kill you," Rob growled, meaning it with every fiber of his being as he marched toward the man who had destroyed Janet and now threatened to destroy Vivienne.

"Stop there, Rob, or I'll kill ya! I mean it." Jack reached into his coat and pulled out a dagger.

"Are you forgettin' something, my buck?" Rob asked quietly as he continued to stalk his opponent, his accent slipping to what it had been years before. "As I once told a client o' mine, I wasn't born a lawyer. I've beaten you in fights before, and by God, I'll beat you now."

"You've got no weapon."

"I won't need one."

There could be no mistaking Rob's determination. Jack saw it, and with his lips pressed together and panic in his eyes, he ran at Rob and lunged.

Rob jumped back, and as he did, it was as if he jumped back into his past, into the boy he had been, the youth raised in the rough world of alleys and back streets, where a weapon was fists or anything that came to hand.

He crouched, his gaze eagerly scanning the narrow passage between stables and houses, seeking a piece of wood or anything he could use as a weapon, all the while aware that Jack had his dagger ready.

They circled warily. "I ain't going to kill you, Rob," Jack assured him, the dagger twitching. "Sir Philip ain't payin' me for that."

"Then put that knife away."

"Can't. I need it. You was always a better fighter'n me, Rob. I have t' even the odds."

They continued to circle like two wolves, teeth bared, eyes watchful.

Suddenly Rob darted forward, deftly avoiding the knife. He grabbed hold of Jack's arm and twisted.

Jack gave a yell and kicked, his booted foot striking Rob hard in the knee. It buckled and Rob fell onto the uneven cobblestones, crying out in pain.

Rob saw Jack's arm rise and he rolled away, out of range of the plunging knife. Staggering to his feet, he crouched again, wary, panting, keeping his eye on the dagger.

"I'm bigger now, Rob," Jack taunted breathlessly. "Not the little runt anymore. I can take you and I mean to, and then your balls are mine. Maybe I'll hang 'em 'round my neck when I go to the New World."

"A savage with the savages," Rob muttered, swaying back and forth, ignoring the burning pain in his kneecap.

"At least I don't pretend to be what I ain't," Jack cried as he sprang forward.

Rob sidestepped him, turning and moving away as fast as his injured knee would let him. As he did, he struck out at Jack, hitting him on the shoulder.

"Feeble, Rob, very feeble," Jack declared as he whirled around. "No more than a flea bite. Remember flea bites, Rob? Remember how we used to pick the nits out o' each other's hair?"

"Of course I remember. Do you? Do you remember how many times I shared my food with you? Or how many times I hid you when your father was on one of his rampages?"

"Ever the kindhearted soul," Jack jeered as he moved closer.

"I did what I could."

"Till you got lucky. Tell me, Rob, is it as they say? Did you let that man diddle with ya?"

"You know better."

"So I always thought—but then, you always thought I admired you. I *hate* you, Rob Harding."

Again Jack lunged. Rob jumped away and gasped at the shock of pain as he landed before he grabbed Jack's arm. He held tight, pulling downward and twisting, determined to wrest the knife from Jack's hand.

There was a loud crack. Jack cried out in pain and the knife clattered onto the cobblestones. Rob pushed him away and reached for it. At the same time, Jack scrambled after him.

Rob got it first. Jack tackled him, trying to grab him.

It was no good. In the next instant, Rob had him on the ground, his uninjured knee pressed against Jack's chest, and the knife at his neck. "I should slit your throat for what you did to Janet."

"Go ahead," Jack panted. "Go ahead and be done with it. I ain't got nothin' to live for."

Rob drew in a great, shuddering breath as he remembered the boys they both had been.

He slowly slid his knee off Jack's chest. "Run away," he commanded grimly. "Get out of here, and out of London." As he rose and tucked the knife in his belt, he looked down on the man who had been like a brother to him. "Consider your life and your freedom my gift to you, as my education was a gift to me."

Clutching his broken arm, Jack eyed him dubiously as he staggered to his feet. "You're letting me go?"

"Because you're right. I should have done more to help you. But this is the end of it, Jack. Now we are even."

Still holding his broken arm, Jack backed away as if unsure that Rob meant what he said.

When Rob didn't follow, he turned and ran down the mews.

As he did, a coach lumbered through the gate, nearly striking him. "Here, you, get out o' the way!" the driver cried while Jack disappeared into the night.

As the coach rolled to a stop, Rob quickly drew back into the shadow of the stable wall, out of sight. He glanced up at Vivienne's window and saw the rope dangling along the wall beside it.

Careless, very careless, Jack, he thought. Might as well have leaned a ladder against the wall.

"Oy, where's the watchman?" the coachman called out.

Rob could hear the sound of doors opening and excited talk as he crept toward the drainpipe. He grabbed it and began to climb, biting his lip to keep from crying out in pain every time he bent his knee.

As he looked up at Vivienne's window, a shadow moved across it.

Chapter 22

~~~ ∽◯◯◠ ~~~

Owens tugged the ribbon from Vivienne's hair so hard, she cried out in alarm.

"Oh, sorry, mistress," the maidservant mumbled. "I'm that put out by the ruckus outside."

"Nobody knows who was fighting?" Vivienne asked.

Their coach had nearly run down a man fleeing the mews, and after they had stopped, the liverymen, stableboys and grooms had all excitedly informed them of a brawl. Reports as to the number of participants varied from two to ten. On one point, however, all were certain: The combatants had disappeared.

"We never had such things go on in my day, when Cromwell was in charge," Owens muttered. "Things have gone to the dogs since Charles got restored."

Vivienne glanced at the window, noting that Owens had drawn the curtains. She was in no mood to argue the merits or demerits of her king. She wanted to open the window and look for Rob.

"Since you seem so upset, you may leave me to finish myself," Vivienne said.

Owens didn't protest.

"Good night, Mistress," she said, hurrying out the door.

Vivienne didn't doubt that Owens would head to the kitchen to discuss the brawl with the rest of the servants. That pleased Vivienne, because the kitchen was far from her bedchamber, so nobody would hear anything.

She went to the window and pulled back the curtains—to see a broken pane of glass and a rope dangling outside.

"Expecting somebody, were you?"

That was not Rob's voice!

"Who's there?" she demanded as she whirled around, peering at the shadows beside her bed.

"Who were you looking for?" Philip said, stepping into the candlelight.

"Get out!"

"Hush, my dear, or you will rouse the house, and I shall be forced to tell them what a harlot you are."

"I don't know what you're talking about."

"Oh, please, Vivienne, don't play the fool. It's

most unbecoming. I know all about Heartless Harding."

She swallowed hard. "How did you get in?"

"The same way as your lover. Or should I say lovers?" he asked coldly as he came farther into the room. "I'd be surprised if there was only one."

"Get out!" she ordered.

"Such righteous indignation. That's quite amusing, coming from you, a woman who will take that guttersnipe into her bed."

"He is not a guttersnipe. He is an attorney."

"Harding was born in the gutter and that's where he should have stayed. Society has no use for men who don't know their place—or women, either."

"Who decides that place? You?"

Philip reddened. "I am going to take that thief to court for misfeasance."

"Misfeasance?"

"Stealing the virginity of his client's intended bride is undeniably improper behavior for a lawyer."

"He didn't steal my virginity. I gladly gave it to him."

Philip's lip curled. "My God, you are a bold whore."

"I would be a whore if I married you."

"Listen to me, you stupid wench. I have a use for your uncle's money, and I intend to get it, and you, one way or another." He strolled closer. "You cannot dismiss me like a servant or that fop Cheddersby. I do not intend to leave before the cock crows and I have had my sport of you."

"I have but to scream—"

"And I have but to tell your uncle about Heartless Harding. How do you think your uncle will feel about that bastard sneaking into your bed? Harding has had you, and since he is not the king, your uncle will not be pleased, to put it mildly. I would, of course, be willing to keep your little secret, if you do as I say."

"I gather my secret is already well-known, if you know about it."

"I learned from a most confidential source."

"Now you listen to *me*, Philip, and listen well. I don't care if all of London knows what I've done."

"I would not be so hasty, my Amazon. Unless you give me what I want, I'll destroy your lover's career as thoroughly as you tried to ruin my chances with your uncle. Don't think I won't—I have the means."

Vivienne's mind raced. Did he have that power, as the king did?

The king. If Philip had been waiting here for her, he could not know what had happened at Whitehall.

A genuine smile grew on her face. "Go ahead, Philip. Have you not heard where I have been tonight? Whitehall. In the king's private apartments."

She saw his scowl and pressed on. "So very well, Philip. Tell the world what you believe. Let us see how Charles responds, shall we? Or what courtiers will pay any heed at all to you when I have the king's ear."

He lunged for her, grabbing her roughly. In the next moment, she felt the cold prick of a dagger against her throat. "I fear you've seriously underestimated me, Vivienne. I do not take kindly to losing anything, not even a whore. Not to that guttersnipe or the king of England." He started to drag her backward. "So it's to the bed, my dear—or I will take you on the floor."

Suddenly a hand clapped on Philip's shoulder and wrenched him away, sending him staggering back.

"What in—" Philip cried as cold air blew in through the open window and the curtains swung in the breeze.

Vivienne was so relieved to see Rob, her knees nearly buckled. And then she realized something else was very wrong.

His clothes were torn and filthy, his face muddy and scratched, and blood stained the knee of his breeches. In his hand he held a long, awful knife.

Rob spoke in a low, guttural growl, with the accent of the poorest pauper of the streets of London. "If it's a fight you want, you bloody coxcomb, I'm your man. Come on, fop, let's see what you can do."

"What are you?" Philip whispered incredulously.

"A guttersnipe son of a whore. Ain't that one of the nicer things they say about me around the Inns of Court?" he replied, his tone chilling Vivienne to the marrow of her bones.

"Good God," Philip gasped as he inched backward.

Rob made a terrible smile. "Get out of here or I'll make you wish you had died at birth."

"He isn't worth it, Rob," she protested, seeing murder in his eyes. "You could go to prison if you kill him."

"Or he will, for trying to rape you."

"No!" Philip cried, climbing over the bed in an attempt to get away from him and to the door.

Tossing his weapon aside, Rob dove at him, pushing him to the ground and wrestling to get Philip's dagger.

Trying to rid himself of his attacker, Philip bucked like a wild horse, while Vivienne ran for Rob's discarded knife. She grabbed it, then watched helplessly as the men rolled over the floor, both of them gripping the dagger.

Philip lashed out and kicked Rob in the knee.

Crying out in pain, he collapsed. That gave Philip the chance to shove him off and grab his dagger. He scrambled to his feet and stood over the crippled Rob. He kicked Rob hard in the ribs and she heard a sickening crack.

Rob moaned.

Philip held up his hand, warning Vivienne to stay back. "Leave him or I swear I'll kill him!"

"No, don't! Please!"

"You are a fool, Vivienne," Philip said, standing over his fallen opponent, a triumphant smile on his face. "Why should you care about this piece of dung?"

Vivienne regarded him steadily, her shoulders rigid with determination. "Because I love him."

"Love is for idiots. Do you think he loves you? He only wants your uncle's money and the prestige that will come to him if he marries you."

She glanced down at Rob, who clutched his right side, his eyes full of pain and anguish and frustration. "And what was it you wanted, Philip?" she retorted. "Wasn't it my uncle's money and a body for your bed? So much more noble, of course."

"Shut that shrewish mouth of yours!" Philip snarled. "What will you do, live in poverty with this gutter brat? He won't be able to earn a living as a solicitor anymore, not by the time I've done with him. And as for your uncle—don't you understand that after what you've done, he'll think himself well rid of you? He's likely to send you to live in the streets."

"I would rather live in the streets with Rob than a palace with you. Now leave this house."

Philip's eyes flashed with anger, then his lip curled with scorn. "Very well, my dear. But look—he's getting up. I do believe he intends to murder me. I fear I must defend myself." Philip raised his dagger to strike.

With a loud cry, Vivienne rushed at him and Rob's knife sank into Philip's body.

Aghast, she staggered backward. Philip gazed at her incredulously for what seemed forever before he slowly sank to his knees, then toppled over onto the floor.

Vivienne gradually became aware that Rob had gotten up and was bending over Philip. "He's dead," Rob whispered, looking up at her.

Feeling that all around her had become like a dream, she gazed down at the bloodied knife, then let it fall to the floor. Rob hurried to her and enfolded her shivering body into his embrace. "I didn't mean to kill him," she whispered, too upset even to weep.

"Vivienne!" Uncle Elias cried from the threshold of the room. "Gracious God, what has happened?" He spied the body on the floor. "It's Sir Philip! Good Lord, he's not—"

Rob pulled away from her, but kept one hand on her shoulder for support, keeping his weight on his uninjured leg. "I killed him."

"No!" she protested, staring at him. "That's not true."

"Mistress Burroughs, please allow me to tell your uncle the facts," he said, once more the coolly determined solicitor. "Sir Philip was attacking your niece, Mr. Burroughs, and I killed him."

As Uncle Elias stopped gaping at Philip's body to regard Rob, Vivienne became more determined to have the truth known. "No, that isn't—"

"I fear Mistress Burroughs is distraught," Rob interrupted, staggering slightly.

"You're hurt. We need a doctor, Uncle, right away."

His formerly pale face flushing, Uncle Elias shook his head. "We need the king's guards, that's who we need. A nobleman murdered in my house. This is terrible. A disaster. A scandal. Vivienne, get out of this room. Wait in the withdrawing room."

"No. I am not going to—"

For the first time since entering the room, Uncle Elias seemed to really *see* Rob. "How the devil came you here, at this hour of the night?"

"Through the window."

"*What?*"

"I invited him, Uncle." *Let everything be known. No more secrets, no more lies.* "He is my lover."

"Your lover?" Uncle Elias gasped. "This . . . this . . . *lawyer* is your lover?"

"Yes. For him, I turned down Philip, refused

to consider Lord Cheddersby, and risked the wrath of the king of England. Philip found out. He attacked me and he was going to kill Rob. I had to stop him."

For a moment, Vivienne dared to hope that Uncle Elias believed her—until his eyes narrowed and his lips thinned. "This is the most ludicrous story I have ever heard. *You* killed Sir Philip? Everybody knows women lack the stomach for such a thing. Now get out of the way, or God help me, I'll pick you up and move you myself!"

"There is no need for such agitation," Rob said quietly. "I will come with no trouble."

"But you're innocent!"

"Mistress Burroughs, please don't upset yourself. I am most grateful for your defense, but as your uncle says, everybody knows a woman incapable of such an act."

"Unless the man she loves is going to be killed." She glared at her uncle. "Why else do you think Mr. Harding is here? *He is my lover.*"

Her uncle's scornful gaze darted between them. "You refused Sir Philip Martlebury and the king for this . . . this sodomite? And even if that's true, how dare he come into my house like a thief and take my niece's honor?"

"I have never been a sodomite, but I will not deny that I have been a thief, Mr. Burroughs. And I will not deny that I have caused Sir

Philip's death. I am willing to go to prison for what I have done."

He meant it. She saw it in his eyes, heard it in his voice. "No, Uncle, please," Vivienne pleaded, her anxious gaze going from Rob to him. "He didn't take anything. I gave it. And he did *not* kill Philip. I did, I tell you!"

Ignoring her, Uncle Elias marched to the door and bellowed, "Send for the king's guard. At once."

Vivienne went to Rob, took his hand and looked beseechingly into his pale and mud-streaked face. "I will not allow you to be imprisoned for something I have done."

He held her hands between his, his intense gaze boring into her eyes. "Vivienne, I have been to Newgate and it is a hell on earth. I will not see you put there."

"But Rob—"

He put his finger against her lips. "Shh, my love, say no more. This was done in defense, so have no fear. In the meantime, let me go."

"Take your filthy hands off my niece," Uncle Elias commanded.

Vivienne ignored him to kiss Rob.

"Vivienne!" Uncle Elias grabbed her to pull her away.

"Don't you dare lay a hand on her," Rob said, his voice quiet, but so forceful it made Uncle Elias let go and back away.

In the next moment, three footmen and

Owens were in the doorway, gawking at the tableau.

"Take hold of Harding," Uncle Elias ordered two of his footmen. "You," he commanded the third, "take Sir Philip's body below. Owens, fetch the watch."

As Owens shuffled with more haste than Vivienne had ever seen her display before, one footman started to drag out Philip's body, leaving a thin trail of blood. The other two warily approached Rob, who limped away from Vivienne.

"Uncle Elias," she said, moving to stand in front of him, "you can't take him. He's innocent, and he's hurt."

"Stand aside, Vivienne, and let these men do what is necessary," Rob said softly.

She glanced at him over her shoulder. He nodded. "Please, Vivienne."

"You heard him, Vivienne. Get out of the way," her uncle barked.

"Because Rob asks me to, I will," she said, finally giving in to what Rob wanted—but only for the present, until the situation could be remedied.

She faced Rob. "Tell me what I must do to free you."

"Speak in my defense if this comes to trial."

"Take him, bind him and hold him for the king's men," her uncle ordered. "A nobleman killed in my house," he muttered. "Very bad for business, very bad."

The footmen grabbed Rob roughly.

"Gently! There is no need to manhandle him," Vivienne cried.

She wished she could go to Newgate with him, hoping he would be freed when the truth became known, or at least the truth that this was done to defend him from death at Sir Philip's hands. Her freedom would be too dearly bought if Rob's was the price.

"Vivienne, be quiet!" Uncle Elias snapped as the footmen led Rob away.

Her heart broke to see him being taken from the room as if he were a criminal.

"You are making a spectacle of yourself!" Uncle Elias continued angrily.

Distraught, angry, fearful of Rob's fate, she glared at Uncle Elias. "I don't care what I look like or what people think. I love him, and he loves me. We are going to be married, whether you approve or not."

"You brazen hussy! After all I've done for you, you dare to speak to me this way? After I took you in, fed you, clothed you—"

"Almost sold me off to get a title and the influence to go with it. You would have gladly seen me the mistress of the king to increase your position in the city. Forgive me, Uncle, if I did not wish to repay you with the rest of my life."

"So instead you humiliate me."

"Instead I fell in love with a fine young man whom you should be proud to know."

"A fine young man who's on his way to Newgate for murder! A fine young man born and raised in the gutters of London, who's notorious for the way he paid for his education with that disgusting sodomite—"

"Be quiet!" Vivienne thundered, her whole body shaking with emotion. "He is a finer, more honorable man than Sir Philip could ever hope to be, or the king, or *you*, Uncle."

"If that is what you think," Uncle Elias retorted, his face purple with rage, "I should send you from my house forever."

"You don't have to send me. I will go, and gladly!" Vivienne cried as she marched from the room, down the stairs past the wide-eyed servants and out into the street.

"Odd's bodikins, what the duce is going on?" a sleep-befuddled Lord Cheddersby asked as he rose from his bed. Outside his closet he could hear voices raised in agitation, and unless he was very wrong or still dreaming, one of them was a woman's. The other, he thought, was one of his footmen's.

Pulling on his thick velvet robe, he noted that it must be a little past dawn, yet still very early in the day. He glanced at his wig on his dressing table, then remembered he wore his nightcap. Sliding his feet into slippers, he shuffled to the door of his closet, and out into the state bedchamber.

"I say, there, Jeffries, what the devil is happening?" he demanded of the servant in the adjoining room whose back was to him.

A woman shoved Jeffries out of the way. "Lord Cheddersby!"

"Mistress Burroughs?" he cried, utterly surprised.

"I am in desperate need of your help."

"Good God, you don't say?"

"Yes! Please, it's about Mr. Harding. He's been taken to Newgate for killing Sir Philip. He didn't, I did, but he lied and—"

Lord Cheddersby hurried toward her and put a brotherly arm around her shivering shoulders. "Hush, Mistress Burroughs, hush," he said gently and with surprising authority. "Come with me to my morning room, where I can better listen. Jeffries, have Marlowe send in some breakfast."

Without waiting for either of them to respond, he placed Vivienne's hand on his arm and led her down the back stairs, then along a corridor.

"Lord Cheddersby," she began breathlessly after she had taken a seat on one of the chairs in a room decorated in peacock blue. "I don't know who else to turn to. We need your help. Rob—Mr. Harding—is innocent of any crime, but my uncle won't listen, and so I have come to you. I know you do not think much of me, but I also know you are a good and kind man. Please do not turn me away."

Lord Cheddersby tugged off his nightcap, revealing a head of tousled light brown curls. "I wouldn't think of it," he said sincerely. "Mistress Burroughs, I am not a clever fellow, as you know. If I am to understand and help you, you must start at the beginning and go very slow."

Taking a deep breath and trying to sound calm, she did.

Chapter 23

"So I tried to tell my uncle the truth, but he wouldn't listen to me. I left his house and came straight to you," Vivienne concluded.

"I'm very glad you did." Lord Cheddersby shook his head incredulously. "Odd's bodikins, what a night! And now poor Mr. Harding is in Newgate?"

"Yes, when I should be there in his place."

"Oh, I don't know about that," Lord Cheddersby began when Jeffries appeared at the door, a tray in his hands and still obviously suspicious. "Your breakfast, my lord."

"Oh, thank you, Jeffries. Put it down there. We'll serve ourselves."

Glancing warily at Vivienne, the servant set out the dishes on the oak dresser, then backed out the room and closed the door.

"Pray, eat, Mistress Burroughs," Lord Cheddersby urged kindly, coming around to pull out her chair. "You are so distraught, I fear you will swoon otherwise, and that would quite unnerve me."

She didn't feel hungry, not when she could envision Rob in a pit of a cell at Newgate, without food or water. However, the smell of freshly crisped bacon and warm bread proved too tempting to ignore.

"I'm sorry to trouble you, Lord Cheddersby," she said after they had returned to their seats, their plates and cutlery in front of them.

"Oh, no, I am delighted!" he cried. "Well, not delighted about the circumstances, but delighted you think I could be of use. I've been useless most of my life. And you must call me Foz."

"You are so kind, and I've lied to you."

"Well, in a good cause, I believe."

"Other than Rob, you are my only friend."

Lord Cheddersby set down the fork and looked at her with a remarkably determined expression. "After a good breakfast and when I am properly dressed, we shall see about sorting this mess out, shall we?"

"Do you think we can?" she asked softly, voicing the first hint of a doubt.

He blinked, looking rather like an owl startled by daylight. "Well, now that I've finally got something important to do, I shall certainly give it my all. Besides, I'm convinced you acted in Mr. Harding's defense or else Sir Philip would have killed him. Your action was not premeditated, so it cannot be considered felonious."

Now it was Vivienne's turn to look surprised.

"Oh, I know a little bit about the law. Not a lot. I only know a lot about Latin—but that's where I learned some law. My tutor Muttlechop made me read the medieval yearbooks, the records of the courts. Pretty dull stuff, for the most part, but I do recall a few things."

She reached out and covered his hand with hers. "You make me feel better, Foz, and I cannot ask for more."

"And if your odious, mean uncle has cast you out, you must stay here," he declared. "Nor should you trouble yourself about money. What's the good of me having so much if I can't share it?"

"Oh, Lord Cheddersby . . . Foz, I couldn't."

"Nonsense. I insist."

"Thank you so much," she replied, grateful for his generous offer, for otherwise she really had no idea where else she could go. "You are truly a kindhearted, generous friend."

"Enough thanks, Mistress Burroughs." He gestured at the room. "This place is far too enormous for just me and my servants, really. We simply rattle around like peas in a barrel. I shall gladly pay your expenses until Mr. Harding is free and able to marry you."

"I will always bless you for helping us," she said, smiling at him with tears in her eyes.

He cleared his throat loudly, his own eyes moist. "Yes, well, you had better try to get a little sleep. In the meantime, I'll get myself dressed and go to Newgate and see that he has the best accommodation that ghastly place affords. And I shall be happy to speak in Mr. Harding's favor at trial, if it comes to that. I daresay there are plenty of others who would, too."

"Will I be able to explain what really happened?"

Foz gave her a sympathetic look. "I'm not sure that would be the wisest course, because you would also be saying Mr. Harding told a rather monstrous lie. Besides, the judge and jury will likely think as your uncle does, that a woman is not capable of such an action." He held up his hand. "I know, I know, very blind of them. But they will. No, I think we should keep to the facts as Mr. Harding has told them. If so, he acted in self-defense, and that is something the court should not only understand, but pardon."

"I hope you're right, my lord,"

"Still, it would save a lot of bother if the king would pardon him."

"He can do that?"

"Absolutely, and in this case, quite rightly." Foz gave her a bright smile.

She flushed. "I fear the king may not be amenable to helping me. He was very angry with me last night because I wouldn't—"

"I know, my dear," Lord Cheddersby interrupted gently. "I, um, happened to be at Whitehall. But the king is a very capricious fellow, and just because he is cross with somebody one day doesn't mean he will be the next. I'faith, if that were not so, the Duke of Buckingham's head would have been on London Bridge years ago. Still, even if the king will not help, I'm sure the judge will see that Mr. Harding was acting in your defense, and so not guilty of murder. Now do try not to worry. There is nothing more you can do, at least for the present."

"I cannot sit idly by while—"

"I fear you must. There is nothing a woman can do in such circumstances," he said. He gave her a sympathetic smile as he went to the door and called for his footman. "Jeffries, escort Mistress Burroughs to the green bedchamber and see that she lacks for nothing."

"Yes, my lord."

Vivienne watched Lord Cheddersby depart, then sat some moments at the table before going with the haughty Jeffries, a gleam of resolution in her vibrant eyes.

* * *

Rob fingered the pebble he had plucked out of the fetid straw of the cell, took his aim at the two gleaming, beady eyes in the crack of the wall and threw, grunting at the sudden twinge of pain from his broken rib.

The rat gave a squeal and the eyes disappeared.

"Still good," Rob muttered grimly.

How many rats had he and Jack caught this way? He couldn't begin to say.

There were other sorts of rats in London, human ones who would enjoy hearing of his fall from grace and then come after his clients.

Slumped against the wall, he surveyed his cell yet again. Of course nothing had changed. The dank gray walls were just as damp, the straw just as odoriferous, the pail in the corner even more so. A bowl of scummy water lay near the door, giving off a smell all its own.

He sighed and glanced up at the narrow window, knowing these surroundings did not horrify and repel him as they would Vivienne. He had known worse places, slept in worse places, been beaten in worse places.

In a sense, he could feel more at home here than he ever could in a fine house like Lord Cheddersby's or Whitehall Palace—but that didn't mean he was comfortable or at all anxious to stay.

Would a judge and jury believe that what he had done was manslaughter, not murder? The punishment either way was severe. Could he dare to hope that they would find he had acted in self-defense, and so his offense was pardonable?

He rested his forehead on his uninjured knee. Or maybe this was the ending always fated for him and he had only succeeded in delaying the inevitable.

Even if he were pardoned, what hope did he have now to provide for Vivienne? Nobody would seek his legal services. He would have to take what jobs he could, and he could not bear to think of Vivienne suffering alongside him. To see the burden of poverty dull her bright eyes, the lack of food destroy her blooming health, the misery of cold and filthy lodgings overcome her joyous spirit.

She had said she loved him and wanted only his love in return. If he doubted that, was that not belittling her love—and being as condescending as all the other men in her life who could not believe she knew exactly what she wanted, no matter the price?

He raised his head and looked at the pale morning light trying to shine through the little window, like the hope struggling through his despair. Vivienne the bold, Vivienne the defiant—she would be insulted if he thought she could not cope without wealth. He could see her eyes flash, the set of her lips, the flush of righteous indignation. . . .

By some miracle, the best and bravest woman

in London loved him. Why should he sit here wallowing in his despair?

Had he not been trained to argue cases? By God, even though he was not a barrister, could he not somehow contrive to argue his own?

"By God, I will!" Rob cried aloud, and then he laughed.

Sitting in the squalid guardroom, two jail-keepers looked at one another and frowned at the sound of a boisterous laugh. The turnkey with a grizzled beard, three teeth and pock-marked face tapped his temple significantly.

The other blinked his rheumy eyes barely visible beneath lank, filthy hair, and nodded glumly while he scratched at one of his many flea bites. "Sounds like somebody's gone off his head, all right, Bill."

"Oy, jailer!" a man shouted, his words echoing off the stone walls. "Turnkey, it would be worth your while to attend to me!"

"What now?" Bill mumbled grouchily as he hoisted himself to his feet.

"If you think he's mad, why go?"

" 'Cause he's got better clothes than most, that's why," Bill explained as he waddled toward the open door. "He might have money to pay for additionals."

"Ah!" his fellow guard said with a slow nod. "Need any help there?"

"No, I can manage," Bill muttered as he made

his way along the corridor, ignoring the stares or hawks of spit of the other prisoners, until he came to stand outside the cell of his most recently admitted prisoner. "What?" he demanded.

The tall man who, although he was also better-looking than most of his prisoners, nevertheless gave Bill a bit of a shiver, stuck his face up to the grill in the door. "I want you to fetch my clerk, Bertie Dillsworth. Tell him to bring paper, ink and quills. Oh, and a small table and stool. Also, I need better food than moldy bread and fetid water."

Bill scowled and scratched his grizzled chin. "Think I'm your servant, do ye? Better take another look."

To his surprise, the man grinned. "I can pay for your troubles."

"Show me."

The man produced a sovereign. "There'll be more. I assure you I have additional funds in my chambers."

"Chambers?"

"I am a solicitor, Robert Harding."

Bill looked as if he had swallowed a bug. "Not the one they call 'Heartless'?"

He bowed. "Your servant."

"God's teeth, you got my old mam them ten pounds that skint owed her! Not much, but she needed it bad. Why the hell didn't you say who ya was?"

"I was not at my best."

"Ha!" the jailer barked. " 'Spose not. Right, then, sir, I'll see you get what you need."

"I shall be very grateful."

King Charles looked up from the very boring document he was supposed to be reading and raised a brow. "Chaffinch, what in the name of God is that confounded racket?"

His page, who was standing closer to the door of Charles's apartments, cleared his throat. "It seems, Majesty, that someone wishes to intrude upon the royal presence."

Charles's eyes lit up. "Odd's fish, really?" Then he frowned. "If it's the Dutch ambassador, tell him we're indisposed and can't possibly see anybody."

"It is not the Dutch ambassador, Majesty," Chaffinch replied. "It sounds like a woman."

"Why did you not say so?" Charles demanded as he got to his feet, then stretched. "That sounds like something we should investigate." He got a wary look on his face. "Unless it's Barbara?"

"No, sire, it is not Lady Castlemaine."

"Ah, then we shall have to see who dares to make so much fuss in our palace."

Again, Chaffinch cleared his throat. "Majesty, Lord Clarendon—"

"Can go to the devil for a little while," the king

declared cheerfully. "We swear, if we are forced
to read any more correspondence from the chan-
cellor of the Exchequer, we shall go blind! Now,
out of the way, that's a good fellow."

The king waved Chaffinch aside and opened
the door, then stepped into the corridor. A short
distance away, two palace guards blocked the
hall, obviously attempting to prevent the
woman in front of them from going any farther.

"Ho, there, what's afoot?" Charles called out
jovially. "An assassin in skirts?"

"Your Majesty, please, I must speak with you."

"Guards, step aside," the king commanded.

They did so, albeit reluctantly.

"Ah, Mistress Burroughs!" Charles said,
frowning. "This is a surprise. We thought you
unlikely to visit Whitehall again."

The lovely young woman, who no doubt possessed the finest breasts Charles had ever seen,
flushed to the roots of her hair. "Your Majesty,"
she said, dropping to a low curtsy that brought
her cleavage into the royal view, "I most
humbly beg your pardon for intruding, but I
come on a matter of utmost urgency—and not
for myself."

"A good thing," the king muttered in an annoyed tone and letting her remain in a sub-
servient position a little longer, "for we do not
forget your behavior during your last visit here."

She glanced up, her really remarkable eyes
flashing with a bold spirit he couldn't help but

admire. "Your Majesty, Mr. Harding is wrongfully imprisoned in Newgate."

"Wrongfully imprisoned?" Charles repeated as she straightened. "This sounds like most serious business, indeed, and the corridor is no place to be discussing serious business. Come, let us retire to my apartments."

He saw her hesitation, noting the way her shoulders stiffened ever so slightly. Nevertheless, she did not protest when he tugged gently on her hand to lead her away.

He barely subdued a smile. He was sure she must be a bold, energetic lover. Robert Harding should count himself a fortunate man.

They entered his private domain, where the dutiful Chaffinch waited. "You may go, Chaffinch. Mistress Burroughs and I wish to be alone."

Chapter 24

Vivienne's heart throbbed wildly as the king's servant abandoned the room, but she would not flee. Her dread and fears were insignificant. All that mattered was getting Rob free. "Majesty, I have come—"

"You are all out of sorts, Mistress Burroughs," he interrupted as he strolled toward the table bearing several decanters and crystal wine-glasses. "Perhaps you would like some wine?"

"No, Majesty," she said, trying to sound calm.

The king poured himself a goblet of rich red wine, the heady scent of it drifting toward her. "We gather you've come about Sir Philip's death?"

She stared at him. "Sire?"

"Lord Cheddersby interrupted our game of tennis this morning to tell us all about it." He took a sip. "The poor fellow was quite indignant that Mr. Harding had been taken to Newgate."

"Quite rightly, sire," she replied. "It is I who should have been taken away, for I did the deed."

The king turned to her with an incredulous look. "You?"

"Yes, Your Majesty. I stabbed him."

"Lord Cheddersby tells us Mr. Harding was defending himself."

"He was defending me, but he was injured and Philip was going to kill him. I had a knife in my hands and I killed him."

"God save us," Charles muttered. "Amazing."

"It is the truth, sire."

"Yet your lover has confessed to the deed."

"Only to protect me, Majesty."

"A most charming sentiment that has, unfortunately, landed him in a terrible situation." Charles cocked his head to regard her shrewdly. "Perhaps you are trying to protect him, too. The law is usually more merciful to a woman."

"Sire, what I say is the truth. Have me taken to Newgate and set him free."

Charles set down the goblet and approached her. "You are far too pretty to go to prison, my dear, and surely too pretty to have killed a man."

Her body trembled and perspiration trickled down her back as she stood before him, afraid but resolute. She would do whatever she could to have Rob freed, and if nobody was willing to believe the truth, she would try another way. "Majesty, if you are not willing to see me in prison in Mr. Harding's stead, then I ask that you pardon him."

"Pardon him?" the king demanded. "Even if we believed you, we are not in the habit of interfering in criminal proceedings, except as they concern treason, Mistress Burroughs. We hardly think this matter requires your sovereign's involvement."

Desperate, seeing no other way, Vivienne swallowed hard and said, "If the truth alone is not enough to persuade you to pardon Mr. Harding, I will do whatever I must to encourage you to do so."

The king ran a measuring gaze over her. "You are willing to barter for his freedom?"

"Yes, Your Majesty, if I must."

"And you would offer whatever we most desire?"

"Yes, Your Majesty."

"So it is a bargain, then, is it, Mistress Burroughs? We shall pardon Mr. Harding in return for . . . whatever we will?"

She nodded.

"Shall we seal our contract with a kiss?"

Again, she nodded, and she closed her eyes as she waited for his unwanted embrace.

"You are most tempting, my dear," the king said, his voice sounding unexpectedly far away, "really most tempting. However, we have enough troubles with women and do not seek to add to them."

She opened one eye cautiously. The king stood by the decanter-covered table again. As he reached for his wine, he said, "We really don't need another mistress."

She opened both eyes.

He frowned with displeasure—but she saw the sparkle of merriment in his eyes as he raised in goblet in salute. "We are not so decadent as to make a woman pay for a pardon with her body, Mistress Burroughs, no matter what you may have heard, although, as we said, you are mighty tempting.

"Lord Cheddersby pleaded the case most eloquently this morning. Really, he was quite astonishing and not at all what one might expect, given his usual bumbling manner. In fact, we think the young man has been hiding his light under a bushel—or should we say, a wig?"

The king chuckled at his own joke, while all Vivienne could do was make a weak little smile.

"As he put it to us," Charles continued, "the facts seem quite clear. Sir Philip intruded into your bedchamber, made improper advances, and a struggle ensued. One way or another, Philip lost."

"Yes, Your Majesty," she confirmed, too confused and uncertain to speak in much more than a whisper.

"So Sir Philip's death was justifiable. However, you tell me now that Lord Cheddersby and Mr. Harding have misrepresented the actual events."

"They did that for my sake, sire."

"We understand that, too. And frankly, we think anyone who believes a lawyer never lies incredibly naive. However, we have it on good authority that Mr. Harding may indeed be exceptional in this regard, as well as very well versed in the law. If so, it would be unfortunate if he were to lose his reputation for honesty. He most certainly would if it got out that he had lied, even if it was to save the woman he loved." His mien softened. "We would dearly like to inspire so much tender feeling in a woman's breast."

Sighing, he set down his goblet. "Be that as it may, we think it best to let the confession stand, and to pardon Mr. Harding, which we had every intention of doing this very day. One of our secretaries is writing the document now and we shall sign it as soon as it is ready."

"Oh, Majesty!" she cried, covering her face with her hands as she burst into tears and sank to her knees.

"Please get up, my dear," Charles said tenderly as he took her elbow. "Really, we are not an ogre, you know. Mr. Harding can take credit for our mercy, too. We have heard of his assistance to those who have been unfairly treated and his attempts to have justice rendered to them."

She wiped her face and tried to stop crying as Charles gently helped her to her feet and led her to a chair. "You . . . you have heard of what he does?"

"Indeed." The king grinned and his eyes twinkled. "Did we not tell you we have plenty of courtiers who dearly love to inform us of so many things? We are glad to hear of Mr. Harding's efforts. If people feel justice will be done, it reflects well on the government, of which we are the head, so it reflects well on us and makes us popular with the people. We do not overlook something that increases our popularity."

He pressed a crystal goblet into her hand. "We really must insist you take a drink."

She did, and wine had never tasted better. She looked up at Charles, who was watching her with paternal concern. "I cannot possibly thank you enough, Majesty. And dear Lord Cheddersby, too."

"Whom we truly believe has been most seriously underestimated," the king remarked. "All finished?"

"Yes, thank you, sire."

He took the goblet from her.

"Your Majesty, I must confess I feared that I had angered you so much, you would hold that against Rob, too."

"Our reputation really is not very gentlemanly, is it?" Charles replied with a wistful expression that made her feel sorry for him. Then he grinned, once more the Merry Monarch. "It was for your sake we did that, Mistress Burroughs, for we fear you are no actress."

"I don't understand."

"We didn't want to damage your reputation any more than it already had been. Everyone at court thinks you are foolishly virtuous for refusing to be the king's mistress, which was part of our plan. But as we said, you are no actress, so we felt we dare not confide in you. As it was, you were beautifully and indignantly angry and distraught. It was quite the talk of the Banqueting House last night."

Although she had had many a dreadful moment since that meeting in the palace, given that Rob was going to be set free, she was willing to forgive the king for misleading her. "You are very clever, Majesty."

"Now, that is a compliment we rarely receive," he said, obviously pleased. He gave her a devilish grin. "If Mr. Harding should ever grow tiresome, my dear . . ." he murmured suggestively.

"You shall be the first to know, sire."

His deep laugh filled the chamber. "We don't believe you for a moment, but we can ask no more."

There was a soft knock at the door. "What it is?" the king bellowed.

The door opened a crack and Chaffinch's head appeared. "Lord Cheddersby has returned, sire."

"Ah, wonderful! Have him come here. And see what's keeping that pardon, will you?" Chaffinch nodded and disappeared.

Grinning gleefully, the king turned toward Vivienne. "This should be excellent! We've sent Foz to fetch your uncle." He clapped his hands like an excited child, then hurried to the table holding the decanters.

The king lifted up one end of the embroidered cloth. "Hide under here and you'll see what we mean about Lord Cheddersby's astonishing and unexpected burst of eloquence, for we shall put him through his paces for you."

"But Majesty, I don't think I'll fit—"

"Of course you will! Hurry, hurry!"

He was the king, she was his subject, and moreover, he was going to pardon Rob, so she obeyed.

She had no sooner managed to get all her skirt under the tablecloth and sit cross-legged on the floor than she heard the door to the room open.

She recognized her uncle's heavy tread on the parquet floor. The other man was Lord Cheddersby, for he spoke the moment he stopped. "Here is Mr. Burroughs, Your Majesty, and a more stubborn man I have yet to meet," he declared.

Even though there could be no mistaking the voice, Vivienne nevertheless raised the tablecloth to peek out and confirm the identity of the very irate, and certainly not stammering, speaker. Lord Cheddersby looked like the very vision of angry righteousness, while Uncle Elias appeared decidedly uncomfortable.

And the king—the king looked more imperious than she had ever seen him, even the night she believed he was trying to seduce her.

She felt of twinge of sympathy for her uncle.

"Your Majesty, I don't know what you've been told—" he pleaded.

"Everything, Mr. Burroughs," the king interrupted. "We know what transpired in your house last night, and we know why—which seems to be something in which you are completely uninterested. However, we assure you that your sovereign is always keen to know all the facts. And," he finished, glowering, "we do not take lightly to wrongful imprisonment, which is a fate we narrowly avoided ourselves."

"But Your Majesty, what else could I do? There was Sir Philip lying there dead, right in my niece's bedchamber, and—"

"You might have asked yourself what Sir Philip was doing there in the first place," Lord Cheddersby said coldly.

Uncle Elias blushed. "And Harding was there, too, where he had no business to be—"

"*Mr.* Harding, if you please," Lord Cheddersby said in a low growl that would have done credit to a highwayman.

Indeed, if she weren't so uncomfortable under the table, she would have been delighted to simply admire the change that had apparently come over the nobleman.

"Didn't your niece explain that to you?" Lord Cheddersby continued. "He was defending her honor."

Uncle Elias flushed as he looked from Lord Cheddersby to the king and back again. "But he shouldn't have been there, either."

"It was a good thing he was, or your niece might have suffered even more than she did," Lord Cheddersby said.

"But . . ." Uncle Elias fell silent.

"But what?" the king demanded.

"But a dead nobleman in my house, sire! My business would surely suffer when that became known. Although Sir Philip was a fool, a fop, and a heedless, impetuous—"

"Impetuous?" Charles roared. "Impetuous? He attacked your niece in her bedchamber!"

"And he died there. What will people think?"

Vivienne couldn't stay silent. Her uncle and Lord Cheddersby regarded her with shocked surprise as she clambered out from under the table.

"Vivienne, what—"

"Uncle, are you forgetting that Philip wanted to rape me and kill the man trying to stop him? What does it matter if you lose some custom? Would you feel better if it had been Rob who died? Is his life less valuable than a nobleman's?"

The king held up his hand for silence. "We are venturing onto swampy and republican ground with such questions. We remind you that your king is well within hearing."

"But sire—" Vivienne began.

"However, without venturing into that swamp," Charles continued, "we must say we value Mr. Harding. His absence would be a great loss to British jurisprudence. Therefore, Mr. Burroughs, we are not only prepared to pardon Mr. Harding, but we believe we must show our appreciation for his work with the less fortunate. We think a knighthood at the very least would be sufficient. Yes, a knighthood—but he must continue his practice, of course." He turned to Vivienne with a warm smile. "What say you to that, Mistress Burroughs? Shall we make him Sir Robert Harding?"

"Oh, yes, please, Your Majesty."

"It is no more than he deserves, sire," Lord Cheddersby seconded, while Uncle Elias looked stunned.

Charles noted that and grinned. "Smile, Mr. Burroughs," he chided. "Your niece is going to get her titled husband after all—and one who is very good at contracts."

"Husband?" he gasped as if he had just lost all his money.

"Why, yes. They are in love."

"I want to marry Rob, and he wants to marry me," Vivienne confirmed.

"Cheddersby, get the poor fellow a drink, will you?" Charles commanded. "Sit down, Burroughs, before you collapse."

As Uncle Elias nodded and did as he was told, Vivienne went to the king. "I don't know how I shall ever thank you, Your Majesty."

He ran his gaze over her. "As long as you come to Whitehall on occasion, we shall consider that sufficient."

He turned toward Uncle Elias. "Think of it, Mr. Burroughs. A solicitor in the family—surely that would come in handy at times. We also understand you deal in silk. You must bring some samples of your merchandise to the palace for the court tailors."

Her uncle's expression altered as the king spoke, from dismayed to befuddled, then to outright joy. "You shall not be displeased, sire. I sell nothing but the finest silk fabrics, and at a good price, I assure you."

Charles surreptitiously winked at Vivienne. "Yes, yes, we are sure of that."

Chaffinch again appeared at the door, this time bearing a rolled document. "The pardon, Your Majesty."

"Ah!" the king cried. "Lord Cheddersby, you had best stay here to nurse Mr. Burroughs back

to his usual robust state of health while Mistress
Burroughs and I make a visit to Newgate."

"Sire?"

Charles chuckled at her surprised expression.
"We would not miss this lover's reunion for
anything less than a declaration of war against
the Dutch."

"Oh, it's wonderful, that's what," Bertie said
as he handed Rob the rolled paper through the
grill. "I don't think the king himself could get
through! They just come, too. After the screw
told me where you was—and more surprised I
never was and hope to never be again—I
thought I'd best keep it quiet. I said you'd been
taken ill. Then old Mrs. Dugall kept insistin' she
was goin' to bring you a nice pork pie and Mrs.
Murphy said she'd fetch you a jam pasty. Well, I
couldn't let 'em do that, could I? So I told 'em—
and next thing I knew, there was ten people outside the office, clammering to know what I was
goin' to do about getting you out. They all
looked at me like I oughter come down here and
break you out! I tried t' explain, but it wasn't
easy, with them all talkin' at the same time."

He stopped to draw a breath, and then pulled
the bottle of ink out of his pocket and handed
that to Rob. He next pulled out some quills,
rather the worse for their mode of travel, from
inside his shirt. These he also passed through

the window to Rob. "So what should I tell 'em when I leave? They'll expect me t'say somethin,' unless you was to come with me?" he finished optimistically.

"You may tell them that I killed a man in self-defense and that I am confident that I will be judged accordingly and released."

Bertie sighed heavily. "Good!"

Rob set the quills beside the ink on the floor. "No stool and table?"

"That turnkey what came for me said he'd see to them, and better food, too."

"How much did you have to pay him?"

"Nothing."

"He's doing all that for nothing?"

Bertie barked a skeptical laugh. "Not him! Your clients took up a collection right there in the street."

These were people for whom a penny might mean the difference between sleeping with a full belly or an empty one. "I shall never forget their generosity," Rob murmured, meaning it with all his heart. "You haven't seen Jack, I suppose?"

"No. Want me to fetch him, too?"

"I don't think we'll see him again. He's probably left London."

"What for?" Bertie cried.

"For his health."

Suddenly there came the sound of many excited voices and hurrying feet, as well as another sound so odd and out of place, Rob thought he must be hearing things.

Who would brings dogs to Newgate?

Bertie peered down the hall.

"What is it?" Rob demanded, wondering if someone was about to be taken to be executed, although it was not the right time of day for that.

"Lord save me!" Bertie gasped.

"What?" Rob asked, holding his injured knee as he tried to get as close as he could to the grill to see who was coming.

His gaze still trained on whoever was approaching, Bertie whispered, "It's the king!"

"The king?" Rob repeated incredulously. "Are you sure?"

Charles would probably have dogs. . . .

"Aye, it is!" Bertie hissed, excited now that the surprise had worn off. "I seen his mustache!" He started to chortle. "The turnkey looks like he's going to collapse. Come out of the guardroom all wobbly."

"Who's with him?"

"The other screw with the—"

"No, no, who's with the king?"

His clerk abruptly disappeared.

"Bertie? *Bertie!*" Rob called out, wondering what had happened. Perhaps the king had suddenly swooned from the smell of the prison, or Bertie had collapsed from the shock.

And then he stopped thinking, because Vivienne was at the door. "My love!" she cried happily.

"Vivienne!" He was so shocked and so desperate to touch her through the opening, he forgot about his rib and his knee, and banged the latter on the door. "Damn it!"

"Really, Mr. Harding, that is not the tender greeting she was expecting, surely!"

"Your Majesty?" Rob choked, trying not to groan with pain as he regarded the man whose face replaced Vivienne's at the grill. Holding his rib with one hand, his other hand on his aching knee, he tried to bow.

The king waved his perfumed mouchoir in front of his face, and the incongruous scent of lavender mingled with the usual prison odors. "Indeed, it is your king," he acknowledged. Charles's merry eyes grew more serious. "You are seriously hurt?"

"Majesty, that is not what is causing me my greatest pain," he explained before the king abruptly stepped back.

The key rattled in the lock. Then the door swung open and in the next instant Vivienne was in his arms. She embraced him tightly, causing him to yelp with pain, yet hold her just as close.

She smelled like spring, and liberty. "Oh, my darling, my love!"

She drew back and surveyed him worriedly.

Meanwhile, the king strolled into the cell, looking about the tiny space as if he were in a museum or gallery.

Outside the cell, they could hear his dogs whining for their master.

Vivienne followed Rob's suspicious gaze. "He was only pretending at Lord Cheddersby's," she assured him in a swift whisper before Charles spoke again.

"That was a much prettier greeting, Mr. Harding," Charles observed approvingly, ignoring the cries of his bereaved pets, and Rob's confused expression.

Rob surreptitiously reached for Vivienne's hand. Smiling at him, she squeezed it. "I meant it from the bottom of my heart, sire."

"And yet some men would call you heartless."

"Ruthless is, perhaps, justified," he replied, "when I am acting in my client's interests."

"We understand your clients do not often have a champion in the courts."

"No, sire."

The king's brow wrinkled with thought. "Well, the courts are run by men, and we are all fallible, so some discrepancies are to be expected."

Rob opened his mouth to reply that such "discrepancies" were injurious to his clients, but Vivienne squeezed his hand again, and he held his peace. After all, he was hardly in a position to argue with the king.

"Which does not mean we condone it," Charles continued, and Rob was very glad he had paid heed to Vivienne. He looked at Robert's knee. "Tell me, are you able to kneel?"

"Majesty?"

"Granted, this place is foul beyond belief, but can you kneel?"

"I think, Your Majesty, the question would be, could he get up again?" Vivienne suggested.

"Ah, yes, we see." Their sovereign cocked his head. "Well, we shall consider this a sort of battlefield appointment, then, shall we, and so shall not stand upon ceremony."

With that, he drew his sword. "Robert Harding, do you swear to be loyal to your king?"

"Yes, Your Majesty," Rob replied, confused. With incomprehension, he turned to Vivienne, who was smiling with delight.

"Mr. Harding?"

Rob immediately faced the king again.

"In token of your efforts on behalf of the least of our subjects in our courts of law, we knight you. Rise—well, stand—Sir Robert Harding," Charles said before tapping him lightly on the shoulders.

Rob was too stunned to move or speak, while Charles smiled magnanimously and Vivienne clapped her hands with delight. She went to hug him again, but stopped. "Oh, I don't want to hurt you."

"Majesty, I . . ." he began.

Charles grinned. "You've just been knighted, man, that's all."

Rob swallowed hard. "But sire, I am only—"

The king regally held up his hand to silence him. "Sir Robert, *we* are the king of England and sometimes we can do as we please."

"Yes, sire."

"Besides, this young lady's uncle seems to set a great deal of store in titles. You *do* wish to marry her, do you not?"

"I most certainly do, Your Majesty."

"Good, otherwise we would have come to this dismal place all for naught."

A dog barked, drawing their attention. "That's Mollypuddle," Charles said. He glanced at them. "She doesn't wish to linger here any more than we do. Come along now, Sir Robert, Mistress Burroughs."

"Majesty, I regret I must point out—" Rob began.

The king chuckled. "Your pardon is signed and sealed, Sir Robert, so have no qualms. You are as free as any man in the kingdom." A winsome expression crossed Charles's face. "Perhaps more than some."

Then his face resumed its usual merry look. "And you've got a very beautiful woman in love with you, too."

"Sire, please, a moment," Rob said. He let go of Vivienne's hand and slowly, carefully, regardless of the pain, knelt in the malodorous straw before his monarch. "Your Majesty, I am humbly grateful for what you have done. Thank you."

A smile of genuine friendship shone on Charles's face as he helped him stand. "We appreciate your words and your action more than we can say, Sir Robert. And we think if there is any man in the kingdom worthy of this young woman's hand in marriage, it is you—and we intend to see to it that her uncle agrees. Now, enough sentiment, or Mistress Burroughs is liable to burst into tears."

"If I do, they will be tears of joy, sire."

"We had better see what's upset Mollypuddle and how that young man is faring. We fear he may have swooned at the sight of our magnificent presence," Charles said with a wry chortle. "Come along."

Charles strode forward and greeted his dogs as if they were his long-lost children, while they responded in kind with yips and barks.

Supported by Vivienne, Rob hobbled out of the cell, and immediately saw Bertie seated on a stool outside the guardroom. His eyes were closed as if he were insensible, until he heard them approach. Then he opened one wary eye, saw the king, and closed both of his eyes so tight, his eye sockets might have been empty.

"Are you ill?" Vivienne asked anxiously after the king had passed by.

Bertie opened his right eye. "I may never be the same again," he whispered gravely. "I was close enough to touch him!"

"So you are only overwhelmed by the king's presence?" Rob asked with concern.

"Ain't you?" Bertie whispered.

The king turned around and Bertie jumped to his feet, swept his cap off his head and bowed, giving the king a very fine view of the top of his head.

"Your Majesty, allow me to present Albert Dillsworth, my clerk."

"Mr. Dillsworth," Charles said in acknowledgment.

Bertie bashfully raised his eyes for a fraction of an instant, then lowered them.

"We trust you appreciate your employer, Mr. Dillsworth?"

Bertie mumbled something unintelligible.

The king winked at Rob and Vivienne. "A most suitably humble subject," he observed before strolling toward the door.

Vivienne smiled and couldn't refrain from exclaiming, "Rob has been knighted."

Bertie's gasp was audible despite the noise of the dogs at the far end of the corridor.

"Yes, it's true," Rob confirmed. "And if it's any consolation, I can't quite believe it myself."

"It's wonderful, that's what!" Bertie cried, his eyes glowing. "Oh, they'll come out of the woodwork for your services now, Rob, indeed they will."

"Meaning that I shall need another solicitor in my chambers even sooner than I planned. You had better study harder so that you can be a solicitor soon, Bertie."

"Truly, Rob?" he breathed incredulously.

"Very truly indeed. Besides, I will not want to work so long into the night when I am married."

"Married?"

"Married," Vivienne confirmed, giving Rob a light kiss.

"You might warn a body," Bertie declared, grinning from ear to ear.

"Sir Robert, Mistress Burroughs, we should leave before my dear dogs add anything more to the unpleasant smells of this place," Charles called to them. "Come!"

"You do not have to wait for us, Your Majesty," Rob replied.

Charles shook his head and waited while they approached, his eyes shining gleefully and, Vivienne suddenly realized, with what looked like great cunning. "Odd's fish, and go out without our newest knight, and all those people who have been demanding your release hovering about? We think not."

He beckoned for one of the guards, who rushed forward. "You might pass the word along that we shall be accompanying Sir Robert

Harding, whom we have just knighted, and ask that the people be so good as to clear the way, for he is injured."

The man nodded eagerly and darted out the door.

The king glanced at Vivienne and Rob, then sauntered forward, slowly enough that they had no trouble keeping up with him, two paces behind.

"I think our sovereign has a better nose for the political moment than I suspected," Rob noted. "Perhaps my knighthood has little to do with me at all."

Vivienne hugged him gently. "I don't care why he did it. You deserve to be honored, my love, for all you have accomplished and for all the good work you do—and I will not hear you say a single word to the contrary."

Chapter 25

Five weeks later, Vivienne's scalp tingled as she combed her hair. She was not sure if it was the pressure of the comb or the fact that Rob, her husband as of this morning, watched her while reclining on their newly purchased bed, still fully clothed and with his head pillowed on his hands.

Or it could be that she was so nervous because they had not been intimate together since that terrible night when Philip had attacked them.

Her mind raced over all the things that had happened since then. The first was the continued good reports of Rob's progress from the physician. He should suffer no serious, permanent injury, although he might have a limp for the rest of his life.

The second was her uncle's unsurprising decision that her marriage to Sir Robert Harding was a wonderful thing. Indeed, he had been quite enthusiastic and given her the same dowry he would have given Philip. No doubt his several visits to the royal tailors with samples and the order of plenty of fabric—as well as having a lawyer to consult free of charge— were more responsible for his generosity and good humor than his happiness at her marriage.

Lord Cheddersby, a true friend, had woefully confided that Uncle Elias should save his rejoicing until he actually saw some money for his goods. She had decided that it would be only right to ensure that her uncle knew this, but he had waved off her concerns. "Providing fabric for the king will ensure good relations with the general public," he had assured her.

She and Rob had spent a few happy hours ordering furnishings for his new chambers, which were now in Chancery Lane. As for the other solicitors who toiled there, Rob was still finding it difficult to accept their friendly overtures. She didn't doubt that while he would unlikely ever be friends with many of them, he would grow to accept his newfound popularity, and not just from his legal associates. Clients of every background now found their way to his door. Despite this, he made it clear that while he would happily represent wealthy people whose cases had merit, he would not abandon those who had sought his help before, or others of that class.

Apparently Lord Cheddersby had decided to put his knowledge of Latin and obscure legal precedents to work. He was going to study law, he declared, and become a barrister.

"I may as well try to do some good with all that learning," he told them, "and I have informed my father that the king approves, so there's a chance I will wind up on the King's Bench someday. I'm not hopeful of such a thing myself, but you should have seen the poor fellow's face. He didn't know whether to be angry or not after that, and he never said another word."

Thinking of Lord Cheddersby reminded her of Nell Gwynn, who had, it seemed, finally attracted King Charles's notice. Smiling in a way that utterly charmed Vivienne, Rob had informed her that Nell was quite happy to return the fascination, so she could wish them both well.

Mentioning the actress, however, had made him think of Jack, who had disappeared. Not one of Rob's acquaintances had seen him after that fateful night, so whether he had fled London for another city in England or sailed away to a foreign land, they did not know.

Jack's betrayal of both his sister and Rob had cut him to the quick, and would likely never cease to inspire Rob's anger and bitterness and self-reproach. Vivienne had assured him over and over again that he could not be faulted for failing to see the evil in his boyhood friend, yet Rob still chastised himself for not suspecting Jack sooner and more for not helping him when he had first been given an opportunity to rise above his poverty. She believed he always would, just as he would always wonder what he might have done had Janet come back to him.

A less honest man would not question his actions, past or present, so she would have to accept his self-recriminations; nevertheless, she would try to help him replace the worst of his memories with pleasant ones.

She put her hand to her belly and smiled to herself, thinking of something that, in a few months, should help her to do that.

"You look very happy."

She twisted to look at her husband over her shoulder. "I am very happy."

"I could watch you comb your hair all day."

Her heart quickened at the deep, intimate timbre of his voice. With trembling fingers, she set down her comb. "That would get very boring, I should think."

"It is such little intimacies you miss when you live alone."

"I suppose." She moved around on the stool so that she was facing him. "But I do not wish to spend my wedding night combing my hair."

"No?" he asked gravely, yet with a sparkle in his eyes that delighted her.

"No, indeed, Sir Robert." She rose and sashayed toward him. "I do not think a virile man like you should want to, either."

"Well," he drawled, smiling, "perhaps not tonight."

"Is it your intention to wear your clothes to bed?"

He grinned. "Not at all."

He sat up, put his feet on the floor and slowly began to peel off his jacket.

"Be careful," she cautioned.

Grinning, he said, "Oh, I shall. I do not want to disappoint my bride."

She blushed hotly. Really, such a reaction was utterly ridiculous. They had made love before. Twice, in fact. And just because they had been married today . . . "Would you like some help?"

"No."

"It is a wife's duty to help her husband."

"Oh, so you would only be doing your duty?"

"No," she confessed softly, going closer. "It would be my pleasure, too."

His eyes glowed with passion as he looked at her. "Then I will accept your assistance, Vivienne."

She stood between his legs and gingerly helped him remove his jacket, letting her hands slide lightly over his strong shoulders and the lean curves of his arms. She laid his jacket over a nearby chair, then undid the ties of his shirt, so that it gaped, exposing bare skin above a wide, white bandage.

His face inches from her breasts, he murmured, "I had best take this binding off, or I fear I may burst it."

She drew back. "Are you sure that's wise? Did the doctor not say you should keep your ribs bound while you are . . . active?"

"He did," Rob replied, tugging her back so that she was between his knees again. "But I think he was lacking in imagination. Otherwise, he might have realized that with such a beautiful bride, clad in such a thin nightgown and bringing her delectable breasts so close to my lips . . ."

He never concluded that thought; instead, he inched forward and nuzzled her breasts.

Arching back, she panted, "I suppose it could be loosened a little."

He stopped kissing her to get to his feet, then stood still while she lifted off his shirt. The binding ran around his chest and back. As she began to work the knot, his only movement was the rise and fall of his chest as she replaced the binding, now somewhat looser.

There was a rise elsewhere, too, which she could not fail to notice.

He saw her look. "As you can see, you had better hurry with this exquisite torture, Vivienne, or I will not be responsible for what my body may do."

She kissed the bare flesh of his shoulder as she retied the knot. "Patience, husband, patience."

She trailed her hand downward. "Do you require assistance with your breeches?"

"I think not."

She put her hand on the buttons. "No?"

"Not when my beautiful wife should be disrobing herself." He smiled wickedly. "If I am going to be naked, I think it only just that you be naked, too."

"I could argue that I could get cold."

"Do you really believe it is wise to try to argue with a solicitor?"

She regarded him studiously. "Perhaps not."

His expression was just as fraudulently grave. "Definitely not, and I think this is something you should bear in mind at all times."

"Especially when you are the most famous solicitor in London."

He stopped smiling and his eyes lost their merriment.

"I'm sorry, Rob," she said, inwardly cursing herself for her impetuous words, wanting to see him smile again.

He shook his head. "I confess it is disconcerting to realize that after all my years of toil, I am now sought out because of a man's death."

"You were already sought out, Rob, by people who knew you were a good and honest man, and a fine attorney—people you are still representing even though you could have your pick of wealthy clients."

He reached out to take her hands. His voice lowered to a husky whisper. "You are my good angel, Vivienne. Whenever I have dark thoughts, it will comfort me to speak them to you. I have never had that luxury—that love—before."

"As long as I live, Rob, you will never lack it."

"Then there is nothing more I could wish." His eyes darkened. "Well, there is one more thing to make this day complete, my lady," he said, his tone sending shivers of delightful anticipation down her body. "I believe it is a husband's duty to help his wife," he murmured as he took hold of the drawstring at the neck of her nightdress.

She held her breath as he undid it, then slowly, torturously, lowered her garment until it puddled in a heap around her feet.

He ran a wondering gaze over her. "You are even more beautiful than I dreamed."

"So are you."

"I am not beautiful."

"Handsome, then. Virile," she said as she caressed his chest. "If I could dress you in anything, I would see you in chain mail like the knights of old. Indeed, my love," she said, reaching up to touch his cheek, "you are as they were, chivalrous and generous. You tried to help a maiden in distress, even if she didn't want you to."

He pulled her into his arms, warm flesh meeting warm flesh. "You aren't a maiden anymore."

"And gladly so," she sighed as he bent to kiss her passionately.

Then she shivered.

He broke the kiss. "Now come to the bed. My bed. Our bed."

Wordlessly, she let him lead her there and she slipped between the clean sheets. In a moment, he was beside her, looking at her with hot, hungry eyes. "I love you, Vivienne," he said as he began to trail his hand over the slope of her thigh.

The sensation was delicious. "I love you, Rob," she managed to gasp before she tugged his head down to her yearning mouth.

They kissed deeply, drowning in the feel and taste of one another, experiencing a heady, dizzying host of sensations engendered by tongue and lips.

She gently guided him back against the pillows. "You are injured."

He looked befuddled.

"Lie still," she commanded huskily.

He looked about to protest, but before he could, she bent and began to tease the hard nub of his nipple with her tongue, the hairs surrounding it tickling her nose.

Instead of speaking, he groaned softly.

Aware of his healing rib, she lightly brushed the other nipple with her fingertips.

He stifled another groan.

Vivienne stopped and glanced up at him. His eyes were closed, his lips pressed tightly together. "We have never truly been alone before," she noted seductively. "I think you may make all the noise you want. I know I shall."

She moved her hand lower ever so slowly, and his moan of pleasure told her he had heard her, and agreed. More than that, it provoked her own yearning.

And then he reached out to caress her. "Your skin is so soft," he said, panting as she licked him. "Like velvet."

One hand stroked her breasts, and her nipples pebbled as his had, while the other roved wherever it could, stroking, caressing, lightly touching.

Every place his fingertips alighted, she burned.

She reached yet lower until she grasped him and another groan burst from his lips. Gently rubbing, she gloried in his virility, a primitive notion that he belonged to her filling her with pride and delight.

Carefully she raised herself and positioned him, then slowly lowered herself. His eyes flew open and he grimaced.

She halted. "Am I hurting you?"

"I . . . don't . . . know," he growled. "I cannot tell. Don't stop."

She hesitated nevertheless. "If I am hurting you—"

He reached around her waist with his lean, strong hands and pulled her lower. "Don't stop."

He slid inside her waiting, moist warmth, filling her, the pressure exciting and yet she wanted more. She moaned and leaned forward so that her breasts brushed his chest, her nipples stroking his.

Arching, feeling her hair down her naked back, hearing his moans and sighs, she felt powerfully, primitively female. She was taking him. Possessing him. Pleasuring him. Making him hers completely. Slowly, deliberately, she reveled in every tantalizing movement as she pressed against him in a way that increased the swelling in her own body and added to the urgency she felt.

Groaning, he gripped her upper arms and

guided her rhythm. He wanted her to go faster and, leaning her weight on her forearms, she was happy to comply.

Tension—indescribable, delicious and unbearable—seemed to thrill along every muscle. She leaned closer, inhaling the scent of him. His hair. His skin. His body. Her body. Her skin. Her hair. She could not sense where he began and she ceased.

He pulled her down for a fierce kiss, thrusting his tongue inside her mouth. But she did not stop moving. She could not stop moving. Not . . . until . . .

She cried out as her own body quivered and throbbed with release, while his agonized groan sounded in her ear.

Her eyes flew open. "Are you—"

He shook his head, smiling at her. "You had best get used to that sound. It has nothing to do with my broken rib or my injured knee."

Very gently and mindful of his injuries, regardless of his words, she eased herself off him, then snuggled beside him and pulled the sheet up to cover them both. "Good."

Holding her against him, he brushed a lock of hair from her face. "I don't deserve you, Vivienne."

"No, you don't," she agreed with a gentle laugh. "My uncle would say you have made a bad bargain, for I am very stubborn and I like to have my own way."

"If you were not, I would not be holding you in my arms at this moment."

She raised herself on her elbow and regarded him with an unexpectedly serious mien. "I will hear no more criticism of Sir Robert Harding, even from you—or what will I tell the baby when it is born?"

He blinked. "Baby?"

She smiled gloriously. "Our baby, that I carry even now."

"Vivienne!" he cried, simultaneously pulling her into his arms and crying out in pain.

"Careful, Rob!"

"Damn my rib!" he muttered, hugging her tightly. Then, with a gasp, he drew back. "Or have I hurt you?"

"Not at all."

"Not even—"

"Especially not then. I am sure of it. Besides, I checked with the physician and he assures me we may indulge ourselves for some time yet."

"You sound as if you were very thorough with your questions."

"I was." She nestled back beside him.

"I was right. You should have been a lawyer." They lay still in each other's arms a moment, before he laughed aloud, a wonderful sound in the intimacy of the dark bedchamber.

"Our baby, Vivienne," he murmured softly. "I thought I was happy when we wed today, but this . . . this is even more wonderful. I have everything I ever wanted, and so much more."

"I feel the same, my love," she agreed, rejoicing in the strength and comfort of his arms. Secure.

And loved, as she had always yearned to be.

Nationally Bestselling Author
CHRISTINA DODD

"Christina Dodd is everything
I'm looking for in an author."
Teresa Medeiros

The Governess Bride series

RULES OF ENGAGEMENT
0-380-81198-7/$6.99 US/$9.99 Can

RULES OF SURRENDER
0-380-81197-9/$6.99 US/$9.99 Can

And Don't Miss

RUNAWAY PRINCESS
SCOTTISH BRIDES
(with Stephanie Laurens,
Julia Quinn, and Karen Ranney)
SOMEDAY MY PRINCE
THAT SCANDALOUS EVENING
A WELL FAVORED GENTLEMAN
A WELL PLEASURED LADY
CANDLE IN THE WINDOW
CASTLES IN THE AIR
THE GREATEST LOVER IN ALL ENGLAND
A KNIGHT TO REMEMBER
MOVE HEAVEN AND EARTH
ONCE A KNIGHT
OUTRAGEOUS
TREASURE IN THE SUN